Jean Saunders began her career as a magazine writer. She has written about six hundred short stories and over eighty novels. She is past chairperson of the Romantic Novelists' Association and she frequently speaks at writers' groups and conferences. She is married with three grown-up children and writes full time. She lives in Weston-Super-Mare, Somerset.

A PERFECT MARRIAGE

Robert Jarvis dies from a heart attack, leaving his wife Margaret a widow at forty-two. Family and friends rally round, but their attentions only serve to stifle her, and with increasing suspicions that her marriage had not been as perfect as it had appeared to be, Margaret longs to get away from it all. Six months later she revisits Guernsey, the scene of her honeymoon twenty-five years earlier. There she meets and becomes attracted to the confident Philip Lefarge, but after a night of torrid passion, Margaret is filled with guilt and indecision . . .

Books by Jean Saunders
Published by The House of Ulverscroft:

LADY OF THE MANOR
GOLDEN DESTINY
WITH THIS RING
DEADLY SUSPICIONS

JEAN SAUNDERS

A PERFECT MARRIAGE

Complete and Unabridged

ULVERSCROFT
Leicester

First published in Great Britain in 2002 by
Robert Hale Limited
London

First Large Print Edition
published 2004
by arrangement with
Robert Hale Limited
London

British Library CIP Data

Saunders, Jean, *1932 –*
    A perfect marriage.—Large print ed.—
Ulverscroft large print series: romance
1. Widows—Fiction
2. Marriage—Fiction
3. Large type books
I. Title
823.9′14 [F]

ISBN 1–84395–192–4

Published by
F. A. Thorpe (Publishing)
Anstey, Leicestershire
Set by Words & Graphics Ltd.
Anstey, Leicestershire
Printed and bound in Great Britain by
T. J. International Ltd., Padstow, Cornwall

This book is printed on acid-free paper

1

'What am I going to do, Robert?'

Margaret looked at her husband, wanting answers, expecting answers as always. This time there wasn't one.

In those first awful, disorientating moments when she felt totally alone, she tried to think how it had come to this. Why couldn't they have seen it coming? They hadn't changed so much over the years. Twenty-four years of marriage hadn't turned them into the kind of people who hardly knew one another any more, who rarely talked about their problems.

She was forty-two years old and he was not yet fifty, and everyone who knew them said they had the perfect marriage. They had a lovely home overlooking the sea in Bournemouth, three so-called typical children, two of whom had fulfilled all their hopes, and one who had . . . well, she chose not to think about Jenny at that moment. Now wasn't the time.

She couldn't seem to think of anything properly. The thoughts churning around in her head had no proper substance at all. The crux of it was that she simply didn't know what to do next. Nobody prepared you for this. Robert was always the strong one, the one who took responsibility, who told her not to bother her pretty head, that he'd see to everything.

Some would see it as patronizing, as putting feminism back fifty years, but she hadn't. Being married at eighteen to a gorgeous man who had literally swept her off her feet and promised to take care of her for ever, had been magical. She had loved the pampering, the feeling that as long as Robert was beside her, everything would be all right.

Years ago, her mother, a globe-trotter all her life, had told her firmly she should be more self-sufficient, and couldn't understand why her elder daughter was going against all that burning your bra had stood for in her young days. But Margaret was happy in just being domesticated, in building a home for Robert and Keith and Ben, and Jenny . . .

And now it was all falling apart like a house of cards, and *she didn't know what to do.*

'Help me, Robert,' she said, her voice breaking with a strange mixture of anger and despair. But of course there was no answer. There couldn't be, ever again. Because he was dead.

★ ★ ★

She heard the swish of a uniform. Did they really swish, or was the noise just in her head, because of the popular image that films and TV programmes had put there? Nurses' uniforms swished. QED. She realized she was sweating, and that shock was fast taking over. OK, she thought, with a weird kind of cheerfulness, maybe I'll just lie down beside you, Robert, and once we get the tangle of tubes and medical paraphernalia out of the way, I'll quietly pop off too.

'Mrs Jarvis — Margaret — please stay with your husband as long as you like, and Doctor will speak to you eventually — '

'Oh really?' Unreasonably, unexpectedly, she lashed out at such consideration. 'And what will he tell me that I don't already know? My husband's had a heart attack and he's dead. What else is there to say?'

She bit her lip, surprised to taste blood, and guessed she had probably been biting it for some time. It wasn't the nurse's fault. She was being kind, the way they all were, but right now she couldn't cope with it. She couldn't yet face the appalling knowledge of having to live the rest of her life without her husband, her lover, her best friend . . . it had happened so fast; this heart attack that was no more than a bad bout of indigestion, according to Robert, who always dismissed illness as something that happened to other people, and never to him.

'Margaret, can I call someone for you? Do you have family? Children? Parents? Close friends?'

Oh yes. She had all that. They were a popular family. And once they all knew about the nightmare that had happened so suddenly, she was going to be surrounded by a wall of love. An *overload* of love. But none of it could replace the only love she could never have again. The only man she had ever loved.

She caught sight of the nurse's concerned face. Nice, plain, worried for her, and felt ashamed of her outburst. And of herself. These things happened to women every day. She wasn't the first widow in the world . . .

God, what a terrible word. As it came into her head, she felt sick. Any minute now and she was going to throw up all over the nurse's clean uniform and disgrace herself.

She dragged up some strength from somewhere.

'I'm sorry. The shock — '

'You don't need to apologize. I'll organize a cup of tea to help steady your nerves.'

Margaret stared at her. Was she completely mad, offering the standard panacea for all ailments in TV hospital programmes? The recipient gratefully sipped the heavily sugared, calorie-laden tea, and suddenly everything was all right again. Well, it wasn't. It bloody wasn't.

She felt the nurse's hand on her shoulder.

'It's not as ridiculous as it sounds, my dear. It will be something to occupy yourself with. And why don't you give me one of those phone numbers to call?'

'No. I'll just have the tea,' Margaret was sullen, caving in. 'But no sugar. I hate the stuff.'

She looked down at her husband when the nurse had gone.

'You see, Robert? My first strike for independence. Tea, no sugar, no matter what they say.'

Tears flooded her eyes. He was still so handsome, despite the grey pallor, his hair as thick as the day they had met all those years ago, his mouth still so kissable. She held the hands that had caressed her a million times. He had what her mother always called pianist's fingers, long and strong . . .

A few minutes later, a younger nurse came in with the tea, looking at her nervously and going straight out again. Probably never seen a dead body before, Margaret thought prosaically. Well, neither had she. Without warning, the cardboard cup in her hands began to shake uncontrollably, and dropped from her fingers, spilling all over the bed. God, how awful. Robert hated mess. He was so fastidious, which was why he and Jenny were always at war with one another.

'She's no daughter of mine,' he'd bellow, whenever he glanced into the unbelievable chaos of her bedroom. 'How can she live in such a pigsty?'

Jenny. Keith. Ben. Margaret found herself reciting their names mechanically in her head. The wrong way round, of course, since Jenny was the youngest. They didn't yet know their father was dead. She felt a keen sadness for them, wishing she could keep it from them. But they had to be told. And she had to be the one to do it. When the nurse came back she stood up, surprised to find her legs still worked.

'Sorry about the mess,' she said jerkily. 'Can you show me where there's a phone?'

There would be others to contact, too, she thought vaguely. Their local vicar, Robert's work people, the undertaker . . . but her first priority was their children. She was still thinking in lists. Her parents, Robert's mother. And their friends. Close friends, good friends, especially John. Oh God, John would be devastated.

In the visitors' room, she dialled Keith's number with trembling hands. They all had mobile phones, and Lord knew how anyone was supposed to keep all those numbers in their head. But since she hadn't done anything as mundane as grabbing her handbag when the ambulancemen had rushed Robert out of the house at three o'clock in the morning, she forced herself to memorize them now.

Keith sounded sleepy, cross at being woken from whatever pit he was in. Hopefully Laura's, unless that situation had already changed. She hoped not. She and Robert liked Laura.

'Mum? Is that you? You sound funny. What's up?'

Her throat began to close up. It was so thick with tears she thought she would never get the words out.

'What's happened, Mum?' His voice sharpened. 'Is it Dad?'

He was more perceptive than she thought. She heard the murmur of another voice in the background, and whoever it was, she was glad he wasn't alone.

'Darling, I'm at the hospital — '

'I'm coming right away — '

'No, *wait*. Keith, I'm afraid it's the worst news.'

She couldn't say it. She just couldn't bloody well say it. She loathed herself for being so spineless, but then Keith said it for her.

'You're not telling me he's dead, are you? Mum, tell me it's not that.' She heard the panic in his voice now.

'It was a heart attack. Massive, they said. Nothing they could do. I'm so sorry — '

'I'll be right there. Have you told the others?'

'Not yet.'

'I'll do it. God knows where Jenny is, but if she's in the country I'll contact her. Don't worry, Mum. Just try to keep calm, and I'll be with you soon.'

His voice had changed to the practical, and he had hung up before she could say any more. He was so like his father, Margaret thought. Taking over. Trying to stop her worrying. Cushioning her.

He was twenty-three years old, and she knew he'd see to everything. She could rely on Keith. It wasn't right, but she was so guiltily grateful right now, she didn't care.

She called her parents, just home from Tenerife. Her mother had never really got on with Robert — always calling him a Flash Harry — but they promised to travel down from London right away.

'Shall I call Robert's mother for you, Margaret?'

'Oh, would you, Mum? Thanks.'

It was passing the buck, but the prospect of all she had to do was suddenly a gigantic mountain she didn't know how she was going to climb. Everything they had built up together was crumbling in front of her eyes. She didn't really know what their financial situation was, nor what Robert had written in his will, nor how she was going to cope with clearing out his study at home.

And his clothes. He liked to dress smartly. Oxfam would be pleased. And his garage with the vintage car he was so proud of. And the workshop at the bottom of the garden where he'd made wooden toys for the children when they were small.

And the garden where they had bought a new plant or shrub from every place they visited, and where they used to have so many summer barbecues for friends and neighbours. They were the successful Jarvises, and now she was alone.

She was still slumped over the telephone when her son arrived. He must have broken speed records, she registered numbly. A fine thing for a police constable to do! And then she was being held tight, and she no longer felt quite so alone as they cried together.

'I've contacted Ben and he'll be here around noon, but I told him we'll be at home by then. Laura's still trying to get hold of Jenny, but I think she must be abroad, and her mobile's not answering. She'll keep trying though.'

He paused, still holding on to her, shock still in his voice, but clearly steeling himself not to break down any more. He had training, Robert used to say proudly. My son, the policeman.

Margaret didn't think Ben would be so stoical. Ben was a commercial artist, working for a glossy magazine in London, and more temperamental. It went with the territory, Robert used to say, not quite sure it was the career he'd wanted for his second son. He'd wanted one of them, at least, to go into the family firm of boat builders with him, but neither had been so inclined. And the only thing Jenny liked about boats was that they could satisfy her wanderlust. She was more her grandmother's child than his, Robert said scathingly.

Margaret realized how much she was thinking in Robert's terms now. Using his voice, his thoughts. Or maybe he was doing that for her. Still guiding her. Still controlling.

She felt a huge shock as the word slipped

into her head. It seemed so disloyal when he had been everything in the world to her. He *had* controlled her though, she admitted, and she had been content to let him.

And what had she done with her life? He'd been old-fashioned enough not to want her to work at all, and at eighteen it had charmed her, but being the grand lady of leisure was more for her mother's generation, and not hers.

Then the babies had come soon after their marriage, so being a wife and mother had taken up all her time. Later, she had taken on some of the secretarial work for the business, because she certainly didn't want to seem like a total sponge. But learning computer skills still foxed her . . .

'Have you called John?' Keith said suddenly.

She shook her head. 'I don't know what to say to him.'

'Say it like it is, Mum,' Keith said brutally. For some reason he'd never had much time for Robert's oldest friend. 'He'll soon be sniffing round you, anyway, wanting to get his feet under the table.'

'*Keith!*' She was stunned at the bitterness in his voice. 'How can you say such a thing? John was like a second father to you children when you were growing up.'

'We didn't want a second father. We already had one.'

They looked at one another, realizing what he had just said, and then hugged one another again. But there was a temporary awkwardness between them that was relieved by the door opening, and the doctor arriving to speak to them.

Not that he could tell them anything they didn't already know. Robert Jarvis, aged forty-nine, had died from a massive heart attack, and no amount of the medical jargon he was spouting was going to change anything.

'Is there anything else we can do for you right now, Mrs Jarvis?' he went on quietly.

He looked so *young* for such a responsible job, Margaret thought illogically. But everyone seemed young now, when she felt more like a hundred years old instead of forty-two.

'My son will want to see his father, and then I think I just want to go home,' she said slowly. 'Is that all right?'

'Of course it is. Whenever you're ready. And may I say how very sorry I am.'

'Thank you.'

He escorted them back to the side ward where Robert lay, and tactfully left them alone, thinking that life was a bitch when such a bloody attractive woman should have to go through this. The husband had been overweight, a heavy smoker and apparently a workaholic, prime candidate for a heart attack. It was the relatives he felt sorry for, and sometimes he hated his job when you felt so impotent to do anything. And then he answered his bleeper and got on with the next one.

★ ★ ★

By mid-afternoon the house overlooking the sea was full of people. Margaret had been hugged and kissed so many times, she wanted to scream. But by now, after what seemed like a million cups of tea and coffee, and endless forays to the biscuit and cake tins, things had settled down a little, and they were swopping anecdotes of happier times with Robert.

Keeping the little widow's chin up, Margaret thought, with a cynicism that wasn't like her at all. But then, she didn't feel like herself. She didn't know who she was any more. But she wasn't little, either.

She wasn't exactly tall, but she had good bearing and an air of confidence when she walked into a room; it was one of the things Robert had always loved about her. She swallowed back a sob, as people glanced her way, watching, caring, smothering . . .

She caught sight of her reflection in the sitting-room mirror over the mantelpiece, and was almost surprised to see that she still looked more or less the same as usual. Apart from the dark shadows beneath her eyes and her pale complexion, she hadn't changed that much in the past twelve hours after all. Not physically, anyway.

Her weekly hair appointment had only been yesterday, her blonde highlights freshly done, so it still looked in reasonably good nick. And she had kept her figure. She could still wear a bikini on the beach . . . and just for one nostalgic moment the scent of a sun-kissed ocean was strong in her nostrils. It was probably just a whispering breeze from the sea through the open French windows, but it seemed to epitomize all the times they had shared together. Robert had worked hard, but he'd played hard too, and their foreign beach holidays had always been magical.

Especially when the children had grown up, and they had become lovers again instead of just parents-with-children on package holidays . . .

'Mum? Where have you gone?' she heard Ben say, his voice full of worry. She gave him a brilliant smile, her eyes bright with unshed tears, and patted his arm.

'Just popped down memory lane, as your Gran would say. Pathetic, isn't it?'

'Of course not. It's what we're all doing today.'

'And not only today, I hope,' Margaret said more pithily. 'We won't forget him that easily, will we?'

As he mumbled something and moved away, Margaret told herself she was coping marvellously. Holding court, being brave, not letting the side down. Her father had been in the military, as he invariably called it, and he'd be proud of her for that. Her sister was eyeing her warily, expecting her to crack at any minute. Well, she damn well wasn't going to, Margaret thought stubbornly. Not until she was alone, anyway.

They were all brave too. Everyone here knew Robert well, and had their own special memories of him. They were all as shocked as she was, in their different ways. But so far they still hadn't been able to contact Jenny, so that was a hurdle still to come. Nor Margaret's best friend Sarah.

But family, other friends and neighbours were here, those who had been contacted so far. Rallying round. Even Robert's aged mother had taken the news better than Margaret had expected. She couldn't make the long journey from Norfolk, but her carer said she wasn't too bad in the circumstances.

John Franklin hadn't arrived yet, which was odd. She knew Keith had phoned him and had told her briefly that he'd sounded pretty cut up. Well, he would. They went back a long way. They'd known each other long before she and Robert met. Been students and drinking buddies together, and gone on some pretty wild benders, if they were to be believed. He'd be here, as soon as he could get away and felt able to face her, she thought confidently.

She caught sight of Keith watching her, and felt the heat in her cheeks, remembering the strange remark he had said at the hospital.

Since joining the police force, Keith had changed from the happy-go-lucky son to someone who'd seen some traumatic things in his time. He was the cynic now, but she'd never expected him to turn against John in that way. Not that there was one iota of truth in what he said. John was their oldest friend, and had never made a pass at her. Thank God. It would be like having your brother fancying you.

She turned, glad to get the thought out of her head as her younger sister walked over to her. Brenda was in public relations, seriously single and intending to stay that way. She worked for a high-powered advertising agency, and they had never been particularly close. Margaret thought her sharp enough to cut herself, and Brenda thought her a dodo to stay at home and do nothing. Once they had cheerfully agreed to differ, they got on better because of it.

'How are you doing, kid?' Brenda asked. 'As well as can be expected, as they say?'

'Something like that. Thanks for not bringing your latest with you.'

Margaret thought him a slimy oaf, and Brenda knew it.

'Oh, Tom's last month's news. Actually I'm off to New York in two weeks' time on assignment. It's a fantastic opportunity.'

She paused, her face quickly reorganizing itself as she remembered where she was and why she was here. 'God, I'm sorry, Mags. You'll let me know when the — when it is, won't you?'

'The funeral, you mean. It's called a funeral, Bren. Of course I'll let you know, but I'll quite understand if you can't make it.'

She saw Brenda's eyes narrow, not expecting this brittle reply from her more docile sister. But she wasn't feeling docile. It was somehow terrible, but as the hours passed and she began to get used to the way things were, she knew she had to assert herself, or she would be swamped by them all. She had to be a person, not a wimp. In her own mind, she had never been that, but she supposed it was how other people might have seen her. It had simply never occurred to her before.

★ ★ ★

By six o'clock some of the friends had moved on. Keith and Ben were staying the night, and Laura was going back to her own place. Thank God. She couldn't have borne hearing them sharing the same room, whether or not they were having it off.

Her parents too, intended staying, though she could have done without them. She longed for her friend Sarah's honest approach. She appreciated her family's bolstering, but she couldn't stand too much of her mother's watchful look, and her father's continual throat-clearing, as if he didn't quite know what to make of this newly bereaved daughter.

It was the wrong order of things, he had been heard to say to an older neighbour. Children shouldn't die before their parents, and a son-in-law was just as much part of a family as one of their own.

Margaret felt as if she wandered around in

a daze, half-listening to people, half-seeing them. She went through the motions of thanking people for coming, while feeling as if she was in one of those old-time movies, where the camera was outside the house, looking in. It followed the movements of everyone inside, watching them talking and laughing, but with no sound. A world that was sepia-coloured, eerie, ghostly.

'My God, Robert, you've turned me into a weirdo,' she heard herself say out loud.

She felt her heart jump as people turned to look at her, and she gave a shaky laugh.

'It's OK. I'm not going crazy. Just having a private word with my husband.'

And if they thought *that* was crazy, to hell with them. She felt suddenly belligerent. This was her house, and Robert was her husband, and you didn't stop communicating with somebody just because they weren't here any more. Even if the conversation was likely to be pretty one-sided in future. Not that she was going to do any of that Ouija-board mumbo-jumbo stuff. No way!

'Wouldn't you like to go and lie down for a while, Margaret?' she heard her mother say.

'No thanks. I'll sleep when I'm tired, and that's not going to be for a very long time yet,' she said.

And where was she going to sleep tonight?

She hadn't considered it. In their bed, where the indent of Robert's head would still be in the pillow?

Where everything of his would still be there, as if he had just gone into another room, which was one of the fatuous remarks people said when someone they loved was dead. But how could she bear to see his clothes, his dressing-gown behind the bedroom door, his books, his presence? Her sense of panic and loss was so sharp it made her senses reel.

'Oh God,' she heard Keith mutter, penetrating her thoughts. 'I thought it wouldn't be long.'

Margaret jolted herself out of her momentary panic, and turned to see the tall figure of John Franklin striding towards her. He looked totally spaced-out, his good-looking face anguished as he caught her in his arms and held her so close she could hardly breathe.

'My God, I can't believe it, Margaret,' he said hoarsely in her ear. 'I simply can't believe it. We were drinking together a few nights ago, and now — '

She couldn't answer. Of all the people she had seen today, John knew Robert better than any of them. He'd known him longer, and more intimately in many ways. Known all his youthful secrets and indiscretions, and shared his passions.

She felt indescribably sorry for him, and mixed up with the sadness was a sudden stab of jealousy. She couldn't explain it, and she didn't want it, and it was gone in an instant. But she had felt it, sharp and strong.

'I'll always be here for you, Margaret. You know that, don't you?' he went on, in best TV drama series language.

She pushed down the awful thought and continued with the play. Acting out the roles they were now being given.

'I know, John. And I know Robert would have wanted that.'

She closed her eyes, wishing she didn't always have to be saying things in the past tense now. It wasn't real, and she had to force herself physically to do it. Because he was still here, all around her, still in this room, in their home, and in her heart.

She was being held too tightly in John's embrace to extricate herself immediately, so she didn't see her mother glance meaningly at her father, and she was too far away to hear her crisp words.

'If you ask me, there's going to be trouble there.'

2

Two days later, Jenny Jarvis breezed into the house fresh from a few weeks' backpacking around southern Italy, her skin tanned and glowing with health. Fun, sun and sex had been the order of the days — and nights.

She paid off the taxi with a handful of coins, ignored the driver's grumbling and tore into the kitchen, breathing in the familiar aromas of fresh coffee and her mother's home baking. She dumped her stuff in the middle of the floor, and yelled to anyone who was around that she was back.

Shushing her, her grandmother came out of the sitting-room with a face like a thunder-cloud, and Jenny groaned. She waited for the usual disapproving lecture, while knowing damn well that Granny Annie was actually green with envy at her ability just to go wherever the spirit took her, thanks to her father's generous allowance. And secretly wishing she'd been born fifty years later to do the same.

'What are you doing here, Gran?' Jenny shrieked now, wrapping her arms around her in a token hug. 'Where is everybody? Where's

Mum? The house is like a morgue.'

At her grandmother's loud intake of breath, Jenny paused. Something was wrong. There *was* no scent of fresh baking, no old-folksy-home smells at all. She was no psychic, but there was definitely something going on here that she didn't like.

'Keith's been trying to contact you for two days,' Annie Vernon snapped. 'Why didn't you answer your wretched phone?'

'Out of batteries. Out of money. What's going on, Gran?'

Her voice was querulous now, and she turned thankfully as her mother came into the kitchen. But one look at Margaret's blotchy face as she silently opened her arms to her daughter, and she knew. The wild child had come home too late.

★   ★   ★

'I always said he smoked too much and let himself get too fat,' she raged, when she'd done her fill of sobbing.

Fury always took over very quickly with Jenny, covering pain, covering the need to be sentimental. Emotions were for morons, and whereas even Ben could cry and not lose one iota of manhood in doing so, Jenny hated any feeling of weakness. Margaret envied her that.

She hadn't been able to shed a tear at the first shock of Robert's death, which some had thought creepy and unhealthy. But now she felt as if she had cried an ocean of tears since then, and much of it was in John Franklin's arms.

'Was it quick?' Jenny asked, savagely needing facts.

'Very,' Margaret said, reliving the moments with a wrench of agony. Wishing she didn't have to, yet still jealously holding on to them. 'He didn't suffer for very long.'

'Just the rest of us, then. If that wasn't typical of Dad. Selfish to the end, wasn't he?'

As her own mother gasped at such brittle callousness, Margaret stilled her with a glance, brushing aside the brash statement, and understanding her daughter's need to lash out only too well. She frequently felt like it herself now. You had to let out your emotions somehow, and if this was Jenny's way, it was better than bottling it up inside. Allegedly.

'Maybe I'm the selfish one for being glad he didn't have a long, lingering illness — ' she said quietly.

Jenny glowered at her. 'My God, Mother, do you always have to be such a bloody martyr? Such a *saint*?'

24

Margaret felt her face flush. 'I'm anything but! But now you're here at last, I'm sure you'll want to see your father.'

'Oh, Jesus, he's not in the house, is he?'

As her voice faltered again, Margaret saw only a young frightened girl, unable to face the thought of death.

Her mother left them, furious at this display of bad manners, crass insensitivity and blasphemy, but Margaret couldn't be angry with her any more. Jenny was still her little girl, scared and bemused by something she couldn't handle. Yes, she thought disgustedly, I *am* a bloody martyr . . .

'Of course he's not here. He's at the Chapel of Rest. It'll be all right, darling, I promise you. There's nothing to worry about. We'll go after tea. You *are* hungry, I take it? And later, when you've got your breath back, you must tell me all about Italy.'

She brought the conversation back to the normal, the mundane. And saw the small spark of relief come into her daughter's dark eyes. They were so like Robert's eyes . . . all the children had his almost Mediterranean sultry good looks and sleek black hair. None of them had what Margaret's father called her cool Grace Kelly looks.

'I'm starving, actually,' Jenny mumbled. 'I ran out of money ages ago. I'm not sure I'd be able to eat anything though. Or should. In the circs.'

'Don't be silly. Do you think your father would want you to starve on his account? If he was here now, he'd be asking for steak and chips, and that's just what you're going to have. And to hell with the calories.'

'Oh *Mum*,' Jenny said, her voice cracking. 'And listen, I'm really sorry I called you a martyr. You're not. You're being very brave, and I never saw it before.'

It was a rare compliment from a daughter who had always been far too indulged and was more used to hurling insults about the place. Margaret didn't think she was being at all brave, and if she was, she knew it wouldn't last. She just did her best to boost everybody else's spirits, knowing that she wasn't the only one who needed boosting. It helped, anyway.

'How's everybody else taking it?' Jenny said later, when she had got accustomed to the news, and was replete with food. 'Keith was being his typical Mr Plod, I suppose, and I bet Ben blubbered as usual.'

'Got it in one,' Margaret said briefly.

'And how about the lovely John? Has he been here?'

'Of course. What did you expect?'

Jenny shrugged. 'I suppose if I'd ever thought about it at all, I've have expected him to muscle in. Don't let him step into Dad's shoes too quickly, will you, Mum?'

'Jenny, I've had to listen to some pretty awful platitudes in the last few days,' Margaret said angrily. 'But I've taken it all, because people don't know what to say in these circumstances. But nobody's been tactless enough to hint at my marrying again. I thought better of you.'

'I'm not saying anything we haven't all thought of. He's a lecher, a creep, and you've never seen it, have you?' she said, hitting out because she knew she'd already gone too far and not knowing how to back out of it now.

'I think we'd better stop this conversation right now,' Margaret said, white with anger. 'You smell to high heaven, by the way, so go and have a shower and change out of those filthy clothes before we go to see your father.'

'It'll hardly make any difference to him, will it?' Jenny yelled, seconds before she hurtled out of the room.

* * *

'I don't know how you stopped yourself from striking that little madam,' Annie said, when Margaret rejoined her. 'I could hear every word. She's disgraceful — '

'No, Mum,' Margaret said wearily. 'She's

27

just young, and she's hurting badly. She loved her father, and she'll be devastated because she never got the chance to say goodbye to him. She needs to spend some time on her own before she can accept it.'

And if only Robert was here he'd know how to handle it. He and Jenny had always clashed, but sometimes voracious verbal fighting was how two temperamentally close people behaved. It didn't mean they didn't love each other.

Tonight was going to be a big hurdle for Jenny, seeing her father at the Chapel of Rest. But until she did, Margaret knew it wouldn't seem real to her. Although she had to admit it still wasn't fully real to her, and wouldn't be. Not yet. Not for a long while yet.

She still expected to hear the sound of his car wheels on the drive, and to hear him calling her name when he came into the house. She missed him so much. Missed his presence, his closeness, the way his arms folded around her in bed each night, when they lay like spoons, his hands on her breasts, his body moulded to hers.

You couldn't dismiss the closeness of twenty-four years of marriage just like that. It was a tangible, almost living thing. She didn't *want* to lose it, she thought jealously. Nor the knowledge that she would never again feel his body warming hers, or the sweet familiarity of his love-making, the heady rush of adrenalin that came from climaxing together.

She would miss sex, damn it. She would just miss sex. It wasn't something you shouted from the rooftops but it had been so very fundamental to their lives together, and its loss was something else nobody understood until they went through the pain of being left alone. She hadn't known about the complex mixture of feelings and emotions to go through until it happened. She supposed the clever pundits would call it a rite of passage. She called it going through hell.

Already, the sense of physical loss was very real. Theirs had been a deeply passionate marriage, a perfect marriage . . . and if it was wrong to be thinking of all that too soon, she couldn't help it, because less than a week ago Robert had been making love to her, and she knew he wouldn't want her to forget his touch, his taste . . .

'Mum, listen, I'm really sorry for the things I said. Forgive me?'

She hadn't heard Jenny come back to the room, but with a start she registered the small, shamed voice as if it came from somewhere on another planet.

She dragged her thoughts back from the abyss, and the next minute they were weeping in one another's arms, if for slightly different reasons, and her daughter was wholly hers again.

★   ★   ★

Nobody could live on a high plane of emotional tension for ever. A couple of weeks after the trauma of the funeral was over, Jenny went to London to stay with her grandparents for a while, to sort herself out, as she called it. And Margaret finally had the house to herself, insisting firmly that she had to get used to it, that she needed space to think.

There were things to do. All the accumulation of a lifetime to sort out; Robert's clothes, his business and personal papers, everything that had made up the minutiae and intimacy of their lives together. She hadn't touched any of it yet. But when she did, she needed to do it alone, to laugh or cry over it as she wished, and it was something too personal to share, even with her children.

Margaret's best friend Sarah saw it differently.

'You should leave it as long as you want to, Margaret, until you feel more able to face it all. I'm sure there's nothing so important that you have to torture yourself with it. My remedy is that we go out and get quietly stoned.'

'Oh, that would be a great thing to do, wouldn't it! What would people say?'

'Who cares what people say? They'll probably call you the merry widow, and good for you for getting on with your life.'

'I am getting on with it. I've got no choice, have I?'

'Has John suggested taking you out?'

'I haven't seen him lately. He's away on a sales conference right now, and then he goes to France on an extended business trip.'

'Well, your friends aren't going to let you wallow in misery for ever,' Sarah said determinedly. 'I don't mean to be brutal about it, Mags, but you know Robert wouldn't want it. I'm not much good at pep talks, but God knows we all miss him. *I* miss him. This place is empty without him. He was a darling man, a big man in every way, but life goes on. Boringly so, for some of us — '

'Well, not for you! You never spent a boring day in your life.' But she was touched by Sarah's passion. She was not normally so serious. She was the scatty one of their group. Happily divorced, she called it, unlike some of the others.

'Nor night, if I can help it,' Sarah agreed with a grin. 'So what do you say? Do we go out and get rat-arsed?'

'Not unless you want me throwing up all over your car.'

'We're still going out. I'll call a couple of the others. Fiona and June — '

'I'm not sure about this, Sarah.' She heard herself dithering and couldn't seem to stop it.

'Well, *be* sure. You need company. And not your kids. They'll pull you down with all their fussing. Your mother's just as bad. Thank God they've left you to find your feet.'

'Is that what I'm doing? Anyway, they all mean well.' She pulled a face. 'And I'm a bloody living cliché, aren't I?'

'We all mean well. I'm calling the others right now, so go and get changed. Wear something glamorous and show 'em you're not dead yet.'

As Margaret's face crumpled, Sarah could have bitten out her tongue. 'Oh God, I'm sorry. I didn't mean that. I'm trying to help, damn it, and I'm just making it worse, aren't I?'

'No, you're not. You're absolutely right. I'm not dead yet.' She said the words deliberately. 'So give me twenty minutes and I'll be ready.'

'Good for you,' Sarah said.

She watched her leave the room, elegant as always, her gorgeous blonde hair pinned up in the topknot she favoured, showing the long lines of her throat and her fine cheekbones. All her friends envied her that model girl bone structure, the wide blue eyes, the mobile mouth. She had everything a man could want in a woman.

Robert had been frequently heard to say as much, and it was no wonder everyone called theirs a perfect marriage. Which made it all the more bloody incomprehensible why . . .

Sarah punched out the numbers on her mobile with vicious fingers. She wasn't going along that road right now. The fact that he'd been oversexed, never satisfed with what he had at home, was knowledge that Margaret didn't have, and was never going to have, if she had anything to do with it.

You thought you knew someone so well, but there were always things you didn't know. Everyone had secrets, and Robert Jarvis was no different from anyone else. But Sarah vowed that she wasn't going be the one to spill the beans.

Anyway, there was no need for any of it to come out, ever. Margaret was to be protected. Unconsciously, she used Robert's words.

★ ★ ★

At the end of it, Margaret decided that the evening had been a mini-success. No, more than that. A turning-point, if you like. It was more than a month since the worst night of her life, but as Sarah, Fiona and June determinedly jollied her out of her miseries, taking her on a pub-crawl and finding anything and everything to joke about, she registered through a haze of wine that people still had fun, grass still grew and the seasons changed.

Spring was already warming up the earth, and Robert's favourite daffodils were in bud. From the day they had bought this house, he had planted them everywhere, in borders, in great clumps around the trees on the lawn, in tubs around the swimming-pool. Soon there would be the annual riot of golden colour to greet her every morning, and she would fill the house with them as she always did. Bringing sunshine indoors, Robert used to call it.

She felt her throat well up again and she deliberately smothered the feeling. Her head still swam from drinking too much Chardonnay, and black coffee sounded like a very good idea. She had to be strong in more ways than one. Firstly, to stop herself from throwing up, and secondly, because it was simply the way she had vowed to be from now on.

Their family solicitor had been agreeably

34

surprised at her resolve. The people who had expected her to fall apart were finding she wasn't made of glass after all, she had thought grimly.

The will-reading had been more or less as expected. The bulk of Robert's estate, the house, shares in the business and various investments, had been left to his wife. There was a bequest to continue his mother's care in the eventuality that she outlived him, generous bequests to his children, several small gifts to certain faithful employees, and a special gift for his long-time friend, John Franklin.

Margaret's mother had sniffed at that, and hadn't been able to resist a snide comment afterwards.

'A bit overdone, if you ask me. I'd have thought the Franklin chap had enough money of his own.'

'Leave it, Mum. It was Robert's wish, and I've no argument with it. There aren't many friendships that lasted as long as theirs did.'

It was true. From childhood, through university and their wild hippy stage and the trek to India to find themselves *à la* John Lennon, to the point where everything had settled down and John had been Best Man at their wedding, she reflected. There couldn't have been any other choice, of course, and he was also one of Keith's godfathers.

'Didn't you ever wonder why he never got married?' her mother went on relentlessly.

'Not everybody does,' Margaret said crisply. 'Keith hasn't, so don't bother giving me your opinion of that.'

'Maybe people don't bother with marriage nowadays, but the Franklin chap's a different generation. He's what? Fifty years old?'

'About that. He and Robert were much the same age. And why can't you ever call him by his name, for pity's sake?'

'Oh well, I suppose it takes all sorts,' Annie said, ignoring the question.

Margaret was exasperated. 'What's that supposed to mean? John's one of the kindest men I know, and he's never been short of girlfriends, if that's what you're implying, Mum. You've been watching too much Channel 5 lately.'

★   ★   ★

Margaret remembered that odd little conversation now, when too much black coffee was giving her an enormous high that she hadn't anticipated. Better than the joints they had tried in their youth, better than sex. Well, almost. But combined with the copious amounts of Chardonnay she had consumed that evening, she was suddenly wide awake and bursting with an energy that had been missing for days.

She knew she wouldn't sleep for hours, and she didn't intend to try. Lying wide awake in the darkness brought back too many memories, sometimes more than she could cope with.

Right now she was feeling strong enough to take on the world, and she didn't want to lose the feeling. So she should do something. Make use of the energy until she was too tired to see straight, then with any luck, she would eventually fall into bed and have the first dreamless night's sleep since Robert's death.

She would tackle his desk. Go to his study and open the door, instead of hesitating with her hand on the door handle as she had done a score of times already, unable to take that first step inside. *Be bold, woman,* she told herself. *Go where no man has gone before* . . . unexpectedly, she found herself giggling as the stupid phrase entered her mind.

She strode through the house to Robert's study and turned the handle, walking inside and taking a deep breath as she did so. Then she coughed, remembering instantly that she had forbidden anyone to come in here, not even Mrs Ashley, her twice-weekly cleaning lady.

Consequently, there was a fine film of dust over everything, and the room was stale, still reeking of Robert's cigar butts in the ashtrays, and the stifling aura of a room that had long been closed up and unused. As dead as its previous occupant.

Without warning, Margaret found herself staggering backwards out of the study, almost gasping for air. She pulled the study door shut behind her, staring at it fixedly, as if she expected the handle to turn at any moment and for the spectre of her husband's ghost to come storming out of the room, furious with her for entering his holy of holies.

If ghosts were capable of storming out of anywhere . . . . The crazy thought was in her head before she could stop it.

But then, enveloped in a panic too wild to comprehend at that moment, she turned and ran up the stairs, leaving lights on all over the house and not caring, until she reached the sanctuary of her bedroom, rushing inside it and slamming the door shut behind her. Shutting out the ghouls of the night.

Her breathing was so fast and erratic it was a physical pain in her chest, and she leaned against the door with her eyes closed for endless moments until it calmed down again.

'You bloody stupid fool,' she told herself savagely, when she could speak at all. 'What the hell is wrong with you?'

She saw the reflection of her wide, frightened eyes in her long mirror, and saw the echo of the small girl who had once been terrified of the dark. The child who was supposed to be a responsible woman now. Wife, mother . . . widow.

And through all the mixture of emotions running through her brain was a bitter awareness that this was what death did to you. Nobody told you this bit beforehand. It was something you had to find out for yourself, this knowledge that death changed you from being a loving partner into someone afraid of your own husband, of being touched by the supernatural.

Those who sought signs from the Great Beyond could have them, Margaret thought savagely. She didn't want them. Robert had been pragmatic about such things. He always said that when you were dead, you were dead, and that was the end of it. All the love in the world could never bring him back to her, and she knew it.

She also knew now, that this had been the worst possible time after all, to think of sorting through any of his things. It wasn't time yet, and she wasn't ready.

She didn't even undress. What did it matter if her outfit got rumpled and creased? Who the hell did she have to impress, anyway? Her head was starting to throb, and she would probably have a hangover of gigantic proportions tomorrow.

But all she wanted to do now was to dive beneath the duvet, bury her head and stay there until daylight. It wasn't the coward's way of dealing with things, she told herself in her last conscious thought. It was the only way.

★   ★   ★

She awoke to the sound of something loud and shrill and horribly intrusive. Her hand reached out to grab it and stop it, and was shaking so much that the telephone receiver fell to the floor. She groaned as she heard the voice calling her name, and knew that if she didn't pick it up and answer it, someone would be round here as quick as blinking.

'Hello,' she said huskily, her mouth feeling full of furry animals, and tasting just as bad.

'Are you all right, Mum?' she heard. 'You sound weird.'

Of course I'm not all right. I've just lost my husband, haven't I? And not at the supermarket, either.

40

She gathered up her senses with a huge effort, considering the state of her head and the rag-bag she was wearing that had once been a gorgeous shot blue silk dress.

'I'm fine, Keith. Just having a lie-in. That's allowed, isn't it?' she tried to be jocular and failed miserably.

'Not for you, it isn't. Well, of course, it's allowed, but it's not normal.'

'Well, nothing's normal any more, is it, darling?' she said, an edge to her voice now as the appalling throbbing in her head took hold.

'No. Of course not. Listen, Laura and I wanted to ask you over for dinner this evening. Will you come?'

'It's very sweet of you both — '

'No, it's not. We want to see you and we don't think you should shut yourself away. You and Dad always had a such a busy social life.'

She sensed that he had to force himself to say the words, and she loved him for it.

'Actually, I went out last night. With Sarah and the girls, which is why I'm feeling so fragile this morning.'

She felt weak tears fill her eyes, knowing how her family always laughed when she referred to her friends as the girls, and calling them more like the Golden Girls. Damn cheek, when they were all in their early forties, and not ready to be put out to grass yet, thanks very much

'So you got pissed, did you?'

'I wouldn't put it quite like that.' She heard herself give a feeble laugh. 'Well, yes, I suppose I would. Shocking, isn't it?'

Keith laughed back, clearly relieved that she wasn't doing anything stupid. He didn't call getting pissed stupid, as long as she wasn't driving.

'Nobody could ever call you shocking, Mum. So what about dinner tonight? Laura's dying to try out a new Thai recipe on you. That's OK, isn't it?' he added anxiously.

She could read him so well. Last year's major holiday for her and Robert had been to Thailand, and she had fallen in love with the food and the country and the culture. Laura would have thought up this meal specially, and she wouldn't be so hard-hearted as to put her down.

'That will be wonderful,' she said mechanically.

'Good. Shall I pick you up around seven o'clock?'

'No, I'll drive. Then I'll be sure to stay sober, since I know you won't let me drive home under the influence, and don't offer me a bed, either. I'm not into a *menage à trois*.'

'That's good. Neither are we.'

Margaret was still smiling as she put the phone down with a clatter, but the conversation had shattered her, and she fell back on the pillows and was instantly asleep again.

3

Laura was a sweet girl who had gone to a lot of trouble. She was a local supermarket supervisor, and had access to all the latest deli and organic foods, which she presumably tried out on Keith. That was as far as the expertise went. In no way could she be called an expert cook, but if the meal wasn't exactly as Margaret remembered, and was rather too exotically spiced, she knew better than to say so.

'I really enjoyed that,' she said finally, dabbing the sides of her mouth with the paper serviette.

Laura twisted her face into a smile. 'Well, I know it wasn't exactly *gordon blue* as my dad used to call it, but we like it that way, don't we, Keith?'

And that effectively shut her out, Margaret thought. She doubted if it was meant that way, but Laura's casual words had the effect of making them a complete unit, an entity, while she was the outsider, the single dinner guest. If the two of them had been here, herself and Robert, the atmosphere would be different. They would have been a chatty foursome, instead of an awkward threesome, with one of them still finding her feet, according to Sarah. As if she'd actually lost them, together with her husband, somewhere along the way.

'More wine, Mum?' Keith said, looking at her anxiously, as her face suddenly became more pinched.

'Better not. I'm driving, remember?'

'You can always leave your car here, and I'll drive you home, Margaret,' Laura put in, helpful as ever.

She only drank non-alcoholic diet drinks. It wasn't particularly noble, she was always at pains to say; she just didn't like the taste of alcohol. It still made the rest of them feel they should be rushing off to AA to get dried out, Margaret thought irritably, not at all sure why she should feel irritable at all, but knowing that she did.

It was something to do with the cosiness of this flat, the complacency of a couple who weren't a proper couple at all, not the way she and Robert had been. Falling in love, getting engaged, then married, then children. The proper order of things. She knew she was being small-minded, and that her divorced friends thought quite differently, and told her she was living in a time-warp. But then, the sexual revolution hadn't touched her. Hadn't needed to, because she had Robert.

'Have you heard from Jenny lately?' she heard Keith say.

Before she could answer, Laura put in her two-pennyworth.

'We thought it so thoughtless of her, going off to London like that. It must have hurt your feelings, Margaret.'

And who the hell do you think you are, to call my daughter thoughtless?

'She has to deal with things in her own way,' Margaret said evenly, her liking for Laura taking a severe about-turn.

'She always did. You were always too lenient with her, Mum. Dad too,' Keith added, siding with Laura.

'I don't know how you can say that! She and your father were more often at one another's throats!'

'She still got whatever she wanted, though, didn't she? More than Ben or I ever did.'

'It's because she's a girl,' Laura said sweetly, as the tension grew. 'Girls always know how to twist men around their little fingers. Especially fathers and daughters.'

Keith laughed, pressing his hand on her shoulder as he poured himself another glass of wine, and instead of feeling glad that his girlfriend could diffuse a situation so diplomatically, Margaret felt more and more annoyed.

God, what was wrong with her? Had she become so insular that now that she was alone, she couldn't bear to watch another couple's happiness? Even her own son's?

'So when's she coming home from Gran's?' he asked next.

'I'm not sure. There was some talk of her staying on and getting a job. She wants to get into journalism.'

The wine bottle banged down on the table. 'Good God, how selfish can she get? You need her at home, Mum — '

'I certainly do not need her at home,' she said shortly. 'You make it sound as if I need a nursemaid to look after me! I applaud her independence, if you must know. She's got more go in her at nineteen than I ever did.'

'But I think you were married at eighteen, weren't you, Margaret? You already had everything you wanted. Jenny's still searching.' Laura looked at Keith, wanting his approval. 'You can't blame her for that, can you?'

Margaret glanced at her watch, unable to take any more of this reasonableness. 'Goodness, I didn't realize it was so late. I must go. I know Keith has an early shift tomorrow.'

She was waffling now, and she didn't care if they knew it. She was just aching to get out of there and be on her own. It was strange, but ever since Robert had died and she had been surrounded by people and the overload of love she had expected, she sometimes longed desperately for solitude and to appreciate the pleasure of silence. It came as a bit of a shock to know it, when she missed the sound of Robert's voice so much. But it was still there in her head, which could account for the reason she didn't miss it half as much as she had expected. He hadn't entirely gone from her, no matter what others might think. And it was in those silent moments with nobody else around, that she could feel him most. If she said as much to anyone, of course, they would think her quite mad, so it was a secret she kept to herself.

'If you really must go, then,' Keith said at last.

'Yes, but thank you both for a lovely evening, and you must both come to dinner with me. When your calendar is free. I know how busy you both are.'

And please leave it vague, she found herself thinking. Too many people tried to pin her down to times and dates, as if she needed to fill her days and moments with things to do.

But she didn't. What she needed was to

re-evaluate her life, giving herself time and space to get used to the new way of things. There were decisions to be mulled over and left until she was ready to deal with them, not pressured into them by well-meaning relatives and friends. She wouldn't be pushed.

The latest thing the girls had hinted at was whether she had thought about selling the house and buying a smaller place. But why should she, when she had the money and means to keep it on? In any case, it was far more than just a house: it was a family home that she and Robert had built up together. It was filled with memories, and there were people to help her keep it as lovely and gracious as ever. There was Mrs Ashley-wot-did, as they had always called her, and dear old Joe the gardener, and the pool man, and the cheerful gang of window cleaners who always had a joke with her.

She let herself into her house and breathed in its welcome. She no longer felt the urge to cry every time she stepped inside the front door. Robert wouldn't have wanted that. It was quiet, though.

Maybe she should get a dog. Something to welcome her with noise and joy and to leap and slobber all over her with unquestioning affection. The children had had a dog when they were young, and they had adored him, and been devastated when he'd had to be put down.

So no. No dogs. No more anticipated sorrow as the pay-off for a few years of company. She felt suddenly restless, and far from tired yet. By now the Thai meal was lying heavily and uncomfortably in her stomach, the spices too much for her constitution. She needed to be active.

She kicked off her shoes, dropped her bag in the hall and wandered up to her bedroom to change out of the smart blue dress she had worn for the evening. Robert always liked her in blue. He said it brought out the colour of her eyes, and she had a wardrobe full of varying shades, from powder blue, through sky to delicate turquoise to deepest royal.

Not navy though. Navy always made her feel insipid. Odd, when she always felt good in a simple black dress dressed up with pearls and high heels. Sophisticated and cool.

And if that dated her, to hell with it. She felt belligerent, and put it all down to Laura, but at least a sense of anger was better than wallowing in misery.

Dressed in a track suit now (defiantly maroon), since she had no intention of going to bed yet, she went down to the sitting-room to find the answering machine flashing. She gave a small sigh. It would be her mother, enquiring after her. Or even Brenda, long back from New York and full of the new man she had met there, and unable to resist giving her as much raunchy detail as she felt right in the circumstances.

Or it might be Jenny, cautious at first, testing the water as to her response before she launched into her doings, and her possible plans for the future, providing her mother didn't object, and *providing* she got the job of her dreams, and *providing* she really, really didn't mind her staying in London with Granny Annie for the foreseeable future . . .

There were two messages on the machine. One was her mother, hoping she was well and coping. And if she wanted anything at all, she was to call her at once.

'*Anything*, darling,' the voice emphasized. 'You know we're always here for you.'

Why did people always say that, when they weren't anywhere near her? Oh, and her father was having chiropractic treatment on his back and he'd found this marvellous man who could work wonders — oh, and she wasn't to worry about Jenny.

Margaret felt breathless by the time her mother's message ended. For someone who'd always been suspicious of answering machines, she seemed to have gone quite the other way.

One of these days the tape would run out and her mother would still be rabbiting on unaware of it, Margaret thought.

The second message was from Ben.

'Hi, Mum. How are you? Sorry I haven't been in touch lately. I've been hellishly busy. Thought about you a lot though. Can I come down next weekend? And if it's not too much of an imposition, I'd like to bring a friend with me.'

Margaret perked up, not sure about visits from strangers, but glad that Ben had found a girlfriend. He was so bloody good-looking, she was sure he could get any girl he wanted.

'Carl's a great guy, Mum. He's dead interested in Dad's vintage car, and I'm pretty sure he'll make you an offer for it. I don't suppose you want to hang on to it, do you? Anyway, give me a call when you get in. It doesn't matter how late it is. Love you.'

When the message ended, Margaret was still staring at the machine long after she had pressed the button to send the tape back to the beginning.

Don't jump to conclusions, she told herself. Just because your head had been instantly filled with the thought of Ben having a girlfriend, didn't mean that friendship with another man meant he was gay.

There was no reason on earth to think it. If

some of her friends thought it questionable that John Franklin had never married at fifty-ish, for instance, she knew differently. Or thought she did. You never knew the heart and soul of anyone unless you were married to them. And not even then. Not *everything*. For no reason at all it was a thought that made her feel sad.

But she had never had any secrets from Robert. She'd had no reason to be secretive. Her life was an open book. A boring, predictable, open book . . . but one in which she had always been happy and fulfilled.

She dialled Ben's mobile before her thoughts went off into realms of fantasy she couldn't comprehend and didn't want to.

'Mum! You got my message then. How are you? I feel so guilty for not coming down before — '

'Don't be. I'm fine. I've been to dinner with Keith and Laura this evening.' She elevated it into a social event.

'My God, what weird concoctions did she try out on you?'

'Actually, it wasn't bad,' she lied. 'Thai food.'

'Oh, great. I think. So what about next weekend? We're both free then. And I know you'll like him.'

'Will I? Well, I'm sure I will, if he's a friend

of yours,' she amended quickly, not having realized before how much of Ben's conversation was peppered with the word 'great'. So much for university education.

And of course, she couldn't ask. Couldn't say: 'What are the sleeping arrangements supposed to be?' And can I condone them? She'd never had to deal with anything like this before. She wasn't sure she could now. It wasn't her style. She was too damn conventional, that was her trouble. But so what? There was no law that said you had to change the ethics of a lifetime to suit someone else.

'He's really keen to see the Frazer-Nash, Mum. Would you be willing to sell? For the proper price, of course.'

'I haven't thought about it. I suppose so. It's no good to me, is it? I've no idea of the value, though.'

'Oh, Carl will know all about that. He's a bona-fide dealer, specializes in vintage cars and motor bikes. Really high-class stuff. Not one of your Arfur Daley types.'

'Good.' She didn't know what else to say. 'I'll see you next weekend then. Friday evening?'

'Great. It'll probably be about nine by the time we get there. And don't worry about food. We'll eat on the way down.'

She hung up slowly. Now that she'd agreed she felt a mild panic. It wasn't exactly big-scale entertaining — she and Robert had done plenty of that in the past, and thoroughly enjoyed it — but it was the thought of having a stranger in the house when she still felt so vulnerable.

'Pull yourself together, idiot,' she found herself saying severely. 'And pour yourself another glass of the wine you didn't have at Keith's place.'

She did as she was told, and took it out on to the terrace overlooking the swimming-pool and the sea. It was a lovely, balmy spring evening, and they had spent so many evenings like this, breathing in the scents of foliage and flowers of the changing seasons, drinking wine, discussing the day's events, the family, the future holiday plans . . .

She caught her breath between her teeth. Among the mass of cards and condolence letters that had arrived in a steady stream, and were only now easing up, there had been various brochures, both business and pleasure, and a whole lot of junk mail that went straight into the bin.

She hadn't discarded everything, but nor had she bothered to open half of it. None of it was important. But the logo on one of the envelopes was suddenly, glaringly in her mind's eye. It was addressed to Mr and Mrs Jarvis, and it came from the hotel in Guernsey where they had spent their honeymoon.

With painful clarity now, she remembered Robert's suggestion that they should go back there for their Silver Wedding anniversary. They had travelled all over the world since then, but Guernsey had been a special place, a magical place, and they had never gone back.

He must have sent off for the current brochure and not told her. It was to have been a surprise. It was just like him. And it would have been marvellous.

But now everything had changed, and she could never go back to that hotel and relive all the memories of their first tentative love-making, of all the joy and laughter that had followed, and the deep, deep love that had grown from such promising beginnings. The brochure would follow all the others and go into the bin.

A small breeze wafted the night scent of narcissus into her nostrils. The endless sky was a beautiful indigo now, the moon-light silvering the distant sea and casting patterns and shadows over their lawns and gardens.

They were the couple who had had everything, Margaret thought, with a catch in her throat . . . and then told herself not to get maudlin, and to remember that she still had Robert's legacy of love. This beautiful home, all their memories, their children.

And Ben's friend, Carl, was interested in buying the vintage Frazer-Nash Robert had so lovingly restored, taking years over it, since something precious shouldn't be hurried.

She poured herself another glass of wine, and took it with her as she wandered around the grounds that had been theirs, and were still hers, drinking in the sweet memories along with the wine, and no longer finding them quite so painful. Finding a strange sort of comfort instead.

'It's early days yet,' wise friends told her. 'It's bound to take time, Margaret.'

And she had wanted to hit out at such banality. But it was true, she thought, reluctantly and sometimes resentfully. With every day that passed, there was a touch more minuscule acceptance that this was the way things had to be from now on. And she was going to be strong, and show these dear and well-meaning friends and family, that she could cope.

She had reached the line of garages. She had put her own car inside when she came home, but the one with Robert's cars was locked, as was the final one housing the 1934

Frazer-Nash. There was a key on a high shelf above the door. She reached for it without thinking, and turned the lock, pushing the up-and-over door open. The car stood gleaming in all its British racing-green glory.

'A triumph of engineering,' Robert had said, as proudly as if he had built the very engine himself.

And so he had, or restored it, anyway. Bringing it back to its pristine magnificence as lovingly as if he brought a woman to climax. At the thought, Margaret drew in her breath, running her hands along the sleek length of the car's wing and closing her eyes as the memories rushed back at her of all the hours he had spent here with his beloved Frazer-Nash.

Her rival, she had called it smilingly. It had been his hobby. The hobby of a rich man, who hadn't needed to do this, but had found pleasure in using his hands and his time in creating something beautiful out of a virtual wreck.

Without warning, she was weeping again, and her clever-clever vow to be strong was slipping away from her so fast she felt her legs dissolve and she was leaning over the car, banging her fists against it, and hating it for every moment it had taken Robert away from her, because she had never known how few of them she had left.

She turned abruptly and slammed down the garage door again. Whoever this Carl person was, he could have the car, she thought viciously. She never wanted to see it again. She went back to the house and dialled Ben's number again.

'Mum?' he said, surprised to hear her voice again. 'Not changed your mind about the weekend, have you? Only Carl's already cleared it with his wife and kids. Mind you, he's had to promise to take them to Florida to make up for it.'

He paused, aware of a peculiar sound coming from the other end. Margaret was surprised to hear it too, and even more surprised that it was coming from herself.

'Have I said something funny, Mum?'

Margaret smothered the almost hysterical relief she felt. Her son wasn't gay! It was the only inconsequential thought running around her head right now.

'No, darling. Just a silly thought, that's all. I just wanted to say that I've thought about the Frazer-Nash, and if your friend makes me a reasonable offer for it, I'm happy to see it go to a good home. Can he do that, with a family to support?'

And oh, the joy of saying it! She hadn't even been aware of her prejudice until it was slap bang in front of her.

Ben laughed. 'He's very well-heeled, actually. Old money and all that crap. I'll let him know tomorrow.'

Not tonight. Not under the duvet, celebrating by doing whatever it was those people did. *God*, she must stop this. It must be the effects of the wine on top of Laura's diabolical Thai dinner, which by now was roaring like thunder in her stomach and quickly ending her charitable defence of it.

'I'll see you both next Friday then, Ben.'

'Great. By the way, you'd better let Carl have my old room and I'll bunk in Jenny's. I wouldn't want him to be blasted into space by her horrendous posters and junk.'

She could hear the grin in his voice, and wondered if he knew, or guessed, at the way her thoughts had been going.

And in the end, it had all been so simple, she realized, somewhat shame-faced. She'd only had to ask.

★   ★   ★

The girls had now decided to take her out of herself one night a week on a regular basis, whether she wanted to go or not. And she discovered that she did, after the first few awkward times when they had met aquaintances of hers and Robert's, who clearly didn't know what to say to her.

'Tell them you've decided to be the merry widow,' Sarah advised again. 'They'll be thinking it anyway.'

'That's what I'm afraid of,' Margaret said. 'I've got my image to keep up, but I have a feeling that the longer I'm with you lot, it's going straight down the pan.'

'Like Laura's Thai dinner,' Fiona said snidely, having heard all about it by now.

'She means well,' Margaret said mechanically, as usual.

'Do you have to be so bloody tolerant of everybody, Mags?' Sarah said, who certainly wasn't.

They had all ended up back at Margaret's house by now, and since June was the designated driver for the night, the others were getting pretty well plastered. Well pissed, in Sarah's words.

'I like Laura — I think. Well, I do. Not sure about her cooking though, and Keith must have the stomach of an ox to cope with it. Oh, and I forgot to tell you, Ben's coming home for the weekend and bringing a friend with him who's probably going to buy Robert's vintage car.'

She said it fast, as she said everything of particular significance now, getting the words into the open without trembling. Jumping another hurdle.

'Good for you,' June said. 'You might as well sell the others too, unless the kids want them.'

'I haven't asked them, and they haven't mentioned it.'

'Still pussy-footing around you, are they?' Fiona said. 'If I were you, I'd just put the cars up for sale and be done with it. Take the money and run.'

'She doesn't need the money,' Sarah put in.

'*Excuse* me!' Margaret said. 'I *am* here, you know. Don't talk around me as if I'm part of the furniture.'

They laughed, and she laughed with them, finding it a healing, healthy sound. They were good, supportive friends, and she had plenty of them. John Franklin was coming home from France next week and had called while she was out, leaving a message on her machine that he couldn't wait to see her, and that he was sorry to have been away so long.

'Anyway,' she went on with a giggle, 'when Ben said he was bringing this friend home, this *Carl*, I had a horrible thought that he was going to tell me he was gay. It totally threw me for a minute. I *know* — pathetic, isn't it? It turned out OK, but I didn't know what to do about the sleeping arrangements, and I wouldn't have known how to handle it.'

'Presumably Carl would have, though,' Fiona said, with a strangled laugh. 'Known how to handle it, I mean.'

Sarah hooted. 'Oh, stop it, you tart, or I shall pee myself. I have to go, anyway.' She rushed off, glancing back at Margaret just before she left the room, hopping from one foot to the other, as idiotic as a schoolgirl.

'Anyway, what if he was a gender-bender? This Carl — or your Ben, for that matter. He'd still be your son, wouldn't he? He wouldn't have grown horns and a tail overnight — '

At which all four of them convulsed, and Sarah was holding herself in the most excruciating way as she fled out of the sitting-room to the downstairs loo.

4

John Franklin was fair-haired, rangy and quietly earnest. He was what older people would call one of nature's gentlemen. It had always amazed and slightly bemused Robert that he had become such an incredibly successful salesman, progressing to sales manager, then director and virtual pivot of his company.

'Why shouldn't he be a good salesman?' Margaret had always argued, defending him. 'Why should it always be the hard sell that does the business? It's sincerity that does it every time, and John has plenty of that, hasn't he?'

'All right, I give in,' Robert had said, laughing, and holding up his hands in mock surrender. 'John's a whizz kid of the spectacularly understated kind, but it certainly gets results, and that's what counts in business these days.'

She had laughed back, always enjoying their mini-arguments. And knowing that despite Robert's powerful personality, he indulged her — especially when he knew that she was right. He was undoubtedly the stronger partner, and she had always been happy to keep it that way, but he never dominated, never made her feel in any way *the little woman*.

She winced now, wondering why these thoughts should enter her mind. But she knew why, of course. It was John's phone call when he finally reached her after the answer-machine message. There had been previous calls to check up on her, as he called it, and postcards from whichever city he was in. But hearing his voice again now, she found herself remembering the discussions she'd had with Robert about him over the years.

Such as: 'We really should find someone nice for John. Go out in a foursome or something. It's such a waste, Robert. He should be married, with children. He'd make a great father. Look how he's always been with ours!'

Or, complacent with her own happiness: 'Do you think John's lonely? He's not — you don't think — '

At which Robert would roar with laughter.

'If you're about to ask in your delicate way if he's a shirt-lifter, forget it, darling. John's as normal as the next man, whatever normal is. He's just a workaholic, same as me.'

'That didn't stop you getting married, did it?'

His arms had gone around her, holding her tight, his voice dropping to a sexy whisper.

'That's because I found you, sweetheart. I was the lucky one. So why don't we just forget John and his non-existent problems and concentrate on us instead?'

★   ★   ★

Margaret shivered now. Was it like this for everyone? she wondered. Did everyone who'd been bereaved have these remembered snippets of conversation bursting into their consciousness when they least expected them? So real that they could remember every detail, every nuance?

Some clever psychologist could probably tell her if it was so, and why. Why *particular* snippets of conversation? She pushed the interesting, if somewhat disturbing thought aside, and remembered John's phone call instead.

'I really do feel guilty for not being in touch lately, Margaret,' his soft voice had said.

His gentle, caring voice. The best friend to them both, over so many years.

'Listen, John, I don't expect you, or anyone else, to keep mollycoddling me,' she had protested. 'I have to get on with my life, don't I?'

'And I admire you for that. I really do. I expected — '

'What? That I would go to pieces? Drown myself in the swimming-pool or throw myself off Bournemouth Pier?'

She was being melodramatic now, and she knew it. But she felt a stab of irritation that it was the way everyone had seen her, had expected her to be.

It filled her with a defiance she hadn't known she had before. She was damn well going to show them. Not that it meant she loved Robert any less. Sometimes she loved him more. And no one knew about the nights when she cried into her pillow until she found herself wondering how anyone had so many tears inside them, until there was nothing left but the exhaustion that only sleep could ease.

'I never thought that of you, Margaret,' John was saying now. 'I always knew you had plenty of mettle, if only Robert would allow it to show through.'

In the small silence while she digested those words, she could hear him breathing. He had always been a little nasal, asthmatic, she supposed, and it was very evident now.

'Hell, that didn't come out the way I meant it at all,' he went on, angry at himself. 'But you must admit that Robert did rather smother you with love. So I wondered — we all did — just how you were going to cope without him.'

'Actually, I'm managing very well. I go out with my girlfriends once a week, and this weekend Ben's bringing a friend down to look at the Frazer-Nash. I'm selling it, of course.'

'Are you? It was always Robert's pride and joy.'

'But not mine, John,' she said, hearing his distress at her crispness and feeling oddly as though he was the one who needed reassuring, not her. 'It's just going to deteroriate if it stays in the garage, isn't it?'

Like me, if I don't move on. Like anyone left alone.

'Well, I suppose you know best, my love. Anyway, I'll be back home soon and thankful to shake off the dust of travelling for a while. I'll come and see you then.'

'I'll look forward to it. Goodbye, John. Take care.'

Take care. And mind you don't have a heart attack in a lonely hotel room with no one beside you to call the ambulance and rush you off to hospital, even if it's too late.

She blotted out the thought and put down the phone, unusually rattled at the phone call. John was their dearest friend, but for once she hadn't been able to warm to him. Perhaps it

68

was because of her family's silly, half-formed insinuations that he wanted to get his feet under her table, when what they really meant was his body in her bed.

She shuddered. However fond she was of John, she could never in her wildest dreams imagine him as a lover. Never had, and never would, so they could all put that in their bloody peace pipes and smoke it.

The childish thought got her smiling again, and she found herself humming as she went upstairs to prepare the bedrooms for Ben and Carl's visit. Actually *humming*, the way she used to when any of the children were coming home to visit. As if she hadn't a care in the world.

She felt the familiar sense of guilt, as if she shouldn't hum. Shouldn't be happy, or smile, or laugh, ever again. And that was totally ridiculous. She had a right to her life, not to be so tied — so *encumbered* — by all she had been to Robert that she couldn't ever be herself again.

'You wouldn't want it, would you, darling?' she said, raising her eyes heavenward. 'If you were here, you'd tell me to go on being me, and not to turn myself into some dowdy gloom merchant.'

She could almost hear him respond heartily that he most definitely wouldn't want that, and she was oddly comforted. And tomorrow, she thought determinedly, she was going to ask Mrs Ashley-wot-did, to take a duster and cleaner to Robert's study and give it a good airing.

And then, when Ben and Carl had gone back to London, she would tackle it herself. It was about time.

Keith had been quite cross with her at hearing she hadn't done any of it yet. It was two months now, and surely there would be things in his father's study that needed to be dealt with. And what about paying the general household bills, in case there was anything outstanding . . .

He had been as tactful as he could, considering his intolerance of inefficiency, but clearly thought this the ultimate in it, and that his mother was a complete airhead if she hadn't begun the task, with or without his help.

'Keith, the bank takes care of all that,' she had told him firmly. 'They always have. Your father arranged direct debits for everything long ago, and the bank simply transfers funds from one account to the other when the bills come in. I daresay there are statements in his study,' she added vaguely, perfectly aware that she should have gone through it all long ago, 'but since I know very well there's plenty of money to cover everything, you really mustn't worry about me, darling.'

'It seems a pretty weird arrangement to me,' he said.

'It's worked very well for twenty-four years, so just leave it, please. Mr Carstairs assures me I don't need to worry over any of it.'

Margaret knew it was so different from the way other people had to manage when they were widowed or divorced, like her girl-friends. And she sometimes felt unnecessarily guilty on their behalf, because she still had so much. She hadn't been left high and dry with nothing. She could do anything she wanted, go anywhere she wanted.

The only thing was, she didn't want to do anything without Robert. But after this weekend, she would definitely tackle that study.

★   ★   ★

Margaret discovered that Carl Tobyn-Black was a delightful man in his mid-thirties who came from a moneyed, practically aristocratic background and was now a very successful entrepreneur.

He was also very much a family man, enthusiastically showing Margaret photographs of his wife and young sons, and of

71

their plans to go to Florida in a few weeks' time.

Ben had swept into the house as noisily as Jenny ever did, aware of a small feeling of embarrassment at having stayed away too long. He dumped his bags and hugged his mother tightly without saying anything, before looking into her face with a sense of relief in his eyes.

'You look better, Mum. I'm glad. I've been worried.'

'Well, now you see there was no need, and I'll be *extremely* glad when everyone stops worrying about me,' she said. 'So how was the trip down?'

'Great. Carl's Range Rover goes like a bomb. And he's itching to see the Frazer-Nash.'

'Well, get your breaths back first, for goodness' sake!' she said with a laugh. 'Wouldn't you like some tea, or coffee, or to put your stuff upstairs?'

'I think a cold beer would be favourite now,' Ben said. 'Right, Carl?'

'Sounds good to me,' he said. 'But Ben's right, Mrs Jarvis. I am itching to see the car. I couldn't believe it when Ben told me his father had restored a 1934 version. And by the way, I really am most awfully sorry for the reason you're thinking of selling it.'

'Thank you,' she said, as she had done a thousand times in answer to similar words.

'So how about that cold beer then, Mum, then we'll go out to the garage,' Ben said easily, taking charge just as Robert would have done. It shook her to sense the similarity in attitude. London had changed him. He was far more assertive now that he was out from under Keith's shadow — and his father's.

She hadn't considered it before, but it was true. Keith was the older brother, the one the others were bound to follow, simply because of the sibling order of things. Jenny had always done her own thing, anyway, but Ben was the in-between, never quite finding himself, until now. She gave them their beer, then put the kettle on, watching them walk out to the garage. Carl had his arm loosely around Ben's shoulders in a friendly manner, and she scoffed at herself for thinking she might have once thought it questionable. He was almost old enough to be Ben's father, anyway.

Not that *that* made any difference if things were what she had falsely supposed. But she was still fervently glad that they were not. Conventional she might be, and conventional she was bloody well going to stay!

She laid up the dining-table with a choice

of tea or coffee, a plate of home-made fruit cake, cheese and biscuits. They may have eaten at some wretched motorway service station or wherever, but if she knew Ben, he'd still be ready for a snack, no matter what the hour. And it wasn't late yet. Barely nine o'clock. They had made very good time from London.

Half an hour later they came back to the house. Carl's eyes were full of enthusiasm, lighting up in a way that reminded her of Robert's, every time he came in from the garage after doing yet another small adjustment to the engine or rubbing down another piece of the bodywork. The distinctive whiff of engine oil was the same, the need to scrub the hands at the utility-room sink with the gunk they used to rid themselves of the smell was the same, and it was at once dear and familiar and poignant to her.

She forced a bright smile when the two of them came into the sitting-room and sprawled out in the armchairs while she poured them their coffee. Tea for her. And as she had expected, cake *and* cheese and biscuits for them both.

'So what do you think?' she asked Carl.

'I think your husband must have been an exceptional man, Mrs Jarvis,' he told her. 'A lot of love went into restoring that car, as well as knowledge and expertise. I'm full of admiration, and if you're willing to sell, look no further.'

'Told you so, Mum,' Ben said, clearly pleased at this reaction. 'So what do *you* think, about selling, I mean?'

Piece by piece, she knew she had to let Robert go. John had reminded her that the Frazer-Nash had been his pride and joy, but in the end, it was just a car, even though she guessed it would be sacrilege to say as much to this nice man.

It was just a car, she repeated deliberately to herself. It was no use to her.

'I'm more than willing to let it go to a good home, and I suspect that Carl would love it as much as your father did. Am I right?' she asked him.

'Absolutely, Mrs Jarvis. My plan is to give it pride of place in my top showroom, with a plaque alongside saying who had restored it, if you approve. Then later, I'd like to move it to my small collection. It's nothing like Montague's Beaulieu place, of course, but interesting enough, I think.'

'It sounds wonderful,' Margaret said, impressed.

They talked long into the night, and she had forgotten what good company Ben could be once he became animated.

She realized again how much Keith — and Robert — had overshadowed him all his life, but not any more. She didn't have to worry about Ben.

Before the weekend was over, Keith and Laura had called round and approved of the plan, and she had felt calm enough to ask Keith to arrange the sale of Robert's other cars — and his boat, since none of them wanted it. Clearing out no longer felt like a betrayal. It made sense. Cleansing, almost. It gave her strength to start again. And it was a beginning.

It was also something of a pleasant surprise to see how well her two sons were getting along now. There had always been a natural sibling rivalry between them, subtly encouraged by Robert, with Keith being more extrovert like himself, and Ben feeling very much the second son.

But since Robert's death, she discovered how often they had colluded over her well-being, keeping in touch, being more together in one sense than she had ever known them before. It was strange. Robert's powerful personality had emphasized the differences between them during his lifetime, and now that he was gone, their mutual concern over her was the unintentional means of bringing them together.

That, and London, as far as Ben was concerned, Margaret conceded, hoping fervently that London would do as good a job on Jenny. She really must call that scatty little madam soon, she thought, and before he left, she asked Ben if he had seen anything of her.

'Went round to Gran's for Sunday lunch last week,' he reported. 'Jenny's OK, Mum, and going after a job on some fashion magazine, I gather.'

'Well, nice of her to let me know!' Margaret said.

'I think she was waiting to spring the surprise on you when she actually got taken on,' Ben said. 'It's quite a good little number, actually.'

'And your Gran approves, does she?'

'Oh yes. Gramps too.'

Well, her mother would approve, she thought, after they had gone, with the arrangements all in hand to collect the Frazer-Nash on a trailer the following weekend.

Her mother and her daughter were two of a kind, Margaret had long realized, with a burst of senseless jealousy. Latent hippies, both of them, and Annie Vernon would probably have agreed to go bungee-jumping if Jenny had suggested it.

Still, there always had to be one conservative in any family. Her sister Brenda thought nothing of hopping on a plane at a moment's notice for New York or wherever the job took her. It was only Margaret who was dull, dull, dull . . .

Her eyes sparkled suddenly, remembering the moment when she had caught a certain look in Carl Tobyn-Black's eyes. It was more than a friendly exchange of glances between new acquaintances. It was the look of a man who recognizes a beautiful woman. And although it had been gone in an instant, and was merely a frisson of awareness, it had existed, taken shape and form, and Margaret had felt a distinct pleasure because of it.

The feeling of warmth in her soul had had nothing to do with sexual desire for this man who belonged to someone else, but a warmth that reminded her she was still a living, breathing, desirable woman. And not dull at all.

★   ★   ★

On Monday, she put her new resolution into action. Mrs Ashley-wot-did had done her job well, and the study now smelled of furniture polish and cleanliness, with no hint of cigar butts or staleness, no screwed-up bits of paper in the wastepaper basket, no anything but a room that needed sorting through.

The desk, of course, was loaded down with papers and letters surrounding the computer and printer; Robert's collection of pens; Post-It memos stuck here and there that almost got her going as she saw her name on several of them, reminding him to do this, get that. But she knew she'd have to face that. Just as she knew she'd be facing the favourite family photos Robert kept in his study, most of them holiday snaps, except for their wedding photo, and the stiffly formal graduation photos of the boys.

Jenny, who had opted out of university, called them their stuffed shirt photos, and Margaret smiled at the remembered sniffiness in her voice.

She took a deep breath and sat down at Robert's desk on the swivel chair that had been his father's. Ben had loved swivelling round and round on it when he was little, until Robert had bellowed at him to stop before it took off and spun him right through the window.

Ben had believed him, too, and had slid off the chair in terror as Keith had hooted at him for being a cry baby.

Oh yes, there had been a cruel streak in Keith in those days, Margaret thought, though it was probably no worse than the way most older brothers treated their younger ones. Anyway, he needed to be tough to be a policeman, with all the terrible things they had to deal with these days.

Excusing him, she realized how many times she forgave people. Sarah was always telling her she was too soft in that direction. In Margaret's book it was just making allowances.

The phone rang on Robert's private line, making her jump. She picked it up and said hello. After a momentary pause, a woman's voice spoke.

'Oh, I thought I had reached Robert Jarvis's number.'

Margaret's heart jolted. When you were caught up in bereavement to the extent of blotting out everything else in the world, you found it hard to believe that there were still people who didn't know . . . still had to be told . . .

'You do have the right number. Who is this, please?'

There was another pause. Then the voice became efficient, almost theatrically so. 'I really need to speak to Mr Jarvis. Would you tell him it's Emma?'

Margaret swallowed hard, knowing that it had to be said. There was no future in slamming down the phone just because this woman didn't know. Nor was it her fault that the sudden turmoil in Margaret's stomach was once again reminiscent of Laura's Thai cooking.

'This is Margaret Jarvis. I'm sorry to tell you that my husband died nearly three months ago. If there's anything I can do to help — '

Since she had no idea who the woman was or why she was calling, she knew it was a fatuous remark to make, but she couldn't think of any other.

'Oh, my God,' she heard the unknown Emma say in a kind of strangled voice. 'Oh, I'm so sorry. I didn't know.'

'It's all right, take your time,' Margaret said, not knowing why she should bother to console her, but doing it all the same. Playing Earth Mother again, she thought cynically.

'I've been in Australia on tour you see, and I've been out of touch for months. I'm so sorry. How did it happen? Was it a car accident or something?'

'Heart attack.' Margaret's reply was more mechanical now. She didn't know this woman, and she wasn't prepared to go into personal details with a stranger over the phone.

'Oh God.'

There was silence again, and Margaret was beginning to lose patience. Beginning to find this woman's call an intrusion into the sanctuary of Robert's study, in which she was only just finding her self-control.

'Can I help you in any way?' she said finally.

'No. I'm sorry. Sorry to have bothered you.'

The line went dead, and Margaret replaced the receiver slowly, still mulling over her words. On tour, was she? In Australia. An actress or something? Whoever she was, she'd obviously known Robert well enough to have his private number, and to sound pretty cut up on hearing about his death.

Just as if . . . an awful, unpremeditated suspicion surged into Margaret's mind and flashed out again just as quickly. They both had many friends and acquaintances, and moved in various social circles and clubs. He didn't know all her friends, and she certainly didn't know all of his, and even their mutual Christmas card list was enormous. She didn't know any Emma, but she wasn't going to let it bother her, either.

But after another half-hour she decided that sorting out the mess on the desk was task enough for one day. The drawers and cabinets could wait for another time. Besides which, the smell of pine furniture polish from Mrs Ashley's outrageously vigorous attentions was giving her a headache.

'Excuses, excuses,' Robert used to tease her, when she opted for a swim in the pool in preference to doing anything remotely like housework. In fact, she never needed to do any, because Mrs Ashley was there to do it for her.

But she had always enjoyed ironing, and especially now. She hadn't told anyone how often she washed and ironed Robert's shirts just as if he was still here, so she could still breathe in the lingering scent of him on his clothes.

★   ★   ★

Thursday was girls' night, and because the weather was so good, they were coming to the house for a swim and a meal. Robert would have suggested a barbecue, but Margaret could never see what was so wonderful about smoke getting in your hair, and eating burnt meat outdoors, so she was cooking sweet and sour pork with lichees. But by the time she had spent the afternoon assembling the ingredients, she was wondering why the hell they weren't going to a restaurant instead.

She had to admit, though, that the aromas

of soy sauce and sherry, the tang of apples and peppers, and the sharpness of root ginger and spring onions combined with the succulent pork, were superbly mouth-watering.

'My God, Mags, I could marry you myself,' Sarah said on arrival, positively drooling.

Margaret laughed, no longer feeling a tug at her heart at such a reminder of her new status.

'Sorry, kiddo, it's only the food on offer. You'll have to wait a while yet, anyway, but the pool's up to temperature, so let's swim.'

Early summer wasn't always as warm as this, but the gods had been kind to them this year, and the pool man had agreed to her plea that she wanted the pool *hot*, not lukewarm the way Robert preferred it as he plunged in to water just off cool, making her gasp and keeping herself well above the bikini line until she had gingerly dunked a dozen times.

Keeping it up to ninety degrees would require more regular cleaning and chlorination and filtering, the pool man had told her disapprovingly. It would mean increased maintenance costs, including his attendance fees, but she airily dismissed such details.

'If it needs it, then do it,' she told him.

Whose pool was it, anyway? And if she couldn't have it just right for herself and her friends, she might as well not have it at all.

'Crikey, Mags, this is wonderful,' Fiona said, sinking straight below the deliciously soft water, as caressing to the skin as a warm bath.

'I know,' she said, smiling. 'And this is the way it's going to be from now on.'

'You're so lucky,' June said, sighing enviously. 'When Ted and I were together we couldn't even afford a paddling pool for our kids, and after the divorce it was as much as he could do to take them off on day trips to the beach now and then. Too busy with his new fancy piece to bother about what happened to us.'

'Yes, I'm very lucky,' Margaret said evenly. 'I only had to see my husband drop dead from a heart attack, not go through all the hairy problems of divorce.'

'Oh shit, you know I didn't mean that. I just mean he left you comfortably off. Or rather, rolling in it.'

'*June!*' she heard Sarah say furiously.

Margaret dived into the pool before she had to listen to Sarah giving her a ticking off for her crassness. She came up gasping, her long blonde hair fanning out on the surface of the water, gleaming like gold in the soft floodlighting Robert had had installed in the surrounding area.

'I know you didn't mean it, June, but you don't need to show your envy so much. I didn't ask to be left all this money, any more than I asked for Robert to die on me while we were still enjoying life.'

She spoke coolly, surprised to find that she could, but realizing more and more that people did her favours to force her into being dispassionate about it. As long as it came from friends and family. Strangers were something else.

'That reminds me. Do any of you know a woman called Emma who might have been one of Robert's acquaintances?'

She trod water as she spoke, feeling the softness of the water lift and support her breasts seductively.

Sarah and June were at the far end of the pool now, still arguing, while Fiona swam by slowly, as graceful as a dolphin, her face beneath the water, the long lines and curves of her body perfectly aligned. She came up, treading water and shaking her head like a cocker spaniel, and the illusion of perfection was gone.

'Sorry. What did you say, Mags?'

5

'Someone called Emma phoned, asking for Robert.'

'You mean she didn't know?' Fiona said, appalled. 'That must have been awful for you, Mags.'

'Well, difficult,' she said, nodding. 'It's silly, but somehow you expect everyone to have heard. I mean, it's not as if Robert was Prime Minister or something, is it? I daresay it was just some business acquaintance. Still, as dear Laura took pains to tell me, the more I say it, the more I can accept it. Quite the amateur philosopher is our Laura.'

'I thought you liked her,' Sarah said, floating towards them on her back, having sorted June out.

'I did. I do. She just gets on my tits, that's all.'

She heard herself using one of Sarah's choice phrases and began to laugh, and as she did so she lost concentration to keep afloat and went under water, coming up spluttering, her mouth full of chlorinated water.

Clean inside and out then, she thought.

'I always thought she was too bloody perfect for Keith. He's down to earth like his father,' Sarah went on. 'I bet she handles it with gloves on.'

For no longer than a blink, Margaret couldn't follow her meaning, and then the four of them began to laugh, and the conversation quickly degenerated into lewd fantasies about what Keith and Laura did or didn't get up to.

Margaret dragged her hands over her eyes to dry the laughter tears, and the pool water made them smart even more.

'I'm sure it's not normal for a mother to imagine her son and his girlfriend contorting while doing the business.'

'What's normal, for God's sake?' Sarah grinned.

She hesitated. The four of them had gathered together in a solid unit now, treading water. Close friends. Intimate friends. Knowing each other well. Sharing a past. Supporting each other in whatever came.

'Do you miss it, Mags? Sex, I mean.'

'What kind of a tactless question is that to ask a poor widow woman, you moron?' she said lightly.

'More like Widow Twanky — or are we back to Keith and Laura again now?' Sarah said, at which they all went off into hoots of laughter again.

'Sarah's off on her favourite subject again,' Fiona said. 'But we've all been there, Mags, you know that. You *do* miss it, and if that's not normal, I don't know what is. And you had it longer than the rest of us.'

Margaret wondered if this was an innocent or intentional innuendo, and decided to ignore it. She wouldn't bite.

But Fiona was getting serious now. 'I mean, you were married to Robert for a long time, weren't you? Twenty-four years is something of a miracle these days. Look at the rest of us. Sarah was divorced pretty quickly the first time, and the second was practically a case of premature ejacula-tion — '

'Yes, OK, thanks,' Sarah put in.

'June stuck it out for twelve years until she got shot of that scumbag of a husband, and Steve and I didn't do much better,' Fiona went on relentlessly.

'But you and Robert, Mags, you had such a solid marriage for all those years, and we all know he was a very physical man, so you must miss it. Sex, I mean. It's natural. And that's all I'm saying.'

'A bloody good thing too,' Sarah snapped. 'You had to go on and on about it, didn't you? You've upset her now.'

'No she hasn't,' Margaret said weakly.

'What's got into you anyway, Fee?' Sarah rushed on. 'Are you so horny you're suggesting we get Anne Summers in and have a sex appliances demonstration or something?'

'You can forget that for a start!' Margaret said, but starting to see the funny side of the four of them treading water and arguing over her and Robert's sex life. More or less. And *that* was private. And however close they might be as friends, they weren't going down the lesbian road either, thanks very much. Thank God they were all of the same mind there!

The welcome smell of cooking wafted out through the open patio doors, reminding her that the swimming party was over.

'I'm getting out,' she announced. 'If we want to eat tonight I'd better check on the dinner. You lot can take your time because it'll be a little while yet.'

She left them to it, rising out of the water like Aphrodite and squeezing the water out of her long hair. She should probably have it cut and reshaped. It would be less trouble. And according to all the magazine Agony Aunts, wasn't that what every woman was supposed to do after a relationship ended, for whatever reason? As if a haircut transformed you into a new, blossoming, independent being . . .

Her friends watched her go, envying her figure, her style, her composure, the amazing strength of character they never knew she had.

'She's bloody marvellous,' Sarah muttered. 'And she was always too bloody good for him.'

She turned and swam away in a determined crawl before the others demanded to know what she meant by that. But they could guess. Robert had always been a Jack-the-lad, but it was only ever harmless flirting. As far as they knew. And they all did that. They were the games everybody played.

⋆　⋆　⋆

John Franklin came back from France looking unbelievably tanned and healthy. His shock of fair hair, which hid any strands of grey so successfully, was summer-bleached now, his body lithe and honed from hours spent on Riviera beaches.

'Did you do any work at all?' Margaret asked him, once they had sized one another up warily, and been relieved to find each of them reasonably whole.

'Plenty,' John said easily. 'But you don't get

91

to be lord of all you survey in business, in a manner of speaking, without making the most of the perks as well.'

'The perks being?' Margaret said with a smile.

His sigh was nearer to a gloat.

'Jesus, Margaret, you should just get a load of the way some of those topless girls are stacked — not that you'd want to — but it's a wonder nature holds them up.'

'Unless it's all down to sticky-backed plastic,' they emphasized together.

Then they were both laughing. Suspiciously bright-eyed together, because it was one of the daft things the three of them used to say in unison along with all her kids. *Blue Peter* had a lot to answer for.

'So how goes it?' he said next. 'Are you bearing up OK without too much interference from the rest of them?'

'I'm doing fine,' she answered, knowing that she was. Most of the time, anyway. And what happened in the rest of the time was her business.

'So where are you going to take me to celebrate, now that I'm back?' he said cheekily, the way he'd always done.

It used to be said to both of them, but apparently he saw no reason not to say it to her now. Neither did she. She had to get out sometimes, socialize, be a person again.

'I don't mind. Somewhere with a lot of noise and music. And dancing,' she said recklessly.

She hadn't danced in ages, of course. She and John used to fancy themselves in the quickstep, while Robert sat it out over his cigars and his Southern Comfort, happily chatting up the waitresses and the singles, and indulging his wife and his friend in their twiddly bits as he called it.

Boring, Sarah called it, but Margaret had loved her old college dance lessons, including the sports mistress with the pseudo Miss Jean Brodie accent, who had such a *passion* for teaching all her *gairls* to dance *properly*.

'Dancing it is, then,' John said, clearly relieved that she wasn't wallowing in misery. 'I'll pick you up around seven o'clock, and we'll go to Luigi's, OK?'

She nodded quickly, before either of them could say that they'd prefer somewhere different.

Sometimes it was best to go to favourite places, do the same old things, in order to exorcise the ghosts of the past. Even lovely ghosts had their place, John reflected. He'd had a hell of a time getting used to Robert's death, but he wouldn't burden her with that now.

Sometime, he hoped they could talk about it properly, the way old friends did, but not yet. It was still too painful. He thought of Robert as the brother he'd never had, and for all his business success and vast acquaintance, he didn't have many real friends, and he had always valued Robert and Margaret's friendship above all others.

'*Go* then,' he heard her say with a little laugh, as he seemed to be staring at her without seeing her at all.

She gave him a playful push, and he felt his face redden beneath the deep tan.

'Sorry, I was dreaming. I like your hair like that, by the way. It suits you.'

'Thanks,' Margaret said with a smile.

It had taken more than a bit of courage to have it done, but she'd made up her mind on the spur of the moment and marched into her favourite salon and told the girl who always did her hair to cut it all off.

'*All* of it, Mrs Jarvis? Are you sure? You have such beautiful hair — '

'Cut the flannel, Gloria. And of course I don't mean *all* of it. I just want a new style, a sort of gamine cut, framing my face. The Audrey Hepburn look.'

Gloria, whose hair was a different colour every week, and was now magenta with silver streaks, looked as if she'd never heard of

Audrey Hepburn. But she quickly flipped open the bible of hairstyles they always kept for awkward customers who didn't know what they wanted until they saw it, and Margaret pointed to the right one.

'Oh, now I know. Oh yes, that will look marvellous on you. You always know what will suit you, Mrs Jarvis.'

And you're not going to get any bigger tip than the usual one, no matter how much you smarm me, kid.

But by the time the girl had finished, and she had been shampooed and conditioned, cut, moussed and gelled, blow-dried and sprayed, she had looked in the mirror and seen somebody else looking back at her. It had been a shock, but since everyone now told her it made her look as if she and her daughter could be twins, she was more than getting used to it. She liked what she saw in the mirror each morning.

'*Elfin*, that's what I call it,' Fiona, with a penchant for fancy words, had told her.

'It gives you a swan-like neck, Mags,' June added. 'It suits you. It's really elegant.'

'If you don't stop, I shall start thinking I should have taken up ballet instead of ballroom dancing,' she'd protested with a laugh.

'Not with those feet,' Sarah said, bringing

her down to earth. 'Some poor sap would soon be falling over them in the *pas de deux*. Of course, you could always grab hold of his box to steady yourself,' she'd added, goggling at the image.

★   ★   ★

Yes, Margaret thought, it would be fun to go clubbing again, even though it would be without Robert. He'd never been interested in dancing, saying it took all his breath away, and he didn't have the shape for it, but he liked to watch.

'You're a bloody voyeur, that's what you are, you lech,' John once told him with a grin. 'You like to see me with my arms around your lovely wife, knowing that you'll get the bloody benefit of my touching her up when you get her home.'

'Damn right, my son,' Robert had always said breezily.

Margaret thought of those little exchanges now as she took a shower and thought about what she was going to wear.

Why hadn't they ever taken Robert's shortness of breath seriously? Why hadn't they paid attention to his diet, or insisted that he took regular medical check-ups, which might have shown that he had high blood pressure, or a dangerously high cholesterol level? Why not persuade him to cut down on his smoking and his addiction for all the wrong kinds of food that the experts told you made for an unhealthy life-style?

And why waste time on stupid regrets now, when none of it did any good, and none of it was going to bring him back?

Margaret blinked the salty tears out of her eyes, and dried herself quickly, dousing her skin in her favourite Samsara body spray and breathing in the heavenly fragrance that always made her feel luxurious and pampered.

Tonight she was going to enjoy herself. There was nothing in the rules to say you couldn't. There weren't any rules at all. You just stumbled through as best you could.

Her mother phoned while she was putting on her final touches of make-up and admiring herself in the new pillar-box red dress she had recklessly bought to go with the new hairstyle. At the time, she hadn't known when or where she would wear it. She had just seen it in a boutique window and wanted it. And since she so rarely wore confidence-boosting red, it added to her sense of being someone else.

'How are you, Margaret?' her mother said cautiously.

'Fine. I'm going out soon, so you're lucky to have caught me.' She spoke brightly, to reassure her mother that she wasn't falling apart, but the minute the words left her lips, she knew it had been a mistake.

'Oh, well that's good. Where are you off to? Are you going somewhere with those girlfriends of yours? Or round to Keith's? He and Laura were on the phone last week for a long chat, and Laura was saying how well you're doing. She's a sensible girl. I hope they'll stay together, but you never know these days, do you?'

When she paused for breath, long enough for Margaret to get a word in, she spoke evenly.

'Actually, I'm going out with John. We're going dancing.'

She would have liked to count to ten before she heard the explosion from the other end, but it was a futile hope. She barely made it to two ... though it wasn't so much an explosion as a reproach.

'Is that wise, dear? Dancing, I mean, let alone with that man. People will talk, you know — and you have your reputation to consider.'

'Mother, has it not occurred to you that we're both unattached now, and free to do what we want with our lives?'

She was annoyed with herself for coupling them together like that, because it was the last thing she wanted to do. It also implied something she hadn't intended.

She heard muttering at the other end of the line, and guessed that her mother was holding her hand over the phone while she reported things to her father. And then she heard another voice in the background, yelling loud enough to be heard distinctly.

'*Is she going out with that sleaze-bag?*'

Margaret didn't bother counting anything now, just spoke into the phone in a voice that would cut steel.

'Mum, let me speak to Jenny, please.'

She gripped the telephone cord tightly, waiting for her daughter to deign to come on the line. The bloody cheek of her, daring to criticize what she did and who she was with.

'Mum?'

'Jenny, when I want your opinion of what I do and who I see, I shall ask for it, and I can assure you that day will be a long time coming. Do I make myself clear?'

Jenny didn't have even her grandmother's minuscule capacity for keeping her feelings in check.

'I never thought you'd be so disloyal to Dad, that's all,' she shouted into the phone. 'You didn't wait long to let that bloke come on to you, did you?'

'My God, for a girl whose morals belong in the gutter, you've got a hell of a nerve — ' Margaret began furiously.

'Fuck you,' Jenny shouted, and slammed down the phone.

The shock of it made Margaret's heart lurch so hard she felt physically sick. Jenny had never used such language to her in her life before. She could hardly believe she had really heard it, and she knew that any minute now her mother would be back on the phone, trying to smooth things over.

She didn't want to hear it. Wouldn't hear it. No platitudes, or apologies, or excuses, or anything else. The ragged sound of her own heartbeats was enough for her. She suddenly retched, and rushed to the bathroom to heave unproductively over the loo until her ribs ached from the effort, tears pouring from her eyes as she realized how far from her Jenny had gone, to react like that. Insidiously, inevitably, Jenny had moved away from her, but to speak in such terms . . . she knew such language was nothing unusual in films and TV programmes these days, more's the pity, but she had never used it. Never seen the need. Her friends often teased her for her puritanical streak, but it wasn't that. The word was ugly and obscene, and she hated it.

She heard the insistent ring of the doorbell and looked at her blotchy face in the bathroom mirror. God knew how long she had been holed-up in here, but one glance at her watch told her it would be John. And far from looking and feeling glamorous, she looked a wreck. A total, shivering wreck.

She went downstairs and answered the door.

'Good God, Margaret, I was about to say you look wonderful, but you don't. You look bloody awful,' he said, with the bluntness of an old friend.

She felt the shimmer of a smile touch her mouth.

'Thanks. And I went to so much trouble,' she said, trying to make a joke of it, and then the shaking took over again, and she was weeping in his arms.

'Your answering machine's flashing,' he said, when she finally stopped, and he had still got no sense out of her.

'It'll be my mother,' she said stonily. 'The machine will have kicked in when I didn't answer the phone.'

She hadn't even heard it. She had been too busy trying to throw up, and she wouldn't have answered it anyway.

'And why was that?' he said, reasonable as

ever. He paused. 'Your father's OK, I hope. And Jenny?'

'Jenny's a bitch,' Margaret said brutally.

'So it's Jenny. What's she done now?'

His voice was tolerant, indulgent, just as Robert had been about Jenny's misdemeanours. Margaret gradually realized that no matter how much they shouted at one another, he had always indulged her in the end. Just as Keith had said.

'Swore at me. With the F-word.'

Unbelievably, she heard him laugh.

'Is that all? So she swore at you. All kids let off steam like that nowadays. I thought it was something terrible.'

She glared at him. Was the whole world happy to curse with every other word, while it was only Margaret Jarvis who was out of sync? If you watched Jerry Springer and heard all those bleeps, you'd better believe it. Why did they cut them out? she wondered, when every other programme left them in? Some weird kind of puritanical streak *they* had?

John was shaking her lightly as her eyes glazed and her thoughts went off at a tangent as they so often did nowadays. She knew it was a way of delaying the immediate problem, but sometimes it frightened her. *Alzheimer's was setting in*, she and the girls always said breezily, but it wasn't so funny when you wondered if it might really be happening.

She told herself not to be so stupid and listened to what John was saying. His voice was firm and deliberate. Taking charge. Doing a Robert.

'What I want you to do right now, Margaret, is to go back upstairs, wash your face and comb your hair, and put on your make-up again. And then we're going out dancing.'

'I couldn't. Not now.'

'Why the hell not? Are you going to let that little madam dictate your life?'

'Of course not.'

'Well then.'

He waited patiently. Patience was one of his strong points. He had it in abundance, which was something Robert never had. Robert had wanted everything instantly. They were complete contrasts in so many ways, which was probably why they had always got on so well. There was no competition. There wasn't now.

'There's always the other possibility, of course,' he said casually.

'What's that?'

'We put on some music, go out on the patio and dance the night away right here, blotchy face and all.'

He was teasing, trying to make her smile, but the scene he described was far too intimate for comfort. It was the kind of romantic evening between two people who knew one another very well that would normally end up in only one way, and she wasn't ready for that. Didn't think she would ever be ready for that, and never with John, despite what her mother and Jenny and anyone else in this effing world might think.

Her small concession to the F-word brought another half-smile to her lips. It was idiotic to be so paranoid about it really. It was just a word.

'I don't think that's a good idea, John. Give me half an hour and I'll be ready.'

'Good girl. Do you want me to vet the answering machine for you while you're gone?'

'I suppose so. When I'm well out of hearing range.'

She was dousing her face in cold water in the bathroom before she remembered, too late, that he might not like what he heard. If her mother went on at length about the unsuitability of going out with her husband's best friend, it might put an extra strain on their relationship that had never been there before. But it was too late now, and by the time she went down to the sitting-room again, more or less restored to her usual serene self, he nodded approvingly.

'Beautiful as ever,' he said. 'And I think you should hear this.'

Before she could argue, he had switched on the answering machine again. She realized he had already rewound the tape, and Jenny's small, contrite voice spoke.

'Mum, I know you'll want to disown me for what I said, but please don't. I feel so awful about it, and I know how you hate that word. Believe me, it's not one of my favourites! I wanted to hit out at the time, but you're the last person I want to hurt. I'm too upset to talk about it any more, anyway. I wanted to tell you about my job offer, and the chance of flat-sharing with two girls my own age. Please say you approve, Mum. At least you won't have to put up with my untidy room all the time. I'll be home at the weekend to talk it over. If you'll have me, of course.'

'Tissues?' John asked as her eyes brimmed over. 'Make it quick, before you undo all the good you've just done.'

'Why did you make me listen to it now then?' she gasped, sniffing and blinking back the dampness in her eyes.

'Because I knew damn well that if it was

left to you, you'd probably erase it without listening to it.'

'Yes, because I expected it to be my mother.'

'And it wasn't. It was your little girl, anxious to come home for your approval this weekend. Will you let her?'

'Of course I'll let her,' Margaret said. 'This is her home, isn't it?'

'Then call her and tell her.'

'Not yet. I'll only ruin my make-up again if I do it now. She thinks I'm out, anyway. I'll do it in the morning.' She drew a deep breath, and gave him the dazzling smile that made him know exactly why his best friend had fallen for her all those years ago. 'So did someone say something about going dancing, or did I get all dressed up for nothing?'

6

As the evening wore on, Margaret knew this hadn't been such a good idea after all. Luigi's catered for all ages, not just teenagers and twenty-somethings. It was as crowded as ever, and people who knew them smiled or said a few words, or turned away in embarrassment. She felt vulnerable, as if she should be wearing a sign on her sleeve that said 'Hey it's OK!' There was no husband around any more, and she was free to date now, and so was her partner.

It was ridiculous, of course, when it had always been the two of them on the dance-floor, and never Robert. But things weren't the same now.

She couldn't look over at their usual alcove table and see wreaths of smoke rising from his cigar. Couldn't hear his throaty roars of laughter as he rounded off some raunchy joke with his cronies, or the women who seemed to swarm around him like a honeypot. He had charisma, as those crushingly twee romantic novels used to say. He also had money and spent it lavishly, and he never lacked for company.

'Do you want to go?' John asked at last, aware that she was mentally drooping.

'Sorry, but yes,' she said, no longer able to pretend an enthusiasm she didn't feel. It wasn't his fault. In fact, he was probably feeling it too.

She doubted if he'd been back here since Robert's death. Or maybe he had. He'd had women friends, though none of them had lasted, and she didn't feel like asking what the situation was now. She wanted to go home, and she didn't know what to do when they got there.

In the past the three of them had always spent a couple of hours at her house after leaving the nightclub, drinking too much and telling ever more risqué jokes, until they all fell into their respective beds in a stupor, leaving their sore heads to be dealt with in the morning.

Would John want to stay tonight? Margaret wondered uneasily. She didn't know how to broach the subject, or if she should. There was an awkwardness between them that was raw and new.

Before, if she'd needed to ask him at all, he'd have made some daft innuendo about a threesome, and Robert would have goaded him on, knowing full well it meant nothing, and that John would end up in Ben's old room as usual, sleeping the sleep of the dead until morning.

She swallowed, feeling him squeeze her hand as they went out of the smoky nightclub into the warm, midnight air. And he had obviously sensed the words she couldn't say.

'If you're asking, Margaret, yes, I'd like to come back to the house and get totally plastered while we talk ourselves senseless about Robert, and then stagger off to Ben's bed to sleep it off. Unless you'd rather I risked killing myself driving home.'

'I can't risk you losing your licence, can I?' she said, tacitly giving her consent without saying anything at all.

She recognized the question in his voice about the two of them being in the house alone. But they both knew there would be nothing wrong in that. She had also sensed his need to talk about Robert with the only other person who knew him as well as he did.

Knew him far *better*, of course, because who knew a man more intimately than his wife did? Even if John had known him far longer. And with the thought came an urge to hear about those days when they were young men, before Robert had taken on the mantle of his father's boat-building business, and come into her life and swept her off her feet.

'We'll go home and talk about Robert,

then,' she said, as they got into his car. 'If you really want to.'

'Do you? Can you bear to? It feels like a good plan to me, reminiscing about him in a way neither of us could do comfortably on the day of his funeral, with everyone going on with their own little anecdotes. Nobody knew him like we did, though, did they? Not even your children.'

'You're right,' she said slowly. It made a special link between them. Between the three of them. The old team, still there, even if one of them was absent.

Just gone into another room came into her mind, and she bit her lips in the darkness, knowing exactly now what that phrase was meant to imply. She was already squiffy with too much wine to dull the senses, which was a state John fully intended to join in later, when he was done with driving.

Ever the careful one, she thought. Keith would approve, even if he didn't approve of much else about John lately for some reason. Probably down to Laura's pious opinion, she thought, unreasonably blaming her for most things nowadays.

'And tomorrow, when you're sober, you can show me how to delete all Robert's computer files. I'm going to offer it to Jenny, and she'll want to start off with a clean slate.'

'What's this? A peace-offering?' John asked.

'Hardly. What have I done for the need to make peace? But I think she'll find more use for it than I will when she starts her new job. Ben told me it's with a fashion magazine.'

He started to laugh, and she laughed back, knowing why. Jenny's fashion sense was bizarre to say the least. Colours shrieked at one another, fabrics clashed, but somehow there was a weird kind of togetherness about it all. It certainly made her stand out in a crowd, like Gloria's hair colours did. Maybe that was what fashion was all about these days . . . and if so, she had missed the boat. Thank God.

As they reached the house the exterior lights came on, welcoming and reassuring. Margaret always left lamps on inside the house too, so that she never had to go inside a dark room. It was sensible as well as a deterrent to any burglars who would see this large house as rich pickings.

She ignored the thought that any local burglar worth his salt would know that a lone woman lived here now. In any case, some years ago, courtesy of Keith's expertise, Robert had installed a panic button to the local police station should she be worried about anything at all. Which was a bit of foresight she appreciated, and hoped she

111

would never need.

'You pour the drinks while I go and change,' she told John. 'Is it too cold for the patio, do you think?'

'Probably. It's cosier indoors anyway.'

She didn't want cosy. But there was always a chill from the sea up here on their side of the hill, so reluctantly she decided he was right.

And just as she always did at the end of these evenings, she went upstairs and changed out of the red cocktail dress into her voluminous silky lounger that Robert always said was as chaste as a nun's habit and about as provocative as a chastity belt. At which John would always remark lustily that she couldn't look unprovocative if she tried.

Well, she was trying tonight, she thought. Provocative was the last thing she wanted to be in the emotion-charged circumstances. And she was certain they both knew it.

When she went downstairs again, he had put on a CD. It was turned down low, and she was thankful it wasn't anything romantic or a particular favourite, just middle-of-the-road Abba background music.

'That's nice,' she said. 'I approve.'

'I thought you might. So let's drink a toast to an absent friend,' he suggested.

He handed her a glass of wine and drank his straight down after they had clinked glasses together. Margaret settled more comfortably into the deep plush armchair that was big enough for her to curl up in, tucking her feet inside the silky lounger until they disappeared, and only her head and hands and forearms showed.

'Are you sure there's somebody in there?' John said with a grin, sprawling out in the opposite chair.

'Quite sure. So tell me about when you and Robert first met. How old were you?'

'Twelve, I think. No, thirteeen. The age when little boys are at their most repulsive and obnoxious.'

'Why do you say that?' Margaret said, knowing what he meant, but wanting to hear it in relation to them.

He was relentless. 'We smoked behind the sheds at school. We bullied the younger kids. We were a pain to our teachers and our parents. We played truant whenever we could get away with it and forged our mothers' signatures to say we were ill. We took home horrible pets and expected everyone else to love them. And we discovered girls.'

'Did you? So young?' she said, laughing at this catalogue of minor faults that most kids went through. And amazed that for all that, they had turned out to be successful, model citizens. It just went to show — well, something or other.

'Oh yes. Robert was always curious about girls. I had a sister — she died when I was young — so I knew a bit more than he did, which he resented, of course. Robert always had to be boss, as you know. So he had to find out for himself.'

Margaret took a long drink of wine and handed over her glass for more.

'He didn't always have to be boss,' she objected.

'Of course he did. All his life. He was the original control freak. And he wouldn't be at all put out at hearing me say so. He revelled in it. Loved it.'

'So you discovered girls. Tell me more,' she prompted, her head not quite at the spinning stage yet, just starting to revolve gently enough to make her feel relaxed and expansive, prepared for anything he might tell her. Prepared to laugh at it all. Laugh a little and cry a little, and to remember Robert with love.

A smaller, sensible part of her asked if she really did want to hear all this. But what harm could it do? It just put the missing pieces of his life into perspective. It was good to be able to talk about him without hurting, and

John was the only person she could do that with.

'Books and diagrams, and the facts of life in rabbits as told in class by a po-faced biology mistress, did nothing for a class of testosterone-fuelled kids, as you can imagine. Not that we knew the word yet. We just knew how we felt, and that certain changes in our bodies had to be there for a purpose. And I'd better not go into graphic detail about that!'

'Perhaps not,' Margaret said.

'Anyway, Robert persuaded one of the girls to do a strip behind the school bicycle sheds. *Ee*, she were a buxom lass, and more than willing,' he said, adopting a pseudo-northern accent. 'Unfortunately we were all caught with our pants down, as you might say.'

'Oh.'

He glanced at her. 'Well, you did ask.'

'I know. I didn't think you meant you actually — at thirteen years old?'

She felt madly put out. It put a different picture on it all. She had been a virgin until she got married at eighteen, and not for any reason other than she hadn't met anyone who even remotely turned her on, until Robert. That, and the fact that her mother would have killed her if she'd got pregnant. For all Annie's liberal tendencies, Margaret knew she would have drawn a very definite line at that.

But Robert had had sex with a girl behind the bicycle sheds at school when he was thirteen . . .

It must be the wine that was making her feel resentful and let down, she thought. It was so long ago. Another life. It was kids' stuff. Even so, some *buxom lass* had known his body before she did. And she didn't like it.

'Wasn't that a terrible risk?' she found herself saying. 'Not just getting caught, but for the girl as well.'

'Oh, we'd discovered condoms by then. Didn't call them that then, though. They were Frenchies. French letters. One of the senior boys let us have some.'

She felt her skin prickle. It all sounded so sordid, so mechanical, so bloody adult . . . Robert had been more street-wise at thirteen than she had been when they married.

'I don't think I want to know any more about that. Move on, please. What about later, when you were older? You stuck together, didn't you?'

'University,' John nodded, taking a swig. He was on the whisky now, mixing it and not caring. It felt right to be here, where he had been a million times before, unlocking memories of his past with Robert's wife. It

116

felt comforting, as if Robert was still here, smiling over them benevolently, still a part of them.

'So? Go on. I bet you got up to some pretty wild times, didn't you?'

Why was she asking this? Almost goading him to tell her of more indiscretions. And Lord knew university students were among the worst, the stuff of future politicians and high court judges and all the rest of the so-called pillars of society. Yeah. Sure. With a past that wouldn't invite too much digging into for some of them.

God, she was beginning to think like Sarah now, Margaret thought. Sarah was the real cynic in their group.

'Cambridge was wild all right,' John said, his words starting to slur. 'If your face didn't fit in one of the private societies, you were quickly booted out.'

'What kind of private societies?'

'You wouldn't want to know.'

'Yes I would. That's why I'm asking, dope.'

He started to laugh. 'Yeah, that too.'

'Seriously? The hard stuff?'

'When you're in a crowd of guys all hell-bent on riotous living and to hell with the consequences, you do things out of character, Mags. Things you wouldn't normally do. We were all exhibitionists in those days.'

She realized he was reverting to uni-talk now. Reliving that wildness, that exhibition-ism. That close-knit group friendship that was beyond anything she had known. He leaned back in his armchair, eyes closed in reminiscent bliss.

'So what did you get up to? Student rags and all that stuff, I suppose?' she asked jealously.

'One year we all got dressed up as tarts and paraded through the town, high heels, tights, make-up, the lot. Those high heels are murder to walk in. God knows how you women do it. Robert made a beautiful bitch, of course. We all fancied him like stink, but he was a one-guy fellow.'

His eyes slowly opened again as he heard Margaret's sharp intake of breath and then the raggedness of her breathing. Her face was deep crimson. And, mortified, John knew how stupidly he'd blundered.

'Jesus, Mags, I didn't mean that the way it sounded,' he said clumsily.

'Yes you did. I know you did. Is it true?'

He tried to bluff it out. 'Come on, Margaret. You know all kids experiment with their sexuality before they find themselves. It's part of growing up.'

'But you weren't kids. You were men.'

She stood up. She wasn't born yesterday,

but this was Robert they were talking about. Robert, who was the most heterosexual man in creation. She knew she was probably being hopelessly old-fashioned now, but she couldn't bear the thought that Robert and some guy . . .

'I'm going to bed,' she said abruptly. 'You know where your room is, and I'll see you in the morning. Unless you decide you need to get away early.'

She gave him the option, but it couldn't have been more pointed. She wouldn't tell him to get out and risk getting breathalyzed, because he had been her husband's best friend, and had been her friend for a long time too.

She didn't know if there had been a one-off or a full-on affair between two male students, and OK, people experimented, but she wasn't damn well asking. She could be jumping to the wrong conclusions, but if not, the thought that one of them was Robert made her sick. And because he was aware of it, not personally involved, she couldn't bear to look at John.

'Don't take it seriously, Mags,' he muttered. 'In any case, it's all history.'

Maybe. But it had still happened.

★　★　★

119

They had both drunk too much, but she must have slept, despite the movement of the room that wouldn't keep still until she eased herself gingerly down in the bed and closed her eyes very, very slowly, as if to fool her brain that she was still awake and not a candidate for spinning into a vortex.

She must have slept, because by the time she awoke it was daylight and the sun was streaming in through her bedroom window. She winced, aware of a head like a bucket and a mouth like mud, and wondered if John's was as bad.

At the thought of his name, her heart jolted, remembering everything about last night, and knew she would have to face him sometime. She moved her head around carefully to look at her bedside clock, and was shocked to find that it was nearly midday.

How could she have slept so long? With all that he had told her . . . ? Or had her subconscious simply shut down on something too difficult to contemplate? But in the light of day, she was also wondering if she'd been over-reacting. As far as a massive hangover would let her she tried to be logical. If she went over his slurred words carefully, he had actually said very little for her to make a fuss about. He hadn't actually *said* Robert had had a gay lover. And she was perfectly sure

Robert wasn't gay. She had simply been thrown over a chance remark.

Men could be good mates without the sex thing. Look at sports fans. Football crowds. Golfing cronies. It was a man thing. Just as women liked their own company. She would trust her girlfriends with her life, and she loved them all, but she certainly didn't fancy them physically.

She dragged herself out of bed and crawled over to her bathroom. She needed a shower to wake her up properly, and help her to get everything sorted out in her mind. And if it *had* ever happened, so what? It was all so long ago. It *was* history, and Robert had been solely hers for twenty-four years. And she'd been a fool for wanting to dredge up a past in which she had no part.

By the time she had dressed in jeans and T-shirt, she felt ready to face John again, hoping they could behave towards one another as if nothing had happened. It was what she wanted, and what Robert would have wanted. Sarah and the others would probably say she was taking the easy way out again, but they weren't going to know anything about this. Whether or not there had ever been anything in it, it was not a secret for sharing.

She went down to the breakfast-room,

expecting to find John already there and eating breakfast or brunch, depending on when he had got up. There was no sign of him, just a large piece of paper pinned to her notice-board.

'Sorry I had to leave early, Margaret. Had an urgent call from the office, and I'm off on my travels again tomorrow. I've left you details of how to erase the computer files in Robert's study, and have deleted a few of them for you before flying off. Thanks for everything. Kisses as usual.'

And that was all. She couldn't help a mixture of relief that he was gone, and a sharp annoyance that he had been in Robert's study. It wasn't exactly a holy of holies, but he should have waited for her. Still, it was done now, and once she got her head together, she would get the files deleted prior to Jenny's arrival next weekend. Then she could take the computer and printer away with her, and that would be that.

★ ★ ★

Technology had never been Margaret's strong point, and she cheerfully admitted it. Her reasoning was why should she bother learning anything complicated, when there was always someone else to do it for her?

She felt guilty about such a negative philosophy now. She had always prided herself on being a positive person. In outlook, she certainly was. How else could she have got through the days and weeks since Robert's death?

Months now, she reminded herself, almost with a little shock. Whatever else happened in life, you couldn't stop time, and the stupid platitude that people made about time being a great healer wasn't quite so inept as she had once thought. It didn't stop the sense of loss and emptiness, it just made it easier to cope with.

'Come on,' she chivvied herself. 'Don't get maudlin now. You've got a job to do, and it's about time you got on with it. Robert wouldn't thank you for being so spineless.'

She didn't *talk* to him quite as much as she had at first, either. Not in any misery-laden way, anyway, but rather to remind herself of what he would want from her. It helped.

She opened the study door and went inside. John had opened the windows, and a fresh breeze wafted in from the garden, bringing the scent of summer roses with it, and the heavenly tang of fresh-cut grass. She could hear the drone of old Joe's motor mower from the slope of the lawn, and she waved to him, seeing him touch his ancient cap in response, the same as he always did. She and Robert had often debated on whether he went to bed in that cap, or if there was anything underneath it. Robert reckoned he was as bald as a coot.

Margaret made herself move forward, knowing she was dithering, and sat down at the computer. She took a deep breath and switched it on, half-wishing she'd had the nous to concentrate more, but then shrugging as she saw John's clear instructions on the pad beside the machine.

There were half a dozen floppy disks stacked up with an extra note on top of them. She read it quickly.

'These are all wiped clean ready for Jenny's use, also deleted from the hard disk, as explained. Any problems, call my mobile before tomorrow, or try Shelley's Computer Service, phone number supplied.'

'Well, thanks, John. I'm sure I could have managed to work that out for myself,' she said. He was treating her like an idiot, and she should be grateful.

She wondered which files he'd deleted, and why he'd bothered. Probably conscience pricking him after last night and wanting to be useful. It was mostly family stuff anyway. Like most computer literates, Robert liked to keep everything on file, names, addresses, important dates, holiday details.

But since Margaret had most of that covered in her own notebook system, it always seemed far less trouble simply to open it up and find whatever she needed. Technology wasn't everything, nor always the quickest route to anywhere, she had once informed Robert when he was still waiting for a relevant file to appear and she had the information all ready.

The hard disk file was hellishly long, and she couldn't waste time checking what was on every one. She just pulled out a few at random, and as she supposed, it was generally family stuff, or things to do with the business.

It had been sold five years ago when Robert had taken early retirement at a ridiculously young age, but he'd stayed available as a consultant. And he obviously hadn't been able to resist keeping a dossier, which was mostly personal comment.

Margaret smiled at his sharp words, knowing he was never one to gloss over faults, and glad he hadn't lost interest. The firm had been in his family since his father had founded it. It was where they had made their money, and she wasn't knocking it, even though she wasn't keen on small boats.

Which reminded her, she must get on to Keith and see if he'd had any progress on the sale of Robert's sailing boat, the Porsche and the Range Rover. She already had a vague idea of dividing the proceeds of the three sales between the children and giving them the money at Christmas.

Oh God, Christmas . . . how was she going to face that? It was still six months away, but she couldn't bear the thought of it. They had always had such huge family parties, and this year it would be heartbreakingly different.

She could go away, of course. Money was certainly not a consideration. Maybe abroad, like one of those pathetic, rich elderly widows who stayed in outrageously expensive hotels where everyone pandered to their needs, and pretended they were having such a good time. *No, thank you!* She hadn't reached that point in her life yet!

But this year Christmas would mean sending and receiving cards with only her name on it, when there had always been two — she always thought one-name cards looked so lonely — except those she sent to her divorced friends.

But that was different. *Very* different, she thought resentfully, and the girls positively revelled in sending her the jokiest, smuttiest ones they could find. It was partly to wind Robert up, Margaret had always suspected. But now they didn't need to.

She switched off the computer. It was no good. She wasn't in the mood for this, and her headache wasn't going away. The best thing she could do would be to have a long, lazy swim and relax in the sunshine.

Besides, Robert had always been meticulous in doing printouts of his files. If there was anything updated she needed to know, anyone's address or phone number she needed to contact, it would be in a folder in a cabinet drawer.

Maybe she could even clarify the identity of the woman who'd called him and had been in Australia on tour — if she was that interested. In any case, the computer could wait, and she would sort it later. Or leave it to Jenny.

7

Margaret decided she wasn't going to be beaten by the computer. Whizz-kids of five and six could use them blindfold, and by the time Jenny came home that weekend she had managed to delete several more files to save her the trouble, and printed out a contact list of names, addresses and telephone numbers. She had no idea who these people were, but in case any of them rang up, at least she wouldn't feel like a dummy as she had done when someone called Emma had called.

There was an Emma in the list. Emma Pritchard, c/o the Gladby Agency. Since the woman said she had been on tour, an agency address seemed to confirm Margaret's assumption that she was an actress. Though why Robert should have had her name on his computer, she couldn't think, and didn't really care. There was only a limited time she felt able to tackle anything in this study, and she had already had more than enough for one day.

The name of the agency tucked itself away in her subconscious though. She'd never heard of it, but then, she'd never heard of so many of Robert's friends and acquaintances. She was only just starting to realize what separate lives they had actually led, when she had always thought them so close. It came to her with a little shock. Together they were a close family unit . . . but once that family went their separate ways, they were also five very diverse characters.

When the children were small, John had once said flamboyantly that they were like the five points of a star. As the memory struck her, Margaret thought it was an interesting observation, because while that star hung together, they were whole, complete, but what happened when those points broke away, became independent and went out into the big wide world? It simply disintegrated.

God, she was going mad, and she must stop it. She closed the door to the study, calling to Mrs Ashley-wot-did that she was going to make coffee and did she want some? There was always time for a gossip and to hear the comfortable doings of Mrs Ashley's world. And the kitchen was firmly her domain.

'Your girl's coming down on Sat'day, then,' the woman stated amicably. 'You'll be glad to see her, I daresay. Bit of company for you, now that — '

She took a deep slurp of coffee, avoiding the end of the sentence.

'Yes. Now that Robert's gone,' Margaret finished.

'She'll be missing him,' Mrs Ashley went on, stating the obvious.

'We all do.'

'Well, of course you do, and that's only to be expected, but Jenny was always Mr Jarvis's special girl, wasn't she? Give her anything, that man would.'

Margaret just managed not to laugh. 'Special girl? Good Lord, even you know how they fought, and he was for ever bellowing at her to tidy up!'

She bit her lip, because the pictures in her mind were suddenly so real, so vivid. Saturday mornings used to be the worst, when Robert was up and out of the house in no time, always with something to do, while Jenny sprawled in bed after a night out with friends, appearing like a zombie at lunch-time.

'Fighting's only another way of showing affection, ain't it? Leastways, that's what *Frasier* says.'

Margaret looked blank, until she remembered how Mrs Ashley was hooked on the TV sit-com with the most mixed-up psychiatrist in creation.

'Oh well, if *Frasier* says so, it must be right then.'

And tell that to the nations forever at war with one another. Not much affection there . . .

'Do you want me to do these bedrooms now?' Mrs Ashley said, when Margaret seemed to be lost in space.

Poor duck, still not over her old man's passing yet, and no wonder, them being so devoted, as she was forever telling anyone who would listen.

'Yes please. And, Mrs Ashley, there's a box of Mr Jarvis's clothes in my room. If you'd care to look through them, please take anything your husband might like, and then I'd be glad if you would take the rest to the Oxfam shop.'

'Of course I'll do that for you, Mrs J, and be glad to.'

Margaret left her to it, unable to face the caring, chattering woman a moment longer, nor to see the undoubted gleam in her eye at the thought of her husband wearing some of Robert Jarvis's expensive clothes. Not that many would fit him since he was as wafer-thin as an anorexic. But healthy. Unlike Robert, who had been overweight and a prime candidate for a heart attack, as everyone belatedly said. Why hadn't anyone said it before, Margaret thought again, with sudden and unexpected rage? Why hadn't *she*?

★ ★ ★

'You're looking good, Mum,' Jenny said cautiously, when she had dropped her various bags, coats and shoes in her bedroom and turned it instantly from Mrs Ashley's tender care into a rubbish dump. 'I like your hair like that. Makes you look younger. You're thinner, but it suits you, and thank God you're not wearing black. I like you in red too. So, have you forgiven me, really?'

Jenny-like, the words came out in a rush. She was mercurial, like Robert, thinking on her feet, saying it like it was, but without his maturity and technique of biting back the words when it was prudent to do so.

'There's nothing to forgive, darling. We were all upset — '

'Yes, but you're not really going to let that guy move in, are you? You know he will, given half a chance.'

Count to ten. 'If you're talking about John — '

'Why wouldn't I be? Or is there somebody else in the running?'

Margaret was exasperated. Five minutes,

and they were already almost bickering. It dawned on her that she had always been the peacemaker when Robert and Jenny were having one of their blistering rows, taking both sides at once, trying to preserve the sweet harmony of family life. She had been the one in the middle, not really involved . . . but now there was no one but her mother for Jenny to rant and rave with here. She had never expected her daughter to miss such spats, but maybe she did. Maybe it was the life-blood of her, this surge of adrenalin that came whenever they were at full flow, the same as it had been with Robert. Maybe Mrs Ashley via *Frasier* had been right, and their fights were a symbol of their affection, because it never harmed the essence of their relationship.

'Are we going to have a quiet weekend, or are we going to argue the whole time?' she asked Jenny mildly. 'I only ask, so that I know whether or not to put on my tin-hat before we have lunch.'

Jenny stared at her for minute and then grinned as she tipped out yet more bags of mis-matched clothes on to her bed. And this was a would-be fashion journalist? Margaret thought, fascinated.

'I didn't know you could be so witty, Mum.'

'Didn't you? Maybe that's because you don't know me at all.'

'What's that supposed to mean?'

'Well, who am I, Jenny?'

'Don't be daft. You're my mother. Keith and Ben's mother.'

'I'm also Robert's wife, or at least I was. No, still am, damn it. I'm also the owner of this house, with many friends and acquaintances, including three very close and dear women friends' — she emphasized the word *women* — 'with whom I go out drinking until we're well and truly pissed and confide all our secrets to one another — including the fact that since I've been widowed — bloody hateful word — I'm missing the very healthy sex life that your father and I once had.'

She caught sight of Jenny's shocked eyes, and realized her daughter had gone very still as she flopped down on her bed.

'Good God, Mum, you said pissed.'

Margaret stared back at her, wondering if she was the only one who was finding this whole situation bizarre. Did this nineteen-year-old girl, as street-wise as they all thought themselves these days, think her mother lived in the Dark Ages? And how come she hadn't picked up on her mother's mention of a sex life? Or was that the next thing to be mentioned?

'*So?*' she said aggressively, in the very way she had hated from the kids when they were growing up and finding their own feet.

Jenny shrugged. 'So, well done. Not such a dinosaur after all, are you?'

Margaret began to laugh, aware that a burst of adrenalin wasn't such a bad thing to experience after all, even in an argument. It was quite heady, in fact. Hardly orgasmic, but it certainly made you feel alive. Even so, the last thing she intended doing was arguing with Jenny all weekend.

'OK, so let's call a truce on one thing. You're not a slob and I'm not a dinosaur. And once you've got some of this chaos sorted out, I'll make lunch, and then you can take a look at your Dad's computer equipment. If you don't want it, I'll advertise it.'

'Of course I want it. It was Dad's, wasn't it? When he first got it, he showed me how to write my name on it in all the weird fonts. I had a great time.'

She turned away, tightening a chin that suddenly wobbled, but not before Margaret had seen a glimpse of the child she had been, adoring her father, before teenage angst and hormones had got in the way.

They were all going to have these moments. It wasn't just Margaret's prerogative. They all had separate memories,

135

excluding all the others. It was like John said: the five points of a star.

'Keith and Laura are coming round this evening. They're going to do a barbecue, since you know how much I dislike doing them.'

The haunted look on Jenny's face vanished at once to be replaced by a scowl. It always amazed Margaret how much her beautiful daughter's face could change in an instant, revealing all her emotions. And right now, it was showing downright resentment.

'Oh, God, must we? What the hell does Keith see in her? She's a self-righteous cow.'

'Jenny, you know it and I know it, but let's try to be charitable for once, shall we?'

And if that wasn't a backhanded reversal of her old peacemaking ways she didn't know what was. But it got Jenny grinning again.

'At least we're on the same wavelength about some things, Mum.'

And after lunch, they would pore over the computer stuff, and the sooner Jenny got it all out of here, the better. The study that had been Robert's was now Margaret's, and she wanted it to house her things, her own favourite photos, her potted plants, her papers and social interests.

For some reason she couldn't explain she hated that black computer screen. It was like an unseeing and yet *all*-seeing eye, staring at her blindly every time she went into the study, hiding secrets, hiding things that belonged to Robert and not to her. Waiting to leap into life at the click of a switch and the insertion of a disk. God, it was almost sexual, greedy, waiting for his touch . . .

She was glad John had wiped so many of those disks, and yet there was a little part of her that wondered why. Why those particular disks? Was there something she shouldn't see? Couldn't cope with? She was ready to admit that her unease all stemmed from that night he had stayed here, when she had forced him to tell her of their early life together, his and Robert's, before she knew them. The childish secrets, the well-stacked girl behind the bicycle shed, the experiments with drugs, the uni parties, the gay friends, John and Robert . . . Robert and John . . .

That part of it was still the epicentre of all her unease. She recognized it for her own suburbanism that was partly a long-forgotten rebellion against having a mother who was a latent hippy, believing, if not practising in free love and all that — though she could no more imagine her stiff-necked military father being a flower-power child than she could fly.

But Grannie Annie, as the kids called her . . . well, it was no wonder Jenny had turned into such a wild child. It was in the genes. Not hers. Her mother's.

'Have you got boxes for all this equipment?' Jenny asked her, once they surveyed how much of it there was to transport back to London.

'I don't know,' Margaret said vaguely.

'Well, *think*, Mum. Where did Dad keep all the stuff that might come in handy *one day*? He'd never have thrown it all out.'

'I suppose not. He was always a hoarder.'

Which was why she had finally had no qualms in disposing of his clothes to someone who could make use of them. The skinny Mr Ashley and Oxfam . . . while she believed in turning out drawers and closets and buying new. The indolent housewife with more money than sense . . . and with so much time on her hands she had turned into a shopaholic. She dismissed the thought. Many of her almost-new clothes had found a good home to those less fortunate too.

'*Mum*, are you listening to me? I said we should look in the attic. That's where you keep the suitcases and all the Christmas stuff, don't you? I bet all the boxes for the computer equipment are up there too — and the cartons the TV and VCR came in, just in case they had to go back for repair!'

'I can't.'

'What do you mean, you can't? You're not afraid of heights, are you?' she asked with a grin.

'I can't go up in the attic because half my life is up there,' Margaret said abruptly. The boxes of Christmas decorations; the old rocking-horse that had been Robert's and seen Keith and Ben and Jenny through their childhood; the stacks of old photographs; the suitcases, large and small, depending on which holiday they were taking; their life together . . .

'Oh well, we can wait for Keith to come and he can sort it,' Jenny said uneasily, privately meaning to remind her brother to keep an eye on her. All this vague retreating into the past might be normal in the first few weeks after someone died, but it was months now. Life went on, and that was something else she needed to talk to her mother about. But not yet. She changed tactics.

'It's so hot today. Why don't we take a swim? Is the pool warm?'

'Can a duck swim?' Margaret said drily. 'So when are you going to tell me what's on your mind?'

'It's a bit tricky, actually, and I don't want to offend you — '

Margaret laughed. 'Since when did that stop you?'

'OK then. I can't stay with Grannie Annie for ever, and I want a flat of my own. Or rather, a girlfriend and I want to flat-share. I know Dad would say it's risky for two people to buy property, unless they're married or in a relationship, and I assure you there's nothing like that about Mel and me! So I want to buy the place and she'd pay me rent. I know Dad would approve.'

There. She had said it now, straight out, ignoring the way her heart was pounding as she awaited her mother's reaction. Cautious to a fault, as Grannie Annie might say scathingly.

Margaret was cool. 'So why would that offend me?' And never mind that her daughter had already voiced Robert's opinion before consulting her.

'I haven't got to the crunch bit yet. I need the money to put down a hefty deposit. You know how expensive London property is, and what Dad left me is in trust until I'm twenty-one. I can't wait two years for it, Mum, not if I'm to be independent. So how do I get round it?'

She looked at Jenny, as dark-eyed and appealing as her father, and as wily as her grandmother, and Margaret sighed, preparing to give in as always. But not immediately. Robert would have given Jenny the third

140

degree while they sparred endlessly before he indulged her, but she didn't need to go that far.

'Have you thought this through? Talked it over with your grandparents?'

'Of course. Grannie Annie loves the place, and Gramps says it's a good investment. I can't lose, and if I sell it eventually, I'll make a bomb.'

'I see you've got everybody's approval before you ask for mine.'

'Not everybody's, only Grannie and Gramps!'

And Robert's, because of course this strike for independence would meet with his approval. So there was no point in pretending an opposition she didn't feel, and was simply too tired to feel.

'I wasn't going to tell you this yet, but perhaps now is a good time. You know Ben's friend has bought the Frazer-Nash, and I'm also planning to sell the boat and your father's other two cars. I was going to divide the proceeds of the sales and give the money to all of you for Christmas. As a kind of present from your father, as well as me.'

She felt her throat well up, and neither of them spoke for a moment, and then Jenny's face was stricken, her voice thick.

'Oh Mum, that's such a lovely idea, but

surely you don't have to do that. Daddy loved those cars, and you loved going out in the boat with him.'

'Actually, I didn't love it at all. I'm no sailor, and I was always glad to get my feet back on dry land. As for the cars' — she gave a shrug — 'what do I need them for? They'll just rot in the garage, and besides, I have my own car.'

After another pause, Jenny said, 'So this is going to happen by Christmas, is it?' She was so transparent that Margaret laughed again, easing the tension.

'It *was*, you acquisitive little wretch, but now that I see your need, I shall ask Keith to set the wheels in motion at once — if you'll pardon the pun. Meanwhile, you'd better tell me how much you need to buy this flat, and I'm sure I can arrange for you to have the funds for the full amount in advance. Much better than just putting down a deposit and paying for ever more, isn't it?'

Astonished, Jenny flung her arms around her mother. 'You know, you never fail to surprise me. Sometimes you can be just as decisive as Dad used to be.'

'Thank you for the compliment.'

'I mean it, honestly. Now I'm just going to take a shower before we have that swim, to get all the dust from Dad's study off me. I swear I could still smell those old cigars of his, even now. Nice though.'

Margaret watched her long-limbed daughter fly up the stairs to fetch her swimming things, and marvelled that she had ever produced such a glorious and vivacious girl. Jenny would never sit around waiting for things to happen. If she wanted to do a thing, she did it. It was no wonder she was so popular. A real chip off her grandmother's block. Which reminded her.

While Jenny was upstairs she punched out her mother's phone number.

'I understand you've vetted this flat that Jenny wants,' she began.

'Now, darling, don't make a fuss and don't put her down just because she's got more spunk than you ever did.'

Counting to ten would never be enough now, so Margaret didn't bother.

'I'm not making a fuss and I'm not objecting, just wanting to be sure that it's a nice place. In fact, I think I'll come back with her and stay with you for a few days, and look it over myself.'

'Good heavens. Just like that?' Annie said.

'Why not?'

'Well, Margaret, it's just so unlike you to make a spur-of-the-moment decision that you took me off-balance. But of course we'd love to have you.'

'Right. That's settled then. Love to Dad.'

She replaced the phone carefully. So unlike her to do anything on the spur of the moment, was it?

They all thought they knew her so well. They all knew Margaret, the one who never did anything outrageous, or out of the ordinary, or unpredictable.

By the time Jenny came down, she was in her swimsuit and had unrolled the cover from the pool. Her daughter smiled with approval.

'You do look fabulous, Mum,' she said suddenly. 'No wonder that rat-fink fancies you. You won't let him take you over though, will you?'

It took a moment for Margaret to register that she was referring to John.

'He's not a rat-fink, and no,' she said automatically. 'In any case, I'm coming back to London with you tomorrow, and staying at Grannie's for a few days. I want to see this wonderful flat you're proposing to buy.'

It was worth it to see Jenny's open mouth at this announcement. It was just as her mother said, Margaret thought, as she plunged straight into the blissfully warm water and streaked beneath it like a lithe dolphin to the far end. Nobody ever expected her to make decisions on the spur of the moment. Well, maybe they were all in for a few surprises.

* * *

'You're doing what?' Laura squeaked, when she and Keith turned up that evening, complete with steaks and chops for the barbecue, and the air was starting to turn blue with the acrid smell of charcoal — and more than a hint of irritation on Margaret's part at the reaction to her news.

'I'm going to London to look over the flat that Jenny's after.'

'Good for you, Mum. It'll do you good to get away,' Keith said, with a warning glance at Laura.

'I'm not ill, Keith. I just want to be sure she's getting a good deal, that's all.'

'My mother, the financier,' Jenny said with a laugh.

'And we all know that a bit of pampering never comes amiss,' Laura added, as if she couldn't see beyond the perfect new hairdo and the immaculate manicure to the woman beneath.

Through the smoke of the barbecue, Margaret glared at them all.

'For pity's sake, will you all stop treating me like a second-class citizen!'

145

Keith looked genuinely astonished.

'When did any of us ever do that, for Christ's sake?'

'When you all thought you knew what was best for me, and tried to guide me into your way of thinking because you thought I was incapable of thinking for myself,' she snapped.

'We never did that. All we wanted was to help you over Dad's death,' Jenny snapped back. Margaret knew it was her way of coping with emotion, but it wasn't helping. It wasn't helping at all, but she also knew that this evening was in danger of turning into a shambles if the bickering didn't stop right now.

'Well, let's just say I've been helped enough, and right now you can cook my steak for ten minutes longer, Keith. Your father may have liked them nearly raw, but I don't.'

Hooray. Asserting her own preferences at last. She may have thought she always did, but now she knew how much she had been influenced by Robert, and she was damned if she was going to let these children do the same.

'Charred meat isn't good for you — ' Laura began.

'It's not good to eat raw meat either, unless you're a cannibal.'

Jenny started to laugh, clearly enjoying this newly resentful mother and her stand-off against Laura. 'Let's all stop talking and just *eat*! I'm starving.'

'So what's new?' said Keith drily.

* * *

Food was always a useful panacea, Margaret reflected, and even the prickly Laura mellowed as the evening progressed. Keith fetched down the computer and printer cartons from the attic, predictably marked and stacked, packed it up right away and put it all in the boot of Jenny's sports car.

'How are you getting back from London?' Jenny asked suddenly. 'Unless you're staying for a week, I won't be able to get away to bring you back, Mum, but you're not planning to drive behind me all the way to London, are you?'

'Do you think I couldn't?'

'Of course not — '

'Ever heard of trains? I'll drive up with you and catch a train back.'

'It's a very long journey, Margaret,' Laura said reasonably.

'Oh, for heaven's sake, I'm not a child. I have travelled on my own before, you know!'

But they all knew she hadn't. Not even as

far as London. The odd journey around town, of course, further afield to have lunches with girlfriends, but for any distance, there had always been Robert. Oh, hell and damnation. Why did these little snippets of anguish always attack her just when she was trying to appear strong and self-sufficient?

'Perhaps Ben will bring you back,' Keith suggested.

She held up her hand. 'Stop right now. I'm going with Jenny and I'm coming back by train. I wish I'd never mentioned the damn trip at all now. And I'm certainly not intending to stay a week. I've got things to do here.'

'Sorry. We're only thinking of you, Mum.' They didn't ask what things were so urgent that she couldn't take a week away to visit her parents.

'Well, don't. I can think for myself. I can plan for myself, and that's exactly what I'm going to do from now on.'

She saw Laura's approving glint, and knew that for all her pseudo-caring attitude she'd probably be glad that Margaret wasn't intending to be a hanger-on in their relationship. And Margaret really couldn't blame her for that.

It was only when Keith and Laura were finally preparing to leave that she thought of something she'd been meaning to ask him. It was something that had been puzzling her for days.

'Keith, have you ever heard of the Gladby Agency?'

He gave a slightly shocked laugh.

'Good God, Mum, don't tell me you're thinking along those lines!'

'Why? What's it all about? It was just a name that caught my eye in a newspaper or magazine, I think,' she said, flannelling.

'Well, I should forget it if I were you. It's an escort agency, and a seedy one at that. Not quite a massage parlour, and always just above the law, but with a certain reputation all the same, if you know what I mean.'

8

Margaret lay sleepless in bed in the darkness, staring at the fleeting patterns made by the moon across the ceiling, trying not to think too deeply of what Keith had said, and yet knowing that the words were burning into her brain.

An *escort agency?* What on earth would Robert be doing with the name of an escort agency on his computer? And even more, with the name Emma as a contact? In her wildest imagination, there could be no call for an escort agency on a boat-builder's agenda.

The sickening unease that had been simmering inside her lately was gathering momentum, no matter how much she tried to stifle it. First John's unwitting revelations, which may or not be true, but which she simply couldn't forget . . . the way Robert had been wickedly flirtatious with any female in the vicinity, even her own friends, always teasing her that the more upfront he was about it, the less Margaret needed to worry . . . and now this. Even if *this* was no more than circumstantial evidence.

In a classic scenario, of course, there would

have been mysterious mourners at the funeral, glamorous females Margaret had never seen before. But although there had been many local people there as well as family and friends, there was no one she could remember seeing who shouldn't have been there.

She caught her thoughts up short. What was she doing, thinking the worst of the man she had loved for a quarter of a century? Especially now, when he was no longer here to laugh at her fears, sweep her into his arms and vow that she was the only woman he had ever loved. To prove to her by his love-making and his charm, that theirs was the perfect marriage she always thought it was.

But that was just it. He *wasn't* here any longer, and the unease wasn't going to go away. Margaret shivered, wondering again just why John Franklin had wiped those computer disks before she or Jenny had had the chance to see them.

Jenny. Just supposing . . . with her heart pounding, the nightmare thought slid into Margaret's mind . . . just supposing there *had* been something incriminating on those disks, and Robert's daughter had opened them, and seen the ugly side of a father she had adored.

'Stop it,' she whispered into the darkness. 'For God's sake, stop it.'

She turned her head into the pillow, blotting out her own thoughts, which amounted to the shameful betrayal of Robert's memory. The name on the list was just a name, no more. Robert may have registered it for someone else, never for him. It would never have been for him. An escort agency? Why on earth would he have wanted such a thing? Why — and when! Logically, it was so unlikely that she found herself smiling tremulously at the absurdity of it all.

★ ★ ★

Driving to London with Jenny was an experience in itself. All the children were good drivers, but that didn't mean travelling at breakneck speed and only just within the legal limits. Gritting her teeth, they were well *en route* on the M3 towards London when Margaret could stand it in silence no longer.

'For pity's sake, I'd like to get there in one piece, Jenny!'

'You will. Dad liked speed, didn't he? I thought you'd have been used to it.'

'Yes, but not in a souped-up sports car where I feel far too near the ground for comfort.'

'Oh, you're quite safe with me,' Jenny said, in a shiveringly real echo of Robert's patronizing words.

Privately, Margaret didn't think she'd feel safe until she was inside her parents' home in Notting Hill, and once there, she had to succumb to the expected scrutiny before she unpacked her bag for the three-night stay.

'You've cut your hair,' her father said, showing his disappointment.

She sighed, knowing how he had always loved her long blonde hair. 'That's because I'm not a teenager any longer, Dad,' she said.

'I like it,' her mother approved. 'I like the new clothes as well. You look surprisingly well, Margaret.'

'Why shouldn't I?'

But the moment she asked, she heard her father's throat-clearing, signalling that either he considered his wife had made a social gaffe, or he simply didn't know what to say. They were so bloody transparent, Margaret thought, with a rush of affection mixed with irritation, but they really didn't need to be careful of her feelings. Robert had been gone for four months now, and she was getting used to being without him — most of the time.

'We've brought back all Dad's computer equipment,' Jenny said quickly. 'Will you help me get it out of the car, Gramps? I'm not going to unpack it yet though, not until

Mum's seen the flat and I've decided to go ahead.'

'*If* I approve,' Margaret said, reminding her tacitly that if she wanted the money advanced for it, that would be the condition.

'Oh, you will,' Jenny said confidently. 'Grannie Annie thinks it's great, and Gramps too — '

'You told me: Gramps thinks it's an investment.'

She was suddenly weary of being manipulated. She just wanted to take a look at the bloody flat, say it was great, get on a train at Paddington and go home.

She was appalled at her own feelings. She hadn't been here half an hour and already she was feeling stifled. It was crazy. This was her childhood home — at least, when her father wasn't away soldiering and carting them halfway around the world — and the minute she was back inside it she felt like a child again.

When she married Robert all those years ago, it had felt so freeing to be an adult and play at house inside her own four walls. She loved her parents, but they had always dominated her in their own way — just as Robert had done — just as her children did now, taking over his mantle. A sense of panic overcame her, and from the sharpness in her father's voice now she knew her face must have paled.

'Are you all right, darling?'

'Car sick,' she gasped, bolting upstairs to the bathroom, and slamming the door shut behind her.

She had never been car sick in her life, but she needed these moments alone before they all smothered her with their bouncy determination to keep her spirits up. *Well, bully off, but my spirits have been far enough up for a while now, especially when Sarah, Fiona, June and I go out on the town once a week and get pleasantly pissed. You're the ones who will get me down if I let you.*

'Mum, are you still in there? Ben's arrived,' she heard Jenny bellow out a while later, and she knew she couldn't sit up here for ever counting Annie's collection of Thai ceramic figurines that adorned the windowsill. She gave the lavatory a token flush and emerged with a bright smile on her face.

'I knew it wouldn't be long before you came to check up on me,' she said, going downstairs and greeting her son with a quick hug.

'Grannie Annie invited me,' he told her. 'Should I go away again?'

'Of course not, idiot,' she said. 'I'm glad to see you.'

'You weren't car sick then,' he said, more intuitively than she had expected. 'So what do you think of Jen's news? Crazy or what?'

'Shut up,' Jenny said. 'You've got your own place, so why shouldn't I?'

'Yeah, but I'm a grown-up.'

As Ben teased her, for one heart-stopping moment it was just as it used to be when they were a few years younger, when the teasing would end in cushion-throwing and Robert would yell at them to watch out for the ornaments or he'd have their guts for garters, in one of his trademark descents into slang whenever the familiarity of the occasion demanded it.

Did he get over-familiar with John — or Emma?

'You'll like the flat, Margaret,' her father was saying steadily, diffusing the unwarranted intrusion of her thoughts.

'If you all approve of it, I'm sure I will,' she said woodenly, knowing that however much she tried to push the ugliness out of her mind, it wasn't going to go away. Every instinct told her to forget it, but she couldn't.

★　★　★

By the time she got on the train back to Bournemouth she felt as if she had been

156

wrung out. She agreed that the flat was wonderful, Mel was a super girl working in advertising, and Margaret had spent ages at the estate agents and on the telephone sorting out the finances in order for Jenny to go ahead.

Robert used to do all this, she thought, mildly resentful that he wasn't here to do it now. And whoever said she was a dinosaur was right, but only because there had never been any need to bother her head with it all. She punched out Sarah's phone number on her mobile, ignoring the disapproving looks of fellow passengers, assuming her to be a businesswoman instead of a bored housewife.

Bored widow.

'Sarah, are we on for tonight?' she said at once. 'If I don't have some company of my own choosing, I shall scream.'

'Right, we missed you the other night. I'll round up the others,' Sarah said, reliable as always. 'You sound as if you need company. Where the hell are you, in a cattle truck or something?'

'On a train, coming home from London. It was a parents and children thing with me in the middle. I'll tell you more when I see you. There's something I want to ask you about.'

'Sounds mysterious.'

'Not really. But I'd rather not say it here.'

The elderly ladies across the aisle had perked up now, and Margaret smiled at them sweetly as she clicked off her phone. Mentioning the Gladby Agency was definitely not something she wanted to say over the phone, but if anyone in her circle had heard of them it would be Sarah.

Her smile faded. She shouldn't be pursuing this at all. If there was anything in it, she would be devastated, and if there wasn't, she would feel even guiltier that she had ever doubted Robert. He had never given her cause. Not once. She could dismiss the way he had always flirted with her girlfriends, knowing it meant nothing. She had always been around when it happened, anyway, at parties, or informal dinners, or social functions.

Which was just about the daftest thought anyone could have, nagged the little demons inside her head. You saw it when it happened, and you indulged it, because it was just friendly banter with your friends, but what about when you didn't see it? Was it always so harmless then?

Although she had been so ready to get away from London, Bournemouth seemed a very long way away now, and Margaret was trapped by a weird sense of never wanting to go back there at all. Not there, or anywhere.

Never wanting to see anyone she knew, or having to ask questions to which there might be the worst of answers. She wished she could flee to where no one knew her at all, where she could dispel these demons once and for all. Forget that any of them existed.

The hell of it was that she knew Robert wouldn't have approved of that attitude. It had never been his way to run away from problems, nor her father's — and it wasn't hers.

At last, stiff and taut with tension, she alighted at Bournemouth station and took a taxi home. Inside, she took a deep breath, appreciating with pleasure the sight of the home that had known such love and happiness. Everything was warm and welcoming, oozing the comfort and stability she and Robert had created over the years, and she knew she could be in danger of destroying it all.

Her answering machine was flashing, and she switched it on automatically while she wandered from room to room, the way you did, even after a short time away; picking up the letters from the mat; filling the kettle for a welcome cup of tea; only half listening to the messages.

'Where are you, Margaret?' she heard Fiona say. 'We missed you the other night.

June's got some news, but she won't tell us until we're all together.'

The bank manager, an old friend, was confirming, with one of his favoured clients, that her request for instant access to funds would be honoured whenever she needed them. Well, she knew that already. Everything for the purchase of Jenny's new flat had gone ahead with such ease in London. She had Robert's financial foresight to thank for that.

Now it was Keith, checking up on her. 'I heard from Jenny that you're enjoying it in London, Mum. Good for you, and I hope the journey home wasn't too horrendous.'

And John Franklin. 'Hi, Margaret. I'm back from my trip. How about meeting for a drink and a chat? Call me.'

She paused with her hand over the kettle. John. John and Robert. John going out on his so-called Singles Nights, which always made her and Robert laugh, since he never elaborated on where or what they were.

Maybe the Gladby Agency was one of his contacts and nothing to do with Robert at all. Emma might have been for John . . . except that she had phoned here and asked for Robert.

Her heart skipped a beat and then thudded haphazardly, and her eyes prickled with tears. How *could* she be so mistrusting, when there might easily be a simple explanation? She still wasn't sure what it could be, but she was willing to snatch at any straw to prove that Robert hadn't been less than the perfect husband she always believed. That had to be it. It was simply some contact Robert had found for his oldest friend. But you could hardly go and ask an old friend if they were in the habit of calling up a girl from an escort agency!

★ ★ ★

'The Gladby Agency?' Sarah echoed that evening, in answer to what Margaret hoped was an artless question. 'Good God, Margaret, if you want a bloke that badly, I think you could do better than that.'

'Don't be daft. I'm not looking for a bloke at all!'

'And if she was, there's always John,' Fiona added.

'Oh yes, I'm sure old reliable won't be slow in coming forward.'

'When you two have quite finished — ' Margaret said with a grin.

Fiona leaned on the bar of the pub in the middle of town. 'Why do you want to know, anyway, Mags?'

'I don't, really. It was just a name I heard

somewhere, and I thought you might know of it. At least, I thought Sarah might know.'

'Thanks! The day I need to go shopping for a bloke, I'll know my time has come for furry slippers and a candlewick dressing-gown.'

'I didn't think you could remember them,' Margaret said with a grin.

'I can't — '

'Does anybody want to hear my news or not?' June burst out, having sat through all this without saying a word.

'You're not getting married, are you?' Margaret said, as a wild guess.

'No. I have to go in for a biopsy next week.'

If there was anything destined to wipe the smiles off anyone's face, that was it. Nobody said a word for a moment, and then Margaret put her arm around June's shoulders, while the other two just stared dumbly.

'Oh God, June — why haven't you said something before?'

She brushed Margaret aside, and her voice was brittle.

'Because this is just the reaction I expected and didn't want. Look at the three of you, already writing me off. Well, forget it. One little lump isn't going to be the death of me, I can tell you.'

'When did you find out?' Fiona said, white-faced.

'I went for a routine mammogram, since it's being offered for the over-fifties and now that I bloody qualify, I thought I'd better show up. What I didn't expect, was that this — this *thing* would show up as well.'

'You always said you were forty-five!' Fiona accused.

'I lied,' June said.

For the first time they all saw the naked fear in her eyes. Without thinking, they closed ranks, their arms around one another, silent, because there seemed no adequate words to say at that moment.

'Blimey, what's this, lezzie night?' a yob yelled out from a far corner.

'Piss off,' Sarah yelled back.

June was shaking, and then they realized it was with laughter. She broke away, and picked up her drink.

'Oh come on, I'm not dead yet. Let's find a table and hear about Mags's trip to London with the old folks.'

'I'd rather hear about *you*,' Margaret said at once. 'Why didn't you tell us about this mammogram before?'

'It was only last week, that's why.'

'And they've arranged a biopsy already?' She didn't want to say it, but she knew it must be what they were all thinking.

'Private clinic,' June said in a clipped voice,

'and I know what I've always said about queue jumping, but hell, when it's your twins you're talking about, and your life, you start seeing things differently.'

'Good for you,' Sarah said. 'The quicker you get it sorted, the better. And it'll be nothing, you'll see.'

'I know,' June said. 'That's what I keep telling myself.'

Margaret raised her wine-glass towards her in silent salute. And right at that moment, a little suspicion about whether or not a husband might have strayed once or twice in his lifetime, seemed very small-fry compared with a life-threatening illness in one of her dearest friends. She put it out of her mind — for the time being, at least. Far more important was bolstering up June with a succession of boob jokes in appallingly bad taste, but which had them all screaming with laughter and behaving more like teenagers than forty-somethings — fifty as far as June was concerned, an undisclosed fact that had hit them all with a little shock.

As far as the kids were concerned they were middle-aged, but not to themselves. Never to themselves. But you had to face it sometime that getting older meant facing all the trappings that went with it. It was something else you never thought about until it

164

happened. Something that as a couple, Margaret and Robert had never thought about, being so young and healthy and in their prime — and all that crap.

But with June's news, it had all returned — all the anguish of that terrible moment when she had realized Robert was dead, and she was alone. There was no worse moment on earth.

And what kind of support was she giving now, practically having one of her best friends dead and buried, just because there was a tiny blip on an X-ray machine, which was how June had described it as she finally got around to explaining it all to them? It was a tiny blip, no more. It might mean breast cancer. It might not. Nobody could be sure until they had done the biopsy. That was what June had been told, and that was what they all had to believe.

It was a ghastly thing to come home to, Margaret thought later, wandering about the house but not yet ready to fall into bed where thoughts became sharper, and often too sharp for comfort. It was a million times more ghastly for June, of course, but for all of them too, because they were all so close. Good friends, through thick and thin and divorce.

It made them all feel vulnerable, because what affected one, affected them all. They were a sisterhood. No men involved. Her thoughts juddered on as she made coffee and forgot to drink it. But it was true. They were all women alone now, and the thought of one of them not being around any more was unbearable.

'Oh, to hell with it,' she said out loud, just to hear her own voice in the void that was this lovely house.

She turned on the TV, and turned it off again, not wanting to watch the starving millions in other parts of the world. She and Robert had always given hefty contributions to charities, but right now she couldn't bear to have it all paraded in front of her in her living-room.

The answering machine was flashing. She flipped the switch automatically.

'So are you home, or have you disappeared again?' came John Franklin's voice. 'I only ask, because I ran into Keith this evening and he thought you were due back from London today. I'm still available for clubbing, dancing, shoulder-crying, or whatever else you may require,' he finished teasingly. 'Miss you, babe.'

Margaret smiled. *Miss you babe* indeed. What did he think she was — a teeny-bopper? It gave her heart a quick lift, all the same. And company was better than wallowing in gloom, even if he wouldn't thank her for calling at nearly midnight. Then again — when had he ever refused to come running?

Before she paused to analyse this, she had called his number.

'I know it's late, and I'm not in the mood for clubbing, dancing or shoulder-crying, but if you feel like talking — '

'I'll be there,' he said.

Margaret hung up the phone. What the hell had she called him for, anyway? Spur-of-the-moment actions weren't really her style, as everyone kept telling her.

But nothing was like it was before any more. She wasn't the same. The way the family treated her wasn't the same, still behaving as if they had to tread on eggshells whenever she was around — except for the occasions when Jenny blew up. And whatever earthy language she used, at least it was *normal*.

And now June wasn't the same. June had to go into hospital for a biopsy, and the thought of losing someone else she loved was starting to feel like an enormous mountain she couldn't climb.

By the time John arrived, she had already poured herself a whisky, even though she didn't care for it much. Robert always said it was good for the nerves.

John took her in his arms and gave her a platonic kiss, then looked steadily into her eyes. 'So how have you been, or is that a stupid question? And I see you've started without me.'

'Never mind hinting that I'm turning into a lush. I'm in need of company,' she said brutally. 'I heard some unsettling news tonight, so just talk, right?'

'OK, but if we're going to talk into the wee small hours, I shall need some fortifying, and that means staying over. If it's going to be a problem, tell me now.'

'Of course it's not a problem. And you can pour one for yourself. I don't really feel like acting the gracious hostess tonight.'

He laughed. 'You can hardly escape that. Even when you're mad, you're still gorgeous, though that hairstyle rather defeats the old Grace Kelly look.'

'Thank goodness,' Margaret said, almost savagely. 'Perhaps people will start taking me seriously now instead of like some blonde bimbo.'

'Grace Kelly was never a blonde bimbo — and she did get her prince, just like you did, sweetheart. So what's this unsettling news you heard tonight?' he went on quickly, realizing he may have overstepped the mark.

But Margaret hardly noticed. 'June — one of my best friends — has got to have a biopsy. Breast cancer's a possibility.'

'But not a certainty. You're intelligent enough to know that, Margaret.'

'I do know it. I just can't seem to handle it.' She was glad he didn't sit beside her on the sofa, and sprawled out in his usual armchair, the whisky bottle on the small table between them.

'It's because of Robert, darling. Everything that happens will seem to be exaggerated for a while. It's only to be expected. Good things will seem bright, and bad things will seem like disasters, but it will pass.'

'You're an expert, are you? You and that bloody *Frasier* who Mrs Ashley thinks is God's answer to sorting out the world.'

'I'm no expert. I just know that time — '

'If you're going to tell me time's a great healer, then don't. It's the sort of crap I've been getting for months now, and it doesn't work. You think you're doing OK, and then something like this happens, and your whole world is suddenly out of sync again.'

'You said as much to June, did you?'

'Of course I didn't! What do you think I am — the angel of death?'

'No. Just a good friend, but Margaret, you can't take everybody's ills on your shoulders.

You have to be objective about this, and I'm sure June will come out of it OK.'

She managed to resist a sharp retort that he considered himself a bloody clairvoyant as well now. She'd invited him here to talk, not to hurl insults at him, but he always said he had a broad back where she was concerned, and he knew her well enough to take it all.

Her head was starting to throb gently now, and she knew she needed black coffee. 'What did Keith have to say?' she asked, changing the subject.

'Not much. He never has much time for me, does he?'

'I can't think why!'

'Can't you? He just told me you'd gone to London and that Jenny had taken all Robert's computer stuff with her. And that he's organizing the sale of the boat and Robert's cars.'

'What do you mean — *can't I?*' Margaret said, ignoring the rest.

'Work it out for yourself, Margaret. Anyway, I'm sure your friend will be all right.'

She was in a contrary mood by now, not wanting reassurances that were no more than platitudes. She'd heard too many of them after Robert died.

'I'm going to make some coffee,' she said abruptly. 'And then you can tell me all about your latest trip and who you pulled. I'm damn sure you never had need of the Gladby Agency!'

It was the most obscure way she could bring it up without actually asking. But she was instantly tuned in to the way his silence followed her out to the kitchen. It was as tangible as if his thoughts were printed in neon-lit letters across the sky: *'How the hell did you get hold of that little bit of information?'*

9

It really didn't matter any more. By the time she brought coffee back to the living-room John was dozing in the chair, or at least making a fair attempt at it.

'Sorry, I must have been more tired than I thought. No reflection on your company, of course.'

'Bull. It was thoughtless of me to call you so late. I think I'll take my coffee up to bed, and you can follow whenever you like. Well, not follow exactly, but you know what I mean.'

He grinned. 'I know. You just like the idea of having someone in the house with no strings attached. Goodnight, Margaret.'

He watched her go, knowing she would be out for the count as soon as her head hit the pillow. Emotion did that for you, and she had probably had a basinful of that tonight, after learning June's news. It didn't take much to knock you back when you were already vulnerable. He wished he dared offer her a different kind of comfort than just a friendly shoulder, but he knew it was much too bloody soon, if ever. He was under no illusion

172

that whatever his faults, Margaret had been madly in love with Robert, and he couldn't be the one to intrude on that idyll. Nor to give any hint of what those faults were.

He had to admit though, that her casual mention of the Gladby Agency had stalled him for a minute. He knew he had deleted all the disks that had the faintest reference to anything best forgotten. Unless Robert had been foolish enough to keep a printed copy of them.

He drank the coffee, and helped himself to a couple more whiskies before he went silently into Robert's old study. It was still very much Robert's domain, even though the computer equipment was gone, and he soon found what he was looking for. Margaret was an artless woman, and wouldn't have thought of hiding a computer print-out away from prying eyes. Nor expect that prying eyes would be searching for something that might be incriminating — not in the criminal sense, but in a way that would harm her perfect vision of her husband. And that was something she must be protected against.

He folded the piece of paper and slipped it into his pocket, breathing in the aura of the room that still held so much of Robert's presence, then giving a silent nod to the photo of himself and his buddy, laughing and

173

smiling into the camera with their arms around each other after a successful golf tournament. Then he left the study and went to bed.

★   ★   ★

Margaret heard the sound of the doors clicking throughout the house, and far from feeling alarmed she felt a hazy sense of security, knowing that she wasn't alone here. This first night, coming back from London, she had felt a deep need for someone else's presence. Even John's, whom Keith didn't trust, for some wild reason of his own.

It was an unreasoning sense of jealousy, of course. Keith, the tough guy policeman, who had naturally expected her to turn to him now that his father was dead, even if Laura might resent this inroad into their lives. But clever though Keith was, he wasn't bright enough to appreciate her preference for people of her own age to take comfort in.

Keith, like the rest of her family, if she gave them half a chance, would smother her. If not physically, then by endless phone calls and penetrating looks whenever they thought she didn't notice.

John was also sensitive enough to know that making breakfast for two was an intimacy she couldn't cope with, and to her relief he was gone by the time she got up next morning, leaving a prominent note by the kettle on the kitchen counter.

'Hope your head's in one piece this morning. We'll go dancing next time you're in the mood. Wish June the best of luck from me. Love, John.'

Margaret smiled. He was nice. He was thoughtful. He'd make any woman a damn good husband. But not her. He didn't do a thing for her in that way and never had. Maybe nobody would turn her on, ever again. Maybe she wouldn't ever want them to. You got used to a man when you lived with him for twenty-five years. You knew his approach, his touch, his taste, his smell, his everything.

She swallowed. She had got up determined to be cheerful, and here she was, already wallowing . . . it was John's mention of June that did it. Reminding her.

'Oh bum,' she said out loud, realizing how often she was doing that these days, the way you did when there was nobody else to talk to, or answer back. Not until Mrs Ashley arrived, anyway, and she was being pathetic if she was looking forward so eagerly to the arrival of her daily. That was the way old ladies behaved, and at forty-two — nearly forty-three now, she reminded herself — she was far from joining their ranks yet, thank you very much. Besides, Mrs Ashley was a good fifteen years older than she was.

The sound of the post dropping through the letter-box made her jump, and she picked up the wad of letters from the mat without much interest. Until she saw the Guernsey hotel logo on one of them again, and her heart leapt. It was addressed to Robert, and she opened it quickly, knowing it was from their honeymoon hotel from where Robert had presumably sent for the current brochure. This was a follow-up letter, hoping that Mr and Mrs Jarvis would be visiting them again for their anniversary, and although they were now under new management, it would be their pleasure to see them on this important occasion.

The kettle screamed out, and she switched it off with shaking hands. It was always going to be like this. How many more letters would there be until the hotel was satisfied that Mr and Mrs Jarvis would not be visiting them this year? The only way to stop them would be to write an explanatory letter — or to get Keith to do it. The minute she thought it, she was disgusted at such weakness.

Wasn't she even capable to writing her own letters now? And what was the effort of writing an explanatory letter compared with the enormity of her friend's medical problem? Such news certainly put everything else in perspective, and by the time Mrs Ashley was due, she had written the reply to the Guernsey hotel and was reaching for an envelope. She knew Robert kept them all in a drawer . . . her hand paused, certain that the drawer was the one where she had pushed the computer print-out with the name of the Gladby Agency on it, and Emma's name. It certainly wasn't here now.

'Coo-ee, anybody home?' came Mrs Ashley's usual greeting.

'In here,' Margaret said, frowning.

It probably wasn't worth bothering about, and she was prepared to admit that she had got a bit absentminded lately. But it was puzzling all the same, and puzzles were, well, puzzling.

'Oh, thank goodness you've got rid of that blessed computer,' Mrs Ashley said at once. 'They're always going wrong, and they take far more time at the bank to add up a few figures than the girl behind the counter ever did. My old man says they're more trouble than they're worth.'

'Familiar with them, is he?' Margaret said with a smile.

'No, he just don't trust them, that's all. But

I always say it's people you can't trust, not machines.'

'That's a bit cynical, isn't it? But I daresay it applies to some people.'

Mrs Ashley beamed. 'Well, nobody around here, I'm glad to say. So did you have a nice time in London?'

London seemed so long ago now that it was hard for Margaret to realize she had only got home yesterday. But she hadn't known then that one of her best friends was about to go under the surgeon's knife. She shuddered, wondering how it must feel to anticipate fearfully one of the worst things that could happen to a woman. However much you cared about a person, you couldn't share that agony. It was something everyone had to do alone. Like dying. And she was fiercely glad that at least Robert never had to suffer the agony of a long and painful illness.

'You all right, Mrs J?'

'I'm fine, just thinking about going to Guernsey sometime, actually.'

Now why the hell had she said that? She had no intention of going there ever again. The words had just slipped out, and the letter in her hand seemed to be burning her fingers. And all the while that she was listening to Mrs Ashley saying how nice it would be for her to get away, she was hearing it as if it was

178

coming through a fog, and asking herself why not? Perhaps she should go back, reliving all the sweet memories — if she could face it again. But not to the same hotel. Definitely not that.

'A holiday is just what you need, and not with the family either,' Mrs Ashley said shrewdly, ever the amateur philosopher. 'You need to sort things out.'

'Well, I might call in at the travel agents this morning, to pick up a few brochures for next year,' she said next, only half meaning it.

'You shouldn't wait that long, Mrs J. You need the break now.'

Margaret shook her head. It was almost September now, and she wouldn't go anywhere until she knew how her friend June was progressing. Margaret's silver wedding anniversary was the 20 October, and she was sure she couldn't bear to be in Guernsey at that time. The month that shouted at her was April, which would be the anniversary of the month Robert died. People said it took a year for you even to start to recover, once you had faced all the anniversaries, birthdays, Christmas . . . weddings.

She couldn't even envisage thinking about Robert having been dead for a year, but she was taking one step at a time, and if a trip to Guernsey gave her something positive for the future — hardly something to look forward to in one way, but a remembrance in another — then she would think about it.

★ ★ ★

'I think it's a great idea,' Keith and Laura said when they called on her, almost as simultaneously as if they were Siamese twins.

'But I agree with your daily,' Keith went on. 'Why wait that long?'

'It's necessary.'

'Not financially, surely,' Laura said, and then reddened. 'Oh, I'm sorry, Margaret, it's no business of mine, but I've heard that they have a real Indian summer in the Channel Islands at the end of the year.'

'Finances don't come into it,' Margaret told her, thinking her one of the most insensitive women on God's earth.

Even her apologies were irritating. And she really knew nothing about Margaret at all. Nothing about Margaret and Robert and their love affair with Guernsey.

Some might think it curious that they had never gone back. But when something had once been so perfect, it might be a risk to go back and spoil the illusion. Was she taking a risk, even thinking about it?

Conversely, she knew that she was not.

Robert would want her to go. And go now. Because he would be there with her in spirit.

As if he could read her thoughts, Keith put his arm around her and kissed her. 'Mum, if you stay here for your wedding anniversary, you'll only mope. You should get away at that time.'

'Actually, I can't plan anything until I know what's happening with June. It would feel as if I'm abandoning her.'

And then of course, she had to explain to them, and it made it all more real and more nerve-racking, and the possibility of losing a friend so soon after her husband brought the reality of mortality screaming at her again.

Not that she was losing her. It was only a tiny lump, not even visible, not even big enough to feel, except by a specialist.

And now Laura was murmuring platitudes about how much they could do these days, and a mastectomy didn't have to mean the end of everything. Even celebrities had them these days, sometimes just for cosmetic purposes, and no one would ever know.

'It's not the same as having false teeth, Laura,' Margaret snapped.

'I know, but it doesn't have to be the end of the world either, does it?'

'Only if it happens to you.'

They glared at one another, or rather,

Margaret glared, while Laura tried to remember that this was Keith's mother, and she was far more scratchy than she used to be, and they had to handle her with kid gloves.

Margaret was glad when they left. They were so smug in their togetherness. She was happy for them. But not for herself. She was just — adrift. It was the only way she could describe it. But she wasn't going anywhere until June was safely through her ordeal, whatever it entailed.

★   ★   ★

They took her to the hospital *en masse*, Sarah saying they definitely seemed more like a junior version of the Golden Girls compared with some of the old dears on the ward, so that should cheer June up. She shrugged, wrapped up in her own world where everyone went when they were faced with something awful.

'No, it doesn't. You can be dead tomorrow, whether you're nine or ninety.'

'Or forty-nine,' Margaret said without thinking.

The others busied themselves with helping June get her things into the locker. The small op was tomorrow, and she would only be in for two nights — *unless* — but that was something they wouldn't consider.

Nobody had asked Margaret whether or not she wanted to come here. It had simply been assumed that they would all be there together.

She had been glad at the time, because it had taken the decision out of her mind, but now that she was here, it all came rushing back; the unmistakable hospital smells; the swish of the uniforms; the brisk and cheerful efficiency; the night Robert died, and the dreadful feeling of emptiness. It was the same hospital, but thankfully, not the same ward. There would be no staff members here to remember her and ask how she was.

A nurse was hovering, clearly wanting to get on with things. There was one thing about it, Laura had commented, cheerfully going in with both feet. When it came to breasts, they didn't waste much time.

'Why don't you all go now?' June said. 'Have a drink on me tonight, and call the hospital tomorrow afternoon, when it's all over.'

There wasn't much point in staying, and June was adamant that she didn't want them visiting that evening. The op was scheduled for first thing the following morning, and she intended getting a good night's sleep before they messed up her twins, which was how she always described her breasts.

'She's being so bloody brave,' Fiona muttered, as they left for the nearest coffee shop. 'I'm sure I wouldn't have that much courage.'

'Yes you would,' Margaret told her. 'You find it when you need it.'

She wouldn't have believed it four months ago either. She hadn't had to face an operation, but it had felt as if part of her had been cut out when Robert died. That's what they said in books, and it was true, every bloody fanciful word of it. But here she was, still surviving, still drinking coffee and buying clothes and having her hair cut, and going clubbing now and then, and finding herself laughing over some of the things Robert used to say. Laughing with warm memories and no longer with quite so much pain or quite such intense grief.

And to their wild relief, June's news wasn't as dire as they had feared. If the surgeon had found cancer right away June had signed a consent form to agree to a more drastic op there and then. But it hadn't been found, and two weeks after the biopsy she went back to the hospital for the verdict, and reported back to the others, waiting nearby, with tears streaming down her face.

'It's OK! They found pre-cancer cells which hadn't yet developed into the real thing, and my lymph nodes were clear, so they're confident that the biopsy removed them all. I have to have regular check-ups and mammograms, and I have to take Tamoxifen pills, but apart from that, no further treatment. God, the *relief*!'

Her voice choked on the last word, and then they were all crying and hugging one another, and a nurse appeared and silently handed them a box of tissues before disappearing again.

'Let's get out of here,' June said finally. 'I don't know how you coped when Robert was brought in, Mags, but the smell of this place is making me gag.'

It was the first time she had acknowledged how Margaret might be feeling, but Margaret didn't blame her. Illness made you selfish, made you turn in on yourself, and so did grief.

She had put any idea of going to Guernsey on hold because of June, but now that everything was all right, apart from a natural soreness and the discovery that the bruising had temporarily turned one of her twins black, June was in good spirits. And Margaret's twenty-fifth anniversary was coming closer.

185

They all knew the date in October, and it was Fiona who mentioned it.

'Are you having any of the family round on the 20th, Mags?'

'Shut up, Fee,' Sarah said at once. 'She doesn't want to be reminded of it.'

'Why wouldn't I? It's hardly something I'm going to forget — or want to forget. Unlike the rest of you, I didn't throw Robert out with the dishwater.'

They looked at her in astonishment.

'Blimey, Mags, it's not like you to be so caustic,' Sarah said. 'And you know we only want to help. If you're not having the family round, how about us? We could hold a private party in Robert's memory. For those who loved him.'

'Especially you,' Fiona told her.

Sarah grinned. 'All right, Margaret knows very well I always had a soft spot for him, and vice-versa, but nobody could help loving him, could they? He was that sort of bloke.'

'It could also be a double celebration on my account,' June added quickly. 'Since I've just decided I intend to live for the next fifty years.'

'When you've all finished deciding for me,' Margaret managed to put in, 'I don't plan to be around here on the 20th.'

'Are you going to London again to see

Jenny and Ben and your parents?' June asked. 'I think that's a good idea.'

'No, I'm not going to London. I don't know where I'm going yet. Just away from here.'

'Why?' Fiona said.

'Don't be daft, Fee,' Sarah said irritably. 'Can't you see why? She'll want to go somewhere where she hasn't been before, a clean slate. But if you want company, Mags, wherever it is, I'll gladly come with you for a week or two.'

'Thanks, but no thanks. I know you mean it for the best — all of you — but wherever I decide to go, I want to be on my own.'

And the last thing she wanted was to have friends around her, even good friends, turning the day of her anniversary into some kind of wake with their separate memories of Robert. They had done that already.

'Well, if you change your mind, you only have to ask,' Sarah said, clearly none too sure about this newly independent and deter-mined Margaret.

'Cornwall's nice at this time of year,' Fiona offered.

'So's Barbados, but I'm not going there either. Now, let's leave the subject, please, and decide where we're going tonight instead.'

★ ★ ★

In the end, there wasn't really any choice of destination in her mind, however much she fought against the idea. It was the only choice.

She didn't tell anyone until it was all cut and dried, and as she had anticipated, Keith couldn't understand her need to be alone.

'You should at least accept Sarah's offer to go with you, Mum.'

'Do you think I'm incapable of spending a few weeks on my own?'

'But this is more than just a couple of weeks. You're telling me you've booked for a whole month! I think it's crazy. Why didn't you come and talk it over with Laura and me first?'

'Why on earth should I? What gives you the right to decide what I should and shouldn't do? You're my son, not my keeper. And when I want Laura's opinion, I'll ask for it.'

'You don't like her, do you?'

'It's none of my business, any more than where I choose to go is any of yours. If it was your father and I taking a holiday, you'd be pleased for us.'

She wouldn't let her voice waver. She damn well *wouldn't*.

'But that's my point. I'm not sure why

188

you're doing this at this time, Mum. And to Guernsey of all places. You don't know anyone there.'

'Well, Keith, that's *my* point. I don't know anyone there, and I simply intend to spend a pleasant, reflective time away from you all.'

'You'll miss your nights out with the girls,' he commented, taking a new tack, even though he didn't particularly approve of the way the four of them acted like scatty teenagers at times.

'I shall miss you all, too,' and she was finally unable to stop the catch in her breath. 'But it's something I have to do, and no one's going to stop me.'

'Well, promise to phone me as soon as you get there. You and Dad always made the rest of us do so the minute we arrived anywhere.'

And now the son was looking out for the mother . . .

'I promise, darling,' she said, leaning forward to kiss him. 'And while I'm away, I'd be really grateful if you would sort out the sale of the cars and the boat, so that they've gone by the time I get back. The last thing I'll want to face when I get back is the sight of prospective buyers looking over them all.'

'It'll be done,' he said.

★ ★ ★

A surprising supporter was John Franklin, who couldn't see anything wrong or macabre in Margaret wanting to spend time in the place where she and Robert had once been so deliriously happy.

'Not in the same hotel though,' she told him. 'I found a place that's at the opposite end of the island from the one where we stayed. It's not so big, but big enough that I can be quite anonymous. And hopefully, it won't be filled with families at this time of year. It caters for singles as a speciality.'

'It puts us in the same category now, then. Being single, I mean.'

Something in the way he said it made her look at him sharply.

'I don't consider myself in any category,' she said carefully. 'I just happen to be taking a break on my own, that's all.'

'Hey, I didn't mean to offend you — '

'You didn't. Just that I'm not exactly going on a *singles* holiday, am I?'

'So what are you going for if it's not a rude question?'

Margaret laughed, aware of the slightly prickly atmosphere between them now, and not wanting it to last.

'Maybe to find myself. That's what the kids call it, isn't it?'

'I wasn't aware that you were lost.'

'Then you're a fool,' she replied flatly, 'if you don't know that I've been lost for the last four months.'

It was only because they knew one another so well, and for so long, that she knew she could say it without hurting his feelings. Nor had he hurt hers. In any case, she enjoyed the way they sparred with one another. It was hardly the aggressive way Robert and Jenny used to do, which often ended in shouts and tears, but this was sparky, making her feel alive.

'Is there anything I can do for you while you're away?' John said abruptly. 'Anything of Robert's you still need sorting out and don't feel like tackling?'

'Hopefully Keith's going to get rid of the cars and boat before I get back. Apart from that, I don't think so. If you want to keep an eye on the place now and then, I've no objection, but you'd better let Mrs Ashley know if you're going to be around, or she might think I've had burglars.'

'And Keith.'

'And Keith.'

'What have your kids got against me, apart from the fact that I adore their mother?' John said casually. Far too casually for comfort.

'Isn't that enough?' Margaret said, laughing. 'Anyway, Ben likes you.'

'Oh well, one out of three isn't bad, I suppose.'

It was a conversation that was going nowhere, and Margaret was starting to feel tired, and more than a little depressed. Once she had made the decision to go to Guernsey she had felt exhilarated, as if Robert was guiding her, telling her this was a good thing, and that he would be with her in spirit if not in body. It was only when she met opposition from everybody else, except Mrs Ashley, that she realized how such opposition could wear a person down.

Perhaps that was why she had always given in so gracefully to any suggestion Robert — or the children — had made in the past. She was simply unused to making momentous decisions — you couldn't count going to the hairdresser or choosing menus for dinner parties — and dealing with arguments. It made her what Jenny would definitely call a twenty-two carat wimp.

Well, now she wasn't. All was right with her world, such as it was, and at the weekend she was taking the high-speed ferry from Poole to Guernsey and starting a month of healing.

10

It was going to be a trip with a difference in many ways. It wasn't just for pleasure, or nostalgia, but as a kind of exorcism, even though that seemed the completely wrong word to use. It wasn't as if she wanted to put Robert out of her life, far from it. But she did need to feel free of whatever hold he still had on her self-reliance. She needed to feel in charge of herself.

That first time they had stayed in an expensive hotel in St. Martin's. This time, Margaret didn't want anything so grand, and had opted for La Roque, a smaller hotel in Castel. It wasn't right on the beach, but set back a little, giving her the privacy and seclusion she sought. As the words entered her mind, she told herself uneasily that she shouldn't think of it as a retreat. She wasn't retreating from the world, just trying to make sense of her particular part in it.

By the time she left, she had been as efficient as Robert would have been; making sure Mrs Ashley would still give the place a thorough going-over once a week, and pick up the mail at the same time; and being assured that Keith would vet any answer-machine calls. She had arranged with the pool man to do the necessary, and for old Joe to continue with tidying up the autumn mess in the gardens. The window-cleaners wouldn't need to come round until just before she came back, and once she had satisfied herself that she had done all the things Robert usually took care of, she began to think about herself.

There were clothes to pack for a month. Since she wasn't expecting or planning to go dancing or socializing to any great degree, there was no need to make a splash. But she had always been an elegant dresser, and there was no way she would ignore dressing for dinner. It was a matter of pride.

Apart from that, she planned to spend much of her time walking in jeans and trainers and fleeces. It would be good for her figure and her health, and some of the long stretches of beaches and pretty little bays were among the loveliest in the world. She and Robert had tramped a few of them, but there were still many to be explored, and she intended to do just that.

'Always leave something for next time,' he would often say. 'Then you'll be sure to come back again.'

Except that they hadn't, not together.

So there had to be a mixture of informal clothes, and a few formal ones. And shoes, lots of shoes, which were her passion, and which she liked to vary frequently for the sake of her feet. And jewellery. She loved jewellery. Margaret found herself smiling as the list went on, and an unexpected feeling of excitement began to sweep through her. Whatever the reason, she was going back to the island she and Robert had fallen in love with all those years ago, and nothing could take away the joy of discovering it all over again.

She sorted through her jewellery boxes. Robert had been more than generous over the years, but she didn't want to take anything too valuable. What Jenny always called 'the good stuff' was kept in the wall safe in the study, and it would be sensible to put the rest of it in there while she was away.

She didn't use the safe often, though she had needed to sort out stocks and shares, insurance policies and house deeds after Robert's death, and she felt a small shiver at opening it again now. But it was nonsense to feel that way. All she was doing was placing some of her second-best jewellery in the safe for security.

At the back of the safe her fingers encountered something that slid through her fingers. It felt like a chain of some sort, and must have been left there in a hurry without being put inside the velvet cases and boxes. She pulled the chain free, and then sat back on her haunches, staring at it.

It wasn't hers, and in any case Robert had had excellent taste, and this was little more than a cheap trinket compared with the costly jewels he had bought his wife over the years. The thin gold chain had a pendant dangling from it, and the pendant was the jagged half of a heart. It reminded Margaret vaguely of something she had seen elsewhere, but she couldn't think where. Curiously, she turned the pendant over.

On the reverse side, one word was engraved: His. And since the pendant was one half of a heart, it presumably meant that there was a matching one somewhere that said: Hers.

Perhaps Robert had picked these things up somewhere, intending to give the other half to her as a fun gift — it was little more than a Christmas cracker gift — and then thought better of it. It certainly wasn't worthy of the gifts he usually bought her, and it might have been simply the sentimentality of the thing that had attracted him. Two halves of the same heart.

Her throat caught for a moment, and she

placed the pendant back into the safe almost reverently, knowing there was no way she would wear it.

Before she got too maudlin about it, she gave up wondering, and finished her packing. She had been tempted to take her car to Guernsey, but then decided against it. She had a whole month to breathe in the clear air of the island, and knowing how narrow the roads were, it would do nothing for her equilibrium if she was constantly watching out for traffic. There were always taxis to take her anywhere she wanted to go, and there were her own two feet, which she intended to use every day.

Sarah had offered to take her to the ferry and she hadn't demurred, knowing that her friend was still a bit off because Margaret hadn't accepted her offer to take the holiday with her, or at least part of it.

'Be sure to keep in touch,' Sarah said, when Margaret had joined the line of foot passengers waiting to join the high-speed ferry. 'You know how we worry about you, and if you change your mind about company, you only have to ask.'

'I'd rather you and Fee took care of June. I wouldn't want her to think we were all deserting a sinking ship.'

'Not quite the best of jokes to make in the

circs, is it, darling?' Sarah said, eyeing the gaping jaws of the ferry that was now accepting cars and lorries.

'Probably not. But thanks for your help, Sarah, and I promise I'll send you a postcard or three.'

'See that you do, and don't do anything I wouldn't do. Or maybe you should. It'll do you a power of good!'

Margaret was smiling as she went on board and found her allocated seat. There was nothing Sarah wouldn't do for a laugh. Margaret often wished she could be more like her, taking every day as it came, and never mind the consequences. But she couldn't, and that was that.

★   ★   ★

A couple of hours later the first sight of the island came into view, and by the time Margaret stepped out on to the balmy Guernsey shore at St Peter Port, she was feeling a mixture of excitement and doubt that she had done the right thing after all. But the journey in itself was an adventure, especially alone. They had gone by plane last time, of course. Nothing but the best for Robert and his bride. And now she was no longer a bride, but a widow.

You never bargained for that. You never saw it coming.

'Are you looking for a taxi, lady?' she heard a voice say close by.

'Yes please,' she said quickly. 'Do you know La Roque hotel, in Castel?'

'Sure, no problem,' he said. 'You get inside and I'll put your bags in the boot. Staying quite a while, are you?'

So she had a lot of luggage. Robert always teased her about never being able to travel light. There was always something to include at the last minute, just in case.

'A month,' she said coolly.

She had a thing about talkative taxi-drivers. It was the same kind of embarrassment she felt in a lift with other people. It was stupid and irrational, but she had never been as garrulous as Robert, who could make conversation with strangers as if he had known them all his life. She couldn't.

'First visit?' the man went on conversationally, eyeing her through the driving mirror as he whizzed the car up through the narrow streets away from St Peter Port. She didn't miss the flicker of interest in his face, and for that she supposed she should be grateful. She hadn't lost it then. But she already knew that. John Franklin could never resist telling her so. She didn't welcome it then and she didn't welcome it now, but it wasn't in her nature to be rude.

'I've been here once before, but it was a long time ago.' A lifetime ago.

'I've lived here all my life,' he went on chattily. 'I was a kid during the Occupation, but I can still remember the shortages — and the way some of the German soldiers took pity on us little 'uns and showed us photos of their own kids at home. You got kids, have you?'

'Grown-up ones,' Margaret felt obliged to say.

She and Robert had visited all the sites of the Occupation during the Second World War, including the German Military Underground Hospital, and found it all pretty chilling. But it was clearly still a topic of conversation to the natives, and one that was now a tourist attraction, if you could call it that.

'Here on your own, are you?' the taxi-driver went on, when she was no more forthcoming.

'For the moment,' Margaret said, not sure why on earth she had said it at all, but unwilling to lie, and say that her husband would be joining her later.

'Won't be long now then,' he said after a lengthy pause, when he spent his time cursing beneath his breath at the traffic. It was minimal compared with the mainland, but since the roads were so narrow, it seemed more of a crush. But then he couldn't resist giving her a bit of local expertise.

'You'll like the La Roque if it's a quiet time you're after. It's not exactly bursting with night life, but comfortable enough.'

'A quiet time is exactly what I'm after,' Margaret said, meeting his eyes in the driving mirror at that moment, and smiling slightly to show him she wasn't being totally stand-offish.

He reported to his wife later that he'd had a real smasher in his car that day, what you might call a lady of refinement.

★ ★ ★

Margaret stepped out of the taxi, breathing in the fresh salt air wafting in from the sea. She was used to that, but the air here was totally different from that of home, softer and sweeter somehow, without all the pollution of the mainland. As they drove along the water's edge before turning into the short road leading to the hotel, she had been instantly enchanted, just as she had been before.

'Mrs Jarvis, is it?' the proprietor greeted her. 'Welcome to La Roque. I'm Louis Stevens and my wife is Anne-Marie. We're very informal here.'

'Thank you,' Margaret said, hoping they didn't expect her to be instantly informal too. She needed to get over the strangeness of arrival, to unpack her things and take a shower before taking a walk outside to get her bearings. And before meeting any other visitors at dinner that evening.

For the first time, she realized what an enormity it was in coming here at all. People didn't normally travel alone without a reason, at least not to holiday destinations, even out of season. People would naturally be curious about her, and the last thing she intended was to satisfy that curiosity.

She filled in the necessary information card at reception, and then Louis Stevens put her luggage on a trolley and took her up in the small lift to her room.

'We don't often get such long-term visitors here, Mrs Jarvis, so we've given you our very best room, with a fine view of the sea. Though I daresay you'll be used to that, living in Bournemouth.'

'I am, but it's not the same,' she told him with a smile, looking round her with pleasure at the extremely comfortable en suite room with its large bay window overlooking a glorious bay. 'It's very nice, thank you.'

He beamed at her. 'Well, if there's anything

you want, you just pick up the phone and call the desk. Otherwise we won't disturb you. Dinner's at seven, and you'll find everything you need to know about the hotel in the brochure on the dressing-table, and there are other brochures about the island there too.'

'I'm sure I shall find everything I need, Mr Stevens,' she assured him, just wanting to be left alone now, with a small threat of depression setting in.

'Righto, and the name's Louis,' he reminded her.

When she was alone she sat down heavily on the bed, wondering in a moment of panic what on earth she was doing here. What on earth had possessed her to think this was such a good idea? She was no good at being alone, not in a strange place, anyway. She could cope with it at home, because she had all her things around her, and people that she knew.

But wasn't that exactly what she had needed to get away from? To be anonymous, and to get through the day that would have been so wonderful for her and Robert, completely and utterly away from sympathetic eyes?

She drew a deep breath and told herself not to be so bloody feeble. If she was going to fall apart in the first few minutes of being here, how the hell was she going to cope with a month of it? But she wasn't going to fall apart. She thought methodically again, thinking in lists. Unpack, take a shower, and then go for a brisk walk.

After she had called Keith. If she didn't, she knew he'd be calling the hotel to check that she had arrived, inferring that she was an incompetent idiot. As if she was a senior citizen, as her mother called it now, instead of in her prime.

Miss Jean Brodie, you've got a lot to answer for.

'I'm fine. The hotel's lovely. The weather's marvellous,' she said, by rote when she heard his voice, as close as if he was in the next room.

'Don't overdo things then.'

What did he think she was intending to do — bungee-jumping?

'And if you get bored, Mum, get on the next ferry and come home.'

'Not a chance,' Margaret said firmly. 'I need some space and this is the perfect place to get it.'

'Right. Well, I suppose you know best.'

Not that he really believed it. And was there a tinge of relief in his voice now? Leaving them all to get on with their lives while the widow woman was being safely taken care of? Margaret bit her lip, wondering how long she was going to go on imagining nuances in peoples' voices that they didn't intend. Perhaps it was one of the stages you had to go through . . . like grief, anger, guilt . . . and not necessarily in that order.

'Grannie Annie called, by the way,' Keith went on. 'Your crazy sister's got married in New York, and she and the new man are flying to New Zealand on some TV advertising project or other they're working on together.'

'Good God!' Margaret said.

Though she shouldn't really be surprised at anything Brenda did. Brenda was the one who took chances — truly her mother's daughter — while Margaret didn't. But marriage had never been on her agenda, and now, apparently, it was.

'That's what I said. Laura and I are taking odds on how long it will last.'

At his sneer, Margaret felt suddenly defensive of her sister. You never knew — it might just work, if the unknown husband had the means of taming her!

'Don't be such a pig, Keith.'

He started to laugh. 'Hey man, don't you know that's what they call us?'

She laughed back, suddenly light-hearted,

and when they finished the call, she was still smiling.

★ ★ ★

Later, unpacked, refreshed and ready to face the outside, she stepped out of the hotel and made for the coast. It was less than 500 yards away, but it might have been in another world from the bustle of an English seaside town. It *was* another world, Margaret thought gladly. It was where she could find herself.

She brushed aside the twee hippy phrase, and amended it to this being the place where she could *be* herself, and even more, make friends with the new self she now was, instead of regarding this alien woman inside her as a freak.

She struck out along the road and then went down to the sandy cove nearby. One of the lovely things she and Robert had noted about Guernsey was the sense of peace everywhere, and the lack of any kiss-me-quick tourists, at least away from the main holiday towns. They had wanted to be alone then, and Margaret wanted to be alone now.

She walked for half an hour and then climbed on to one of the rocky outcrops in this particular stretch of sand. It was still warm for mid-October, and she closed her eyes for a treacherous moment, imagining that Robert was about to put his arm around her, and that she was about to snuggle into his embrace.

The touch of something soft and damp and warm on her hand made her toes curl with fright. Her eyes flew open, to meet the brown soulful gaze of a large shaggy English sheep-dog, his tail wagging furiously with blissful pleasure.

'Bruce, come here,' she heard a man's voice call out, and the next minute her solace was broken into as its owner came into view.

If it was true that people began to resemble their dogs, or vice versa, then this one was a good example, Margaret thought, in a flash of assessment. His sand-coloured hair was unkempt, his face so rugged it was almost ugly, and he wore cord trousers and a sweatshirt that had seen better days. Beside him — though she *wasn't* beside him, of course — she felt as immaculate as a queen.

'I'm really sorry about that,' the man apologized. 'Bruce adores strangers, and we don't see so many of them at this time of year, at least not solitary ones. He probably thought you were in need of a friend.'

He gave what was presumably meant to be an engaging smile. If this was a chat-up line, Margaret thought, unaccountably annoyed, then it missed by a mile. She didn't care to be seen as a lonely old trout sitting on a rock, either by a friendly dog or a rather disreputable-looking man.

But the unbidden image of herself forced an unwilling smile to her lips. It wasn't in her nature to be rude to people, and she shook her head quickly.

'It's all right. I quite like dogs. It was just unexpected, that's all. I was day-dreaming.'

He smiled again, ruffling his dog's head as he did so. She turned away. The animal clearly adored him, which was supposed to be a good sign in a man. Though since animals became attached to villains or heroes, she always thought it was a daft assumption. Dr Crippen could have been a dog-lover.

'It's a good place for day-dreaming,' the man agreed.

Margaret started, already absorbed in watching a small boat bobbing about on the near horizon.

'I'm sorry?'

'I said it's a good place for day-dreaming. I come here often.'

'Really,' Margaret said, making a mental note to try a different cove tomorrow. She knew she was being stand-offish, but she hadn't come here to strike up an instant friendship with one man and his dog . . . As the phrase entered her head, her facial muscles relaxed.

'Phew, that's better. I began to think we had really offended you in some way. I'm Philip Lefarge, by the way, and you've already met Bruce.'

He held out his hand, and it would be churlish to refuse it, so she put her hand in his for the briefest moment.

His palm was quite rough as if he was used to manual or outside work, which certainly went with his image. And since he was obviously waiting for an introduction, she made it grudgingly.

'I'm Margaret Jarvis. It was nice meeting you.'

She turned away again, hoping he'd get the message. She didn't want company. She didn't want anything except to be left alone, at least for these first few days, while she came to terms with why she was here, and overcame the strangeness of it all.

'See you around then, Margaret Jarvis,' he said, and the next minute he was striding back the way he had come, with Bruce barking joyfully at his heels.

She could almost hear Robert's words in her head.

'He's not our sort, Margaret. You couldn't see him done up in a tux for an important dinner with an influential client, could you?'

And Sarah's giggling aside.

'Always imagine them without their clothes on, darling. That cuts them down to size. Or not.'

From the undoubted phsyique of Philip Lefarge, she couldn't imagine that being without his clothes was going to diminish him in any way at all . . .

She stopped short, shocked at even thinking such a thing, and before she left her rock she smoothed down her jeans, picking off the inevitable dog hairs from where Bruce had left his calling card.

In the early days of their marriage she had fancied having a dog, but Robert had always been against it. Too messy. Too much of a tie. Too much of a nuisance in their busy and ambitious lives. *His* busy life.

She could have looked after it, and the kids would have loved it.

But since none of it had any relevance in her life now, it was pointless to waste energy thinking about what might have been. They had had a perfect marriage and a perfect life together, and nothing could take that away from her.

★　★　★

After a couple of days it was surprisingly easy to fall into the habit of using the Christian names of the hotel proprietors, and they were now calling her Margaret without her ever realizing whether she had asked them to do so or not. But since she would be here for a month, by the end of it they would probably feel like old friends. Other guests came and went on a two or three-night basis, so Margaret was never obliged to get into deep conversations with any of them.

She sent postcards to family and friends, and one to Mrs Ashley, who would want to be sure her lady was doing all right and not moping. Which she wasn't. She had a scrappy letter from Sarah, who said they were missing her already, and not to forget that if she wanted company . . . that they were off on a pub crawl that night and seeing who they could pull, and what a shame she was missing out.

Margaret smiled at that. With time and place distancing her, she already felt as if Sarah's shallow nonsense was from another planet. It was odd how you never saw it until you were away from it.

As the strangeness of simply being in Guernsey wore off, she spent her time contentedly tramping the beaches and byways. You thought you knew a place, but there was always some new discovery to find, and she and Robert hadn't visited this side of the island often. One thing was the same, though: they had fallen in love with it then, and she was falling in love with it now.

'Have you been shopping yet, Margaret? St Peter Port has some good dress shops,' Anne-Marie commented on the fourth evening, when she was serving Margaret her speciality of fresh mackerel in a herb sauce.

'I might go there sometime, but I'm happy enough just walking.'

The woman smiled approvingly. 'I can't argue with that, but you wear such lovely clothes, I just thought you'd be interested, that's all.'

'Thanks. What I must do, though, is send my mother some flowers for her birthday next week. Is there anywhere near here where I can get them?'

'Try PL's place. They'll arrange everything for you, and you can walk there easily enough from the hotel.'

She didn't twig it at all, until she was given a business card at the end of her meal. The PL Market Garden, Castel, Flowers by post, All year-round selection, Freesias a speciality. Owner Philip Lefarge.

As his image came into her mind, she wasn't going to let the little matter of having met him — and his dog — put her off. This was something she had to do. Her mother might be unconventional in many ways, but she set great store by birthdays, and Margaret would never live it down if she forgot. Annie would get a real kick from receiving flowers by post from the Channel Islands.

Tomorrow morning she would find the place and get it organized.

★ ★ ★

If she had expected to be greeted by the same rugged man she had seen on the beach, she was mistaken. He was nowhere to be seen in the vast greenhouses with The PL Market Garden emblazoned above the entrance to the site.

It was impressively large, and presumably thriving. As well as vegetable and fruit sections, there were the flower hot-houses, with detailed descriptions of all the flowers available, prices, styles and so on, there was a gift shop selling vases and plastic gnomes, pottery frogs, and carved house names by request.

Margaret knew that such places sold a little bit of everything, cashing in on the tourist market — and she didn't blame them for that. There was a small section of children's

213

toys, books about Guernsey, and a jewellery section, nothing fancy, just the sort of thing you might see on a market stall. Cheap and cheerful trinkets, Christmas cracker stuff . . .

She caught her breath as one of the items caught her eye. Or rather, two of them. Two thin gold-coloured identical chains, each with half of a ragged heart pendant dangling from them. The explanatory leaflet beside them read:

His and Hers pendants. Give your heart to the man in your life — or better still get him to give his heart to you.

It was the same pendant she had seen in Robert's safe. At least, one half of the pair. As her heart began to hammer painfully in her chest, she knew at once where she had seen its matching half.

11

She couldn't have said why she bought it, nor what she intended to do with it. It burned her fingers all the way back to the hotel. If the pendant in Robert's safe had had any significance at all, then it would probably be better not to know, and to leave the past undisturbed. But she had him to thank for her persistence, she thought bitterly. He would never have left a mystery unsolved. In reality, she really *didn't* want to know, not if it meant tarnishing his image, but the seeds of doubt were too strong to be denied now.

She stood at the wide bay window of her room, gazing out to where the stretch of sandy cove was so inviting that morning with the sun glinting on the gently rippling tide. It was perfect, like their lives together. Or so she had thought. Until now. And this was the very worst time to be having doubts, when she was here on this island where they had first known love, twenty-five years ago.

But she wasn't quite as naive as everyone thought she was. She might not be as sophisticated as Robert and John, nor as street-wise as Sarah and the girls, or her own children — or her *mother*, for God's sake, but she wasn't stupid either. Maybe she had been going around blinkered for all these years, but her eyes were opening wider now.

'Circumstantial evidence is no evidence at all,' she remembered hearing her father say, applying his military logic to any situation. 'If you can't face a criminal with the facts, you might as well forget it, because criminals will always be wilier than you are. Always one step ahead. That's the nature of the beast.'

Except that Robert wasn't a criminal, nor a beast; he was a loving husband and father, and there had to be an explanation.

Only he wasn't around to supply one, and Margaret didn't like the gnawing suspicion inside her, and wished desperately that she was able to blot it out.

She turned abruptly, aware that the room was stifling her. She needed to be outside again where there was space to breathe, and she strode purposefully along the coastal paths joining the various coves together, walking for miles as if to rid her mind of everything ugly that had no place there. Finally, she turned and walked back more slowly, ending up at the cove nearest the hotel. By now her stomach was telling her it was well past lunchtime, but food was the last thing on her mind.

She walked right to the water's edge, gazing into the crystal-clear water for a long while, as if it could reveal secrets. Then, with an uncharacteristic sense of rage, she pulled the twin pendants out of her pocket, and hurled them as far as she could into the Atlantic Ocean.

The next minute she was almost knocked off her feet by something heavy lunging against her. She screamed, losing her balance, and would have gone headlong into the water if someone hadn't hauled her back and into his arms.

'I'm so sorry about that,' she heard Philip Lefarge say in alarm. 'I told you Bruce liked you the other day, but I didn't think he was going to fall for you quite so literally — or that it was going to be the other way around.'

Margaret realized the oaf was laughing in relief now that she was all right, and she struggled out of the embarrassment of being held tightly in his arms.

'Can't you keep that damn great dog under control?' she snapped.

'I do my best, and I'm sure there was no damage done, except to startle you. Bruce obviously thought you were throwing pebbles into the sea, which is a game we play quite often.'

'The dog throws pebbles into the sea, does

he?' Margaret said sarcastically, quickly removing herself from his arms.

He looked at her thoughtfully. 'If you'd climb down off your high horse for a minute, I'd invite you out to dinner as a peace offering.'

'And what makes you think I would want to have dinner with you?'

He stepped back, holding up his hands. 'My God! My mistake for being sociable. It's just that I thought I saw you at my place this morning, and you always seem to be alone. But I wish your husband well, coping with that temper.'

It was all she needed. Not to enrage her more, but to make her crumble. It was just like the books said. Your knees did feel as if they were turning to water, and right now there was no way they could hold her up. She simply sank on to the soft, warm sand, and the dog obligingly licked her face to offer her comfort.

'Get off, Bruce,' she heard Philip say, and then he was hauling her to her feet again and holding her against his fleece jacket.

'I'd prefer not to have to apologize every time I see you, Margaret Jarvis,' he said gravely, 'but I've clearly done something to upset you. Whatever the problem is, it's always halved when it's shared.'

218

She looked at him mutely. He couldn't know, of course, but if only he hadn't used that one word — *halved*. Like a jagged heart.

'It's private, and I don't want to talk about it,' she said, her voice tight and tense. '*Can't* talk about it,' she added for good measure.

'It's often easier to talk to a stranger, and I'm a good listener, especially over dinner. Unless Mr Jarvis would object.'

Oh God. How persistent was this!

'He couldn't. I'm a widow.'

There. She had said it. Used the hateful word. Now what? Would he make a play for her? Pretend a sympathy she didn't want? Or shy away, wondering if she would end up being the one on the make?

'And I'm divorced. So that makes the score even. Dinner then? I'll pick you up at seven, if you tell me which hotel you're staying at.'

Was there no stopping him?

'La Roque,' she said abruptly.

⋆   ⋆   ⋆

She hadn't meant to agree, any more than she had meant to throw the cheap trinkets into the sea, or to dress carefully that evening. Since he had only seen her wearing casual clothes, she didn't want him to think she always slopped about in jeans and trainers.

219

She didn't want to give him the wrong impression either, and as she was bound to tell Anne-Marie that she wouldn't want dinner that evening, she made what she hoped were subtle enquiries about Philip Lefarge.

'Oh, he's a lovely man, divorced from that dreadful wife of his years ago, and we're always saying he should get married again. Why do you want to know?'

Well, not because I'm applying for the post!

'I've run into him a couple of times, that's all.' Then she sighed, because since they would recognize him when he came to pick her up, there was no point in not saying that he was her dinner date for the evening.

'You're honoured then. Philip doesn't date much,' Louis put in.

Perhaps *he* was the one being honoured, Margaret thought, slightly miffed that they seemed to regard Philip Lefarge so highly.

But she had to admit that when he called for her, he was almost unrecognizable from the beach bum she had first thought him to be. He was smartly dressed, the ugliness made almost handsome by the transformation, and he took her out to a sleek yellow sports car that would more than rival her daughter's for style.

'Where are we going?' she said, more nervous than she had expected. 'I came to Guernsey once before, but it was a long time ago.'

'La Banquette,' he told her. 'Have you been there?'

She shook her head, relieved that it was not a place she knew.

'You'll like it. It's very elegant. And afterwards we'll go back to my place for coffee, and you can tell me what's troubling you.'

'I think not!' she said indignantly.

He laughed at her tone. 'Only teasing. My God, I've never known anyone as prickly as you.'

'I've never known anyone as pushy as you on such short acquaintance!'

'It's called being concerned.'

'It's called being damn nosy.'

For some reason Sarah came into her mind just then. Sarah would be telling her right now to 'Go for it, girl', that he was definitely interested, and what did she have to lose? Sarah, the slag.

She swallowed, feeling the prickle of tears behind her eyes and dashed them away angrily. If what she suspected was true, then not only had she lost the trust she had always felt in her husband all these years, but her best friend, too. It was a double betrayal. A double whammy. But it had to be a mistake, and she wouldn't believe it. Not until she heard it from Sarah's own lips.

The thought was there instantly. It was obvious really. She had to know. Which meant she had to ask.

'You've gone into retreat again,' she heard Philip say, casually. 'So maybe we'd better get something out in the open before I put my foot in it completely. Is there some special reason for you being here?'

As they drove around the coast road, she kept her eyes straight ahead. She couldn't say *I'm here because I'm starting to suspect that my husband and my best friend had an affair*, because such a thought had never occurred to her before she came and found that damn trinket in Philip Lefarge's shop.

It would explain the lack of mysterious women at his funeral, though. Why bring on the cavalry when the traitor was already there at the graveside?

'I think I'm going mad,' she said.

'Nonsense. You're as sane as I am — and no comments, thanks! So if we discount madness, what's the real reason?'

'You're bloody persistent, aren't you?' Margaret said, nettled.

He put his hand over hers for the briefest

moment. 'Only because you intrigue me, and I hate to see a beautiful woman so troubled.'

She registered the compliment, ignored it and took a deep breath. 'My husband died six months ago. Next week would have been our silver wedding anniversary, and we spent our honeymoon in Guernsey.'

And if that wasn't enough to put any man off — to dampen his ardour as June would say delicately — or squash his love tackle as Sarah would add — she didn't know what was.

'Right. Now we know where we stand.'

Margaret looked at him now. In profile he wasn't nearly as ugly as she had first thought. A bit Kirk Douglasy in a way.

'Do we?'

'Well, since I'm sure my good friends Louis and Anne-Marie have mentioned the fact that my wife ran off with somebody else, I think we do.'

'It's not the same at all.'

He was infuriatingly patient. 'I didn't say it was the same. Just that we know where we stand. I'm over it — a long time ago — and you still have to come to terms with it. It's a ritual we have to get through, whether it's through death or divorce. A rite of passage, if you like. But just for tonight, why don't we both leave the past behind us, and enjoy what

La Banquette has to offer in the most wonderful seafood you've ever tasted?'

'I'll go along with that,' Margaret said, just as keen to get beyond all this talk of past history and behave like new acquaintances with no baggage.

Though the way this man seemed to have sussed her out so perceptively made him seem more like an old friend rather than someone she had only met a few days ago. At least, in the way he had so quickly reached parts of her that others had tried and failed. The vulnerable parts of her. But it was true what he said: there were times when it was far easier to talk to a stranger than to those who were nearest and dearest.

And La Banquette, a beautiful restaurant perched on the cliff's edge, certainly lived up to its reputation. They ate a superb meal of lobster and squid, smothered in the creamiest and most piquant sauce Margaret had ever tasted.

'I don't know what was in that sauce,' she said later, when they were drinking coffee and liqueurs on the terrace overlooking the sea. 'but I'd give anything to be able to stun my family with the recipe.'

'You wouldn't get it,' Philip said with a smile. 'It's a speciality, heavily guarded by the chef, and has been in the family for generations. If anyone new applies for a job in the kitchens, they have to swear never to reveal the ingredients. You'll find such traditions everywhere here.'

She laughed, guessing it was probably true. 'That's what I love about islands like this. They have their own quaint traditions.'

'We're not quaint, madam,' he replied in mock hurt. 'We're perfectly normal. It's everyone else who's quaint.'

'So how long have your family lived in Guernsey?'

'For ever. My grandfather started the market garden in a small way, so you might say it's in my blood. I could never imagine living anywhere else.'

'I can understand that. It's so beautiful here.'

'Then why go back?'

Margaret began to smile. 'Good Lord, I'm only here on a visit. Of course I have to go back. I have commitments.'

She paused abruptly, realizing that she didn't, not really. Not any more. There was no Robert to go home to. The children weren't children any more, and didn't need her. Her parents wouldn't thank her for suggesting they needed looking after, and Robert's aged mother was mostly off in some never-never land in her mind nowadays,

Margaret thought sadly. She certainly didn't need her. There were others to care for her professionally now.

What else did she have? Friends, of course . . . she swiftly moved off that subject for the moment. The social rounds, the charity dinners she and Robert used to support, all very worthy, but all superficial compared with the way a person really needed to be needed, by a loving, passionate life-partner.

'You see?' Philip Lefarge said, when she had been silent too long. 'You don't really have any commitments at all, do you?'

'Are you a mind-reader now?' she said shortly.

'You have a very expressive face, Margaret, and if I dare risk a slap-down, a very beautiful one.'

'I wouldn't be so rude after such a lovely meal. But it still doesn't give you the right to try to see what's in my mind. You can't go there. Nobody can.'

'Fair enough. But you'll find, as I did, that the world's a very lonely place if you shut everybody out. But I can see that you've had enough of my playing the father confessor for one night. Shall we call it a day?'

'Yes, please.'

And not one word about going back to your place, thanks very much . . . He didn't say it, and he left her at the door of her hotel without a single mention of ever seeing her again.

★ ★ ★

It was strategy, Margaret thought, as she lay on her bed in her nightdress an hour later, aware that she had eaten far too well and that her skirt had begun to feel uncomfortably tight by the end of the evening.

He hadn't said anything about seeing her again, or tried to make out with her. He had acted like a friend, though hardly in the same way that John Franklin would have done, aiming to ensure that she wasn't unduly distressed by anything he said. Philip wasn't at all like John. He was brash and forthright, seeing in her a kind of kindred spirit because they had both been bereaved in different ways.

She'd never really thought about that before, but she couldn't deny that the wronged party in a divorce must feel a kind of bereavement. He wanted to help, without cushioning her the way Robert always had, and John, and friends and family. But it was strategy all the same.

Instead of saying he wanted to see her again, she was the one who wanted to see him. She drew in her breath, knowing it was true, if only because these brief times together had made her feel suddenly alive again, and human, not a walking zombie unable to exist on her own.

But she couldn't forget that ludicrous statement about her having no commitments, and implying that if she wanted to stay here, for a while longer, or for ever, then what was to stop her?

Well, not marriage. Not money. Not anything really.

'Oh, damn you, Philip Lefarge, for putting such a crazy idea in my head,' she said crossly, out loud. 'I've got other things to think about.'

But those other things culminated in nightmarish dreams about infidelity and false friends whose faces she couldn't identify, but who disturbed her sleep so badly that she awoke with a splitting headache next morning.

There were a couple of letters for her. She had given everyone the name of the hotel, knowing she would get no peace unless she did so. One letter was from Keith, and the other envelope was in Sarah's scrawling handwriting. Keith's was little more than wishing her well and asking her to call him to let him know that she was all right. As if she was a blessed schoolgirl away on a school trip, Margaret thought irritably. When did the children take on the role of the parent?

She couldn't open Sarah's letter until after breakfast and in the privacy of her own room. Even then, it took a while before she could bring herself to do it, feeling the same sense of rage she had felt yesterday when she threw the heart trinkets into the sea. Suspicion was an ugly emotion, and between them, her beloved husband and her best friend had stirred it all up in her.

She ripped open the envelope and read Sarah's words.

We thought of coming over and suprising you on a day trip, Margaret, she read. *But June was feeling a bit down and decided she couldn't face it. Shame really, you'd think she'd be pretty cheerful now, but the doc says it's probably post-biopsy reaction, if there is such a thing. Anyway, you said you wanted a restful time, though I hope it's not being too restful. What's the talent like?*

Margaret felt her stomach tighten, ignoring the little jibe behind the fact that she wanted a restful time and no company. What was more important was that June was feeling down. She had been through a traumatic experience lately, but as always, Sarah was able to overlook such details and turn her mind to the male population of Guernsey. She read on.

Honestly, June says she's fine, just not up to travelling, so we're going clubbing instead. That's a scream, isn't it? She'll wear herself out on the dance-floor far more quickly than sitting on a high-speed ferry!

There was more of the same, prattling on about what clothes Sarah had bought lately, and how she was changing her hairdresser because there was a trendy new salon opening up, with *the* most divine male stylist you ever saw. Sex on legs was the way she described him.

Margaret stuffed the letter back into its envelope. She didn't want to visualize Sarah's gleaming little eyes whenever she thought of a man. Predatory wasn't the word for it. Why hadn't she ever noticed it before? Well, she had, of course, but never in relation to Robert.

But what if she was wrong? Maybe it wasn't around Sarah's neck that she had once seen the other half of the pendant in Robert's safe.

The telephone in her room rang, and she picked it up quickly. And then her fingers tightened around the handset as she heard Philip Lefarge's voice.

'I know you won't want me hanging around all the time, but Bruce and I would really like to see you again. We take a walk every morning, so if you're interested, we'll see you on the beach. If not, it was nice knowing you, Mrs Jarvis.'

The line went dead before she could say a word, and she fumed at the nerve of the man. Putting the ball very firmly in her court, practically giving his dog the role of matchmaker, for God's sake!

She realized the way her thoughts were going. Matchmaking meant two people having a future together, and that was very definitely not on the cards for her and Philip Lefarge, or anybody else. He was a nice man, a very nice, straight-talking man, she amended, but that was all. He didn't make her heart race. He wasn't Robert.

But if she ever *did* fall in love again — and right now, she couldn't see it ever happening, it would have to be someone totally different from Robert. Someone she couldn't ever compare him with, and who was beyond compare.

She became aware that her heart was starting to beat faster. Because this man, whom she had only known a few days, and yet who seemed to have got under her skin and through to the heart and soul of her so easily, was surely the most complete contrast to Robert.

He must be dynamic in his own way to own and run a thriving market garden, but she sensed that he didn't have the kind of ruthlessness that normally went with business. His attitude was too laid back for that. Seeing him walk that ridiculous dog along the beach, he could easily pass for the beach bum she had first thought him. And she hadn't expected the sensitive side of him to become as evident as it had when he was talking about bereavement, whether as a result of death or divorce.

There was more to him than showed on the surface, and she guessed that his wife's desertion had hit him very hard. Certainly too hard for him to have married again, or even to date very often, if the hotel manager was to be believed.

And what the hell was she doing, creating this character assessment of him, and turning him into a definite proposition, as Sarah would say, when she probably wouldn't see him again, anyway? She would be taking a different walk tomorrow, because there were still plenty of sandy coves to explore.

★ ★ ★

'So you came,' Philip greeted her.

'Look, I don't want you to make anything of this,' Margaret said, automatically caressing Bruce's shaggy head as he adored her with his eyes. 'It's just a walk, that's all.'

'What would I make of it? You're only here for a few weeks, I like your company, and I think you like mine. So let's enjoy it while we can.'

He paused, and she looked at him sharply. 'And?' she said.

'I was on the brink of adding that we're a long time dead, but it would have been a bit tactless, wouldn't it?'

'Well, you've said it now, and it wouldn't be tactless at all, since it's true, and something that none of us can escape.'

She spoke almost brutally, then caught her breath, wondering where the hell these philosophical utterances were coming from. They weren't her style at all.

'Has it been very painful?' Philip said.

'What do you think? And *that's* tactless! And I'd rather not talk about it.'

'That's fine by me.'

He fell into step beside her as she began to walk along the soft sand of the cove to the far end where the rocks had become smoothed and rounded by the erosion of wind and rain and time.

'Of course it was bloody painful,' she said finally, as if goaded into it by his silence. 'It was very sudden. Totally unexpected. A massive heart attack. One minute I was a happily married woman with everything in the world I wanted, and then there was nothing.'

They had reached the rocks and Margaret sat down abruptly as he handed her a wad of tissues. Not just one, she noted, so he was clearly expecting floods.

'Except irreplaceable memories of all the years you shared together.'

She glared at him. 'Well, of course I had — have — those. Nothing can take those away from me, but it's not the same — you must know it's not the same — ' Her voice faltered, her face crumbling as the enormity of that terrible night when Robert died swept through her again, sharp and painful, and brought back so vividly by this probing man who had no damn right to interfere in her grief.

It was hers. Hers alone, and she had no intention of letting him in. Everything else was forgotten right then but the pain of her loss that she guarded as if was her only lifeline.

'It's all right to cry, you know. I did my share after Angela left.'

Oh God, what was this, confession time? She didn't want to know about his so-called dreadful wife who had left him for somebody else. She didn't want to explain about Robert who had been her first and only love. She just wanted to be alone with her feelings.

'I think this was a mistake,' she said stiffly, wiping her eyes and stuffing the rest of the tissues in the pocket of her jeans for later, just in case.

'OK, so let's have dinner again on Saturday night. I make a marvellous duck casserole with onions and apples.'

Margaret was exasperated now. 'You don't give up, do you?'

'Not when I see something I want. So what do you say?'

'You mean dinner at your place,' she stated, unable to resist a small smile at his damn cheek. Ten out of ten for that, at least.

'Well, I wasn't suggesting taking over La Roque's kitchen for the evening. Of course I mean at my place. I'll show you around the market garden at the same time providing you arrive in daylight. I promise I won't eat you, Margaret.'

His eyes challenged her, as if he could see right through to the suburban little housewife there might still be lurking beneath the veneer of twenty-five years of marriage to a successful businessman.

'Well, as long as that's a promise,' she said abruptly, and they both knew it was her way of saying yes.

12

From their arch, and sometimes not so arch remarks, Louis and Anne-Marie were obviously starting to see a romance blossoming between her and Philip Lefarge, and Margaret was quick to put them right.

'He's good company,' she agreed, 'and now and then it's nice to have someone to share a walk with. But I'm certainly not looking for romance and I'm sure he's aware of that. I'll be going home in a couple of weeks, anyway, and it's unlikely that we'll ever see each other again.'

She was smiling as she spoke, not wanting to give offence, and left the hotel for her morning walk. It was almost a surprise to realize she had been here nearly half her time already. Her mother had phoned to thank her for the Guernsey flowers, and the day of her wedding anniversary had come and gone. It shocked her to think it hadn't been the traumatic experience she had expected it to be.

She could thank that reaction partly on the knowledge that perhaps Robert hadn't been as devoted to her as she had been to him,

Margaret thought bitterly, but she was trying to put all that on hold until she could deal with it properly.

And partly because life went on, however trite it sounded. Time did heal, and here, of all places where no one had wanted her to be right now, she had found a kind of peace she hadn't anticipated. And a kind of pleasure.

She wouldn't deny it. She found Philip's company stimulating and exciting, bringing out elements of herself she hadn't known were there. Or which had been kept dormant all these years. It wasn't romantic, but it made her feel alive, as if she hadn't died when Robert did after all. There was still someone inside her that wasn't just an appendage to Robert Jarvis, successful businessman.

She didn't really think anyone had ever seen her in that way, least of all Robert himself, but it was only now, with time and distance away from the cloying and well-meaning help of friends and family, that she was able to be herself. For now, she was no one's wife, mother or daughter. She was simply Margaret.

And right now she felt a little glow of pleasure as she saw Bruce come bounding up to her, scattering sand with his great paws, barking loudly and wagging his tail furiously in greeting.

'Somebody's glad to see me,' she said laughing, as Philip reached her.

'That goes for dog and owner. You look positively sparkling today. Has something happened?'

'Nothing special, except that I think I'm finally getting used to relaxing and taking life one day at a time.' She hadn't intended saying anything so emotive, but somehow he seemed able to bring it out of her without even trying.

There were still two days to go before dinner at his place, and she could still say no. But she wouldn't, of course.

'That's a pretty good way to be,' he agreed. 'So, shall we walk?'

'You were going the other way,' she pointed out.

'So I'll change direction. It's much more fun walking with somebody than walking alone, don't you think?'

And why did she get the idea that his words were barbed with hidden meanings? Or maybe she was just being ultra-sensitive in seeing them that way.

'Oh, much more, providing it's the company you want,' she quipped back.

'And I do.'

She refused to rise to the bait as he fell into step beside her, pausing every few minutes to pick up a pebble and hurl it in the sea, where Bruce raced after it frantically, barking at the shimmering waves in an impossible hunt.

'That's mean,' Margaret told him. 'He can never find the pebble.'

'But he loves the thought that he might. Dogs aren't much different from humans in that respect. He loves the chase.'

She turned to look at him squarely.

'Even if there's no future in it?'

'But that's just it. There's always the hope that there might be.'

Margaret felt a shiver run through her. She wasn't sure where this was going. As far as she was concerned, it wasn't going *anywhere*. But if he thought that it was . . .

'I think we should get one or two things straight, Philip,' she began.

He caught her hand. 'And I don't think we should do any such thing. For once, just go where fate takes you, Margaret, and today, if you stop putting up these ridiculous objections, it will take you to a quaint old fisherman's pub for lunch. How about it?'

'Don't you have work to do, and a market garden to run?'

'Hey, I'm a successful businessman,' he said, in a clear echo of Robert for that instant, and then the illusion that he was in any way similar to Robert faded. 'I own the place, but it doesn't own me. I have others working for me, who know and love the work, and if you can't enjoy the life you've created, what was it all for?'

'I can't argue with that,' Margaret murmured.

'Right then, so it's lunch, and then you can tell me more about yourself.'

'There's nothing else to tell.'

'Then tell me about your family.'

She wasn't sure if it was the third degree or a natural curiosity about his fellow beings, but he certainly had a way of dragging things out of her. Over lunch in the darkened cellar of the old pub with its fishermen's accoutrements everywhere, and a few glasses of scrumpy cider, she told him about Keith and Ben and Jenny, and her mother who was far more eccentric than any of them, and her father who belonged to the military school of keeping a stiff upper lip and your emotions to yourself.

'My mother would love your sports car,' she added for good measure. 'I'm surprised she hasn't driven Jenny's around the streets of London yet.'

He laughed, leaning towards her as if every word she said was interesting, when she really wasn't interesting at all. She could describe other people's lives amusingly, because there was nothing substantial in her own. Not now.

Without warning, the façade crumbled, and her eyes glistened.

'Sorry,' she muttered. 'I told you I was a bore.'

'Did you? I don't remember, and if you did, you were wrong. You're delightful, and I wish I'd met you years ago.'

'Please don't say those things to me,' she said, knowing she sounded like a panicky Victorian virgin, which was crazy in a woman of her age. But she had to admit that apart from John Franklin, who didn't count, and any others whom she simply hadn't noticed, it was the first time a man had shown this much interest in her. Or come on to her so blatantly, as the kids would have it. As Sarah would have it.

'I think I should be getting back now.'

'Of course. You have so much to do,' Philip said, in amusement.

'I do. I have letters to write,' she said, glaring. 'And I'm going to take a bus around the island and do a bit of sight-seeing. And I don't need company for that,' she added.

'I wasn't offering. I must get back, too. I have accounts to write up this afternoon, but lunch with a lovely lady certainly helps to put off the evil moment.'

After they parted, Margaret went back to

the hotel to check up on the bus times. There was a circular tour, and she could stop off where she chose, and pick it up again later. This was something she had not intended to do, since it would remind her too much of some of the places she and Robert had visited, but now she knew she had to do it, if only to prove to herself that she could stand on her own feet, looking the past in the eye and letting it go. And who cared if she was mixing her metaphors, as long as she knew what she meant.

★ ★ ★

But the day had exhausted her, and by the time evening came, she wanted perversely to hear a familiar voice. Or maybe it wasn't perverse at all, because Robert had been so vivid in her mind as she walked the places they had walked so long ago, that she needed to talk to Keith, whose voice on the phone was so very like his father's.

'I'm sorry, Margaret, he's not here right now,' Laura's efficient voice came on the line. 'Is anything wrong?'

'Of course not. I just wanted a chat, that's all,' Margaret said, feeling the usual irritation.

'Do you want to hang on? He should be home any minute.'

And I don't want to waste time with you either, Margaret thought feelingly, hearing the impatience in her voice.

'No, don't bother. Just tell him I called and give him my love.'

She hung up, knowing there would be a call from Keith later. Checking up on her, just to be sure. Treating her like an invalid. It would be just the same when she went home. She felt a frisson of annoyance, knowing it would be a long while before they let her behave as a normal human being again. They would never believe that she could get over Robert.

With a small shock she realized how much she resented that fact, although weeks ago she would have agreed with them. But you had to move on, however much you longed to cling to the past. When you were left alone, you had to make a new and different life, because there were a lot of years ahead of you, and like someone had almost said, you were a long time dead.

It was already half a year since Robert died. The little ripples, like tiny electric shocks attacking her, continued. Half a year. If you said it like that, it made you accept the passing of time, together with all those trite phrases everybody tripped out about time being a healer. You never wanted to believe it at first, because acknowledging it filled you with an unnecessary sense of shame. It implied that you were forgetting the great love of your life.

But, of course, it seemed that Robert could forget it pretty easily.

The shock was spreading to an ugly sinking feeling in the pit of her stomach now. She had to know the truth, of course. She had to confront Sarah when she got home, however much she hated the thought of it. But if she didn't, the suspicion would fester inside her for ever.

Her mobile shrilled out, making her jump.

The display panel told her at once that it was Keith, so it hadn't taken him long, she thought cynically.

'Are you all right, Mum?'

'Of course I'm all right. I just thought I should report in, before you all think I've emigrated, that's all,' she replied, before he got the chance to say anything more.

He laughed. 'You don't emigrate to Guernsey, you just go there for a couple of days and when you get totally bored, you come back.'

'You've never been here, have you, Keith? So you won't understand why I may decide to stay on an extra week.'

'You're joking, aren't you? What the hell is

there to do all day?'

'I take long walks, I socialize with people, I go sight-seeing — '

'I'd have thought you could see all there was to see in a day.'

She stopped bristling, because it just wasn't worth it. She had only said it on the spur of the moment. Of course she had no intention of staying here longer than a month.

But the questioning little voice inside her asked: *Why not? What do you have to go back to?*

The answer was her family and friends, of course. Her family who didn't need her any more, and her treacherous friends. One of them, anyway. As far as she knew.

'Are you still there, Mum?'

'I'm still here,' she said brightly. 'Give my love to everyone, Keith, and I'll keep you informed about my movements.'

'You'd better! Mrs Ashley won't know if she's coming or going if you stay away any longer than you planned. Oh, and by the way, it looks as if we've got buyers for the cars and the boat with no price haggling. They should be gone by the time you get home and the money deposited in the bank as you requested.'

As he rabbited on for a while longer about high interest accounts and all the rest,

Margaret realized she was starting to feel oddly detached from it all. As if this was the real world, and that other one that she had known all her life, especially the life with Robert, was becoming fainter, like a dream in water-colour . . .

She dragged her thoughts back, wanting to end this conversation and think about everything that had been said. Had she really been so uninterested about the sale of Robert's pride and joy — and had she really mentioned the fact of staying on in Guernsey longer than the four weeks she had planned? And if she did so, would anybody really miss her?

But that damn little inner voice was at it again, asking her what she was running away from, and what was the point of putting off the moment when she tackled Sarah and faced up to whatever reality came of it? One thing was for sure: once she demanded to know if Sarah had ever had an affair with Robert, it would change their relationship for ever. She risked losing not only the unsullied memory of her husband's love, but her best friend. She needed to know — but the cowardly way was to put off the moment as long as possible.

Over dinner that evening, she spoke casually to Anne-Marie.

'Do you continue to get visitors late in the season?'

'Oh yes. With our climate we stay open all year round, except when we take our annual holiday in January, and it's rare that we're totally empty.'

'Then if I wanted to stay on longer than a month, would there be any problem?' she said, before she stopped to think.

'No problem at all; and we'd be delighted to have you, Margaret.'

'I haven't actually made up my mind, and it's no more than a thought at the moment. But it's good to know the option's there.'

★　★　★

She should have known it was a mistake to mention it to Philip Lefarge the following morning. The morning walk was becoming a regular occurrence, and she couldn't deny that she looked forward to it.

'That's great news. I knew Guernsey would weave its spell on you.'

'I haven't said it's certain yet; my son thinks it's a mad idea.'

'You don't have to answer to him. Isn't he a big boy now and capable of looking after himself?'

The thought of Keith needing her in any

way was enough to make her laugh.

'If you saw him, you wouldn't have to ask. He's a policeman and built like a battleship.'

'And your other son and daughter are busy with their own lives, so what's to stop you? Though I suspect that whatever the reason, and despite your denial, you've already made up your mind, haven't you?'

His eyes challenged her, and she shrugged, wondering why he always seemed to get right to the heart of things so effortlessly. The heart of her. She moved away from him as they walked along the sands, warmed now by the late morning sun.

'I hope you're not going to read anything personal into this, Philip.'

'Would I do that? The fact that you're the most exciting woman I've met in years, with whom I'd happily spend the rest of my life, should do nothing at all to influence your decision, and I know how bloody independent you are, so I'm quite sure it won't.'

She stopped walking, wondering if she'd really heard those words, and wishing she hadn't.

'That's exactly what I mean,' she snapped. 'I'd rather you kept your distance, and didn't make crazy remarks about spending the rest of your life with me when you've only known me for five minutes.'

'In real terms, maybe, although it feels like forever. But since it annoys you to get personal, I'll leave that subject alone for the moment. What do you plan to do with your time if you're staying here an extra week — apart from making my life happier, that is? If you're looking for a temporary job, I'm sure I can find something for you. Do you have green fingers?'

She was laughing again by now. He was impossible. He was a control freak, but not in the aggressive way Robert had been. He was undoubtedly charming. And he was gorgeous. How had she ever thought him ugly?

She drew in her breath. Against her better nature, she was starting to find him too darned attractive, but with the realization came an unexpected sense of freedom. It was true what he had told her before — they were both free agents now, and if they liked one another's company, there was nobody to get hurt. It didn't have to go any further than that, but even if it did . . .

'Well? Am I tempting you?' Philip said with a smile, and no idea of the raging surge of desire that suddenly flooded through her.

'Tempting me?' Margaret said faintly.

'The job. Working with flowers? Or in the shop? Or the office? How are your computer skills?'

'Absolutely zero. And why on earth would you want me working for you? Haven't you got enough staff already?'

'Plenty, and the offer of a job is just a ruse, of course, though I'd invent one for you like a shot. What I really want is to be sure to see you every day.'

'You practically do that already, so make the most of it, because in the end I'm going home,' she said, more sharply than she meant to, because this whole conversation was starting to alarm her.

'I never doubted it. Just say you'll stay on a little longer, so we can get to know one another better.'

'Don't you have friends and family? I don't see you as a lonely person.'

He was far too sociable for that, and Anne-Marie had said he was a lovely person of the marrying kind, so there must be women friends.

'I've got a couple of cousins and an aged aunt on the other side of the island in St Martin. And friends, of course. Doesn't everyone?'

Margaret immediately thought of hers. Sarah and Fiona and June — and John. Maybe all of them were involved in the conspiracy her brain wouldn't quite leave alone. As soon as she thought about it, she knew she was going to tackle John first. John, who had gone all colours of the rainbow at mentioning a youthful male episode that Margaret found ugly and obscene. She couldn't help her feelings about that, and she found no reason ever to apologize for her reactions either.

'You've gone somewhere again,' she heard Philip say softly.

'And that's just what I'm about to do. I'm going to visit the Fort Grey Shipwreck museum today, and I'm also considering hiring a car.'

He whistled. 'Wow. You're really coming out of your shell, Mrs Jarvis. But it's good to be independent. I'll see you on Saturday evening then.'

She watched him walk back along the beach with Bruce yapping adoringly at his heels. He *was* a nice man. A man who should be married. But not to her, because she was already married, even if it was only to a memory.

But six months — going on seven now — was no time at all to exchange the memories of a lifetime for the uncertainty of making new ones. She could just imagine her family's faces if she even hinted at it.

She was filled with anger at the way her thoughts were going. She didn't want to think of Philip Lefarge as a possible lover . . . and yet she *did*. The thought was in her mind so swiftly that she felt her heart turn over. Not literally, but just as dramatically. And it was thudding now, as erratically as if she was a teenager. She swallowed the dryness in her throat, and told herself to get a grip.

Hopefully this dinner at his house on Saturday night was going to put a stop once and for all to any wild fantasies about a man she hardly knew. Once she saw his home, still with the hallmarks of a wife who had once lived there, the foolishness would vanish.

★ ★ ★

She could have walked there, as she had done before, but by then she had hired a Mini, which she was told was perfect for negotiating the island's narrow streets, and decided to drive. Besides, she was wearing strappy high heels and she was dressed to kill, and she didn't want to ruin the effect by arriving hot and bothered. In any case, she was that already.

Philip's eyes widened when he saw her. 'Come into my parlour, Mrs Jarvis. You look the proverbial million dollars.'

'Thank you,' she said, glowing at the compliment, and her heart flipped as he slowly assessed the slinky green dress and long emerald ear-rings.

'And you drove here,' he noted. 'So if I ply you with too much wine, as I intend to, there's no way I shall let you drive back to the hotel. You'll just have to stay the night.'

'Now, hold on,' she said, starting to laugh uneasily.

This was going too fast. Much too fast.

He laughed back. 'Darling, I'm teasing. Whatever happens between us — or doesn't happen — it will always be your choice. I'll drive you back myself if necessary, or call a taxi, and you can pick up your car in the morning. Does that please your puritanical little mind?'

She ignored it all, refusing to bite on any of the comments. Instead, she sniffed the air, and her mouth watered as she remembered his talk of a duck casserole with onions and apples.

'Something smells marvellous. Are you a gourmet chef as well?'

As well as being just about the most charismatic man I've met in ages.

'I'm not bad,' he said modestly. 'But first I'll show you around the place and then we'll have a drink to celebrate a new beginning.'

'Philip, please — '

'All right, I'm sorry. I'll try to contain

myself, for now, anyway.'

He led her into the large sitting-room, where Bruce leapt up from the hearth at once to greet her joyously. Margaret looked around with a woman's experienced gaze, seeing how casually untidy it was, with vases of what were undoubtedly his own hot-house flowers livening it all up. And no hint of photographs anywhere, as was to be expected if he had had an acrimonious divorce. And no children.

A thought startled her. If she ever married again, she was still young enough to have children. And he — the man — whoever he was — might want them.

'What's up now? You've frozen on me again,' she heard him say.

'It's nothing. Just a silly thought that crossed my mind.'

He ran a cool finger around her cheek, and she resisted a shiver at his touch.

'I'd be fascinated to see into that complex mind of yours, Margaret. There are so many things going on inside it.'

She was genuinely surprised. 'It's not complex at all. I'm the least complicated person I know.'

I don't have secrets, or a hidden background, or anything to be ashamed of. I don't betray my husband or my friends . . .

'Why don't you tell me about it?' he asked

gently, minutes after they were sitting on his comfortable sofa and she was sipping a glass of pre-dinner sherry.

'About what?'

'About the real reason you've suddenly decided to stay on another week before going back to reality. I don't flatter myself it's solely because of me.'

'You shouldn't be stirring all this up,' she said tightly. 'It's personal, and who said it was even remotely to do with you?'

'Isn't it?'

She felt her face go hot. Of course it was because of him, partly or solely, and she hadn't worked that one out yet. But it was also because of Robert, and Sarah, and twin hearts, and someone called Emma and an escort agency, and John with his careful deletion of Robert's computer disks, and all the mistrust that was slowly and insidiously filling her mind, and threatening to destroy her if she let it.

She was breathing heavily now, and her palms were damp. She felt Philip take her sherry glass from her before holding her hands tightly, and she couldn't look at him.

'Since you persist in probing so much into my personal affairs, let me probe into yours,' she said, praying he wouldn't find any innuendo in her words. 'How did you feel when you discovered your wife had been unfaithful to you?'

'So is that what this is all about?' he said, after a moment's silence.

She was in his house, and a guest should always be polite, but they had gone far beyond all that, Margaret thought in a sudden rage. And he had no right to quiz her unless he was prepared to give as good as he wanted to get.

'Are you afraid to tell me?' she demanded. 'Too macho to admit that you felt like hell when it happened, as if it was a huge slap in the face, as if your world had suddenly stopped, and nothing was real any more, and everyone probably knew already and was laughing at you?'

She stopped, knowing she was talking about herself as much as him. More than him. And she couldn't even be sure whether or not he had told her some of this already. But before she could stop her whirling thoughts, he had pulled her into his arms, and was holding her so tightly she could hardly breathe. Kissing her so hard that she could only respond by kissing him back as if there was no yesterday and no tomorrow, only today, only this and only now.

13

'Well!' Philip said, when at last they drew apart. 'Now that we've got that out of the way, I'll go and check on the casserole.'

Margaret opened her eyes slowly, wondering if his quick departure was to give them both a breathing space. She hadn't been kissed like that in a very long time. More than half a year, in fact . . . and she had forgotten how good it felt. How bloody fantastic it felt, she corrected.

As soon as she felt calmer, she found the dining-room. Everything was ready, the table elegantly set with good china, flowers in the centre, wine decanted, and lamps throwing a soft glow over all. The perfect seduction scene.

She went through to the kitchen, and asked, in a voice husky with emotion now, 'Do you want any help, or do you prefer to be left alone?'

Philip turned, and the cartoony plastic apron he wore now made her laugh out loud, breaking the tension of the last few minutes.

'I can manage, thanks. The starter's just about ready, so go and make yourself comfortable, Margaret.'

'What is it?' she said, the piquant smell making her mouth water.

'Brie parcels with mango sauce.'

'Gosh,' she said. 'I'm impressed.'

'So go. Sit!'

As obedient as Bruce, she did so, and in seconds he brought the two small dishes to the table with a flourish, having whipped off the apron like a magician. She wasn't aware that the CD player had been switched on, but the sensual music filled the room.

The food was marvellous, from the brie parcels to the succulent duck casserole and the fresh strawberries with cream that followed.

'If you always cook like this, you'll make some woman a wonderful husband,' Margaret observed with no ulterior motive.

'Oh, it's more often egg and chips for one, but when there's someone special to cook for, I like to make an effort. I've been out of practice lately, though, so I'm glad it all came up to expectations.'

'More than,' Margaret murmured, perfectly aware of the double meaning behind his words. Viz: he hadn't had anyone to cook for lately, and she was the someone special.

'We'll have coffee and liqueurs in the sitting-room, and then some more wine, I think. The woman who comes in once a week can take care of the dishes in the morning, so don't you dare ask.'

'I didn't intend to,' Margaret said with a smile, more relaxed than she had felt in ages. Relaxed, and yet hyped up at the same time. It was a heady mixture. An hour later, replete with food and wine, they had fallen into an even more companionable state of relaxation, and Philip spoke casually.

'I'd like to show you the view from the upstairs windows, but at the risk of sounding like some old gigolo offering to show you his etchings, I'm afraid you might think it's a come on.'

'Even if it was, what makes you think I wouldn't want to see your view — or your etchings?' she asked lightly.

'I'd better warn you, though — if you come upstairs with me, I might never want you to leave,' Philip added, more seriously than before.

'I might never want to, but we both know that I must,' she said.

He held out his hand and she put her own into it, knowing what it meant, and that she wasn't going to refuse, or back out, or cry rape. She wanted this as much as it was evident that he did. She was no longer Margaret Jarvis, respectable wife and mother, but a desirable woman who ached to be fulfilled.

His upstairs office faced the sea, and was such an untidy mess she couldn't think how anyone could operate in it successfully. It looked beautifully and endearingly inefficient, but by now Margaret knew such chaos belied the shrewd businessman he was. The view through the large picture windows was probably magnificent. It was too dark to see it clearly now, save for the moonlight glinting on the sea, and the lights from the nearby town framing the shoreline.

'It's even better from the bedroom,' Philip said softly.

She went without protesting, her heart hammering in her chest, as gauche as a schoolgirl on her first date. Or her tenth, because you didn't go to bed with a guy on your first date, did you? Not in her day, anyway. Unless you were Sarah.

She went straight to the window, as if to put off the moment she both longed for and which was unnerving her. She had never made love with anyone but Robert. She had never known another man's touch. According to some people, street-wise like her daughter and her friends, she was amazingly naïve for a woman of forty-two.

'I should be seeing this in daylight,'

Margaret said in a strangled voice.

'Like after breakfast.'

'Yes,' she said.

She felt his arms go around her as he turned her towards him. He hadn't put on any lights, so that she could see the view reasonably well, but then she wasn't seeing anything at all, because her eyes were closed as she felt his mouth on hers, kissing her gently at first and then with mounting passion.

And then they were moving towards the bed, tearing off their clothes as they went, until there was nothing between them but skin, and he was covering her with himself, filling her and loving her.

'Jesus, Margaret, I'm sorry about that,' he gasped into her throat a while later. 'I hadn't meant it to be so swift, or so unrestrained. I meant to take things slowly, and now you must think I'm a bloody animal — '

'You didn't hear me objecting, did you?' she whispered back, wrapped around him so closely they were like one person. 'If it didn't make you big-headed, I'd say that I think you're wonderful.'

'It won't make me big-headed at all,' he said, and she could hear the smile in his voice.

'Then I think you're wonderful,' she

repeated like a rote.

He laughed, his arms tightening around her even more, his face nuzzling into hers, the taste of wine on his lips, mingling with hers.

'Stay, Margaret,' he said more urgently. 'Stay here for ever, and to hell with the rest of the world.'

'You know I can't do that. I've never been a reckless person — '

'No? Then what was this? Don't tell me you're a calculating woman who intended this to happen all along?'

She moved slightly away from him, seeing his face dimly silhouetted in the light from the window, unsure whether or not he was joking. And then she felt his laughter against her breasts, and she gave an answering laugh.

'Of course I did!' she teased him. 'You didn't know my middle name was Jezebel, did you?'

★   ★   ★

Sex could be fun as well as passion, Margaret decided sleepily a very long while later, when he had made love to her all over again, at a much slower and more intimate pace, until there was no part of her he didn't know, nor she him. Sex *should* be all of those things, which was something Robert hadn't always

263

considered for many years.

Still dizzy with wine and the outcome of this evening, she deliberately pushed Robert out of her mind. He was no longer here, and she was coming to life again as she had never expected to do after his death. Her spirit was alive again, and so was her body, even though the sensible need for sleep was fast catching up with her now. She turned her head towards the craggy face of the man beside her, and her mouth curved into a soft smile.

Thank you, she whispered silently. *Thank you for reminding me that I'm still a woman.*

★　★　★

The sun was streaming in through the uncurtained window when she awoke properly. For a moment she couldn't remember where she was, and then she caught sight of her naked self, and the scattering of her clothes that someone had picked up and draped across a chair, and her whole body burned with shock.

Her friends had always called her a bit of a prude, and so she was, compared with them, and now the full weight of that jibe came back to her. How could she have done this?

Her head jerked around as the door opened, and she snatched up the duvet to cover her nakedness. Philip Lefarge was bringing in a tray of coffee and croissants, and on it was a delicate vase of freesias. He smiled when he saw the involuntary gesture.

'It's a bit late for that now, darling,' he said lightly.

'Please don't remind me,' she began clumsily.

'Why not? Wasn't it worth remembering? It certainly was for me.'

She tried to relax. What kind of an idiot was she, pretending it hadn't been bloody marvellous? And why should there be one iota of guilt about it, either? She wasn't cheating on anyone. But . . .

'Lord knows what Anne-Marie will think when she realizes I didn't go back to the hotel last night,' she groaned.

'No problem. I phoned her. Now, why don't you eat this for starters, then when you're dressed, we can have a proper breakfast downstairs. The bathroom's through there, by the way. You'll find everything you need.'

'Do you do this often?' she couldn't resist asking, half teasing, and half annoyed that he seemed so competent this morning, when she was a bag of nerves. Especially now that Louis and Anne-Marie would be well aware of where she had spent the night. It was practically Shirley Valentine stuff, she thought resentfully, and look what happened to her when her Greek bloke had finished with her.

'You're the first,' Philip said, and left her to it.

Half an hour later, showered and refreshed, and feeling ludicrously overdressed in last night's glitter, she went downstairs, where an aroma of eggs and bacon was starting to make her mouth water. She never normally ate much for breakfast, but sex made you hungry, and right now she was ravenous. And suddenly nervous, remembering just how abandoned she had become last night.

As if she was sex-starved . . . which she was, but that wasn't the point. She hardly knew this man . . . but looking at him now, wearing that corny-cute plastic apron again, she had to admit she knew him more intimately than anybody.

'What?' he asked with a smile, slapping down a plate of sizzling eggs and bacon in front of her.

'You know what,' Margaret said.

'No, I don't, but let me guess. Is it recrimination, regret, embarrassment — or let's do it again?'

The glint in his eyes brought a smile to her lips, and a swift memory of how good it had been.

'While you think about it, let's eat,' he went on.

'I'm certainly not thinking *let's do it again!*' Margaret stated. 'I have to get back to the hotel, if I can possibly go back there wearing this dress without looking as if I've never been to bed.'

'I can vouch that you did,' Philip said drily. 'But if it will make you feel better, you can borrow a long jacket, and before you ask, it didn't belong to my ex-wife. The woman who cleans for me leaves it here in case she gets caught in a rainstorm.'

'Thanks,' Margaret said. But the mention of his wife, ex or not, had the effect of deflating her, and so did the idea of sneaking back to her hotel wearing a borrowed coat. Suddenly she couldn't wait to get out of there. She wasn't cut out for this kind of thing. She wasn't Sarah.

She pushed back her chair. 'Philip, I'm sorry, but I don't think I can eat this. I really do want to get back.'

'Fair enough. But before you go, don't let feelings of remorse spoil things. We're both free agents, remember.'

He left her for a moment, then brought back a long black coat which she tied tightly around her. For the first time since she had arrived here, a fine drizzle of rain was falling as she went out to her hire car. He walked with her, putting his arm around her shoulders before she slid inside the driving seat.

'I'll see you soon, Margaret.'

She nodded, put the car into gear and shot off along the road towards La Roque, feeling unaccountably tearful. She should be jubilant, happy, glowing, but somehow she wasn't. He hadn't asked her to stay, and she hadn't wanted or expected him to. He hadn't said they must do this again, or asked her out to dinner again, and she was so mixed up inside she didn't quite know what she was feeling. Rejected? Used? Hardly that, since she had wanted him to make love to her as much as he had wanted it.

She parked the Mini at La Roque and miraculously got up to her room without seeing anyone. She changed out of her evening clothes quickly and once she was wearing a sweater and jeans, she felt better. She also started asking herself why she was being so damned provincial over spending the night with a man.

'Oh Margaret, I didn't know you were back,' Anne-Marie greeted her when she went down to reception a while later. 'There was a phone call for you early this morning. The lady didn't leave her name, but she said she'd call again later.'

Margaret thanked her. She had left her mobile switched off, and there were only a few people who knew the name and phone number of the hotel, but she didn't want to speculate which one of them it might have been, or to wonder what had been important enough for someone to get in touch with her.

She went back to her room and switched it on, and almost immediately it rang out. It wasn't Sarah or Jenny or Laura: it was her mother.

'Margaret, I don't want to worry you, but your father's been taken ill. With Brenda being so far away, Keith insisted that I should let you know — '

'What's wrong?' Margaret said at once, her heart jumping, as the awful night when Robert died came searingly to her mind. And if Keith was so insistent, it must be something serious.

'Now, don't get upset, but it's a suspected heart attack. A very *small* one, and they're not even sure if it's that,' Annie stressed, completely unfazed. 'We thought it was indigestion, but just to be on the safe side, I called the doctor and he sent your father to hospital. It's most likely angina, and if all is well, they'll keep him in hospital for a few days, then he'll probably go on the rehab course, take some pills, and that will be that.'

Knowing her mother, she would have got every bit of medical information out of the doctors before she left the hospital . . . but how could she be so bloody *blasé*, Margaret thought in a sudden rage. Why didn't she leave a message for Margaret to call her *immediately*?

'When did this happen?' she stuttered.

'Last night around midnight.'

When she had been making love with Philip Lefarge.

'I'm coming home right away.'

'I knew you'd say that, but your father would tell you not to be ridiculous, Margaret. You know what he's like. Besides, Keith and Jenny and Ben are here.'

'I'm still coming home,' Margaret said, already mentally packing.

Especially if Keith and Jenny and Ben were there.

She should be there too. He was her father, not theirs. For one second, an image of childish sibling possessiveness swept through her mind. Herself and Brenda, squabbling over who was getting the biggest hug from their father, and their mother laughing over their scrambling nonsense.

She smothered a sob. She might be getting on with her life, getting over Robert, even wondering if she could be falling in love again, however briefly, and now she was thrust right back into uncertainty again. Brenda was well out of it, she thought with an unreasoning resentment. And that started the guilt inside her again, knowing that Brenda would be just as upset as she was if the unthinkable happened. But it wouldn't. It musn't. Her father was as strong as an ox, always super-fit with his army training and sensible diet. It wasn't fair. It just wasn't fair.

★　★　★

'Oh, Margaret, I'm really sorry,' Anne-Marie said, when she went to settle her bill an hour later. 'But you know where we are if ever you want to come back, and we'll always be glad to see you.'

Margaret had already phoned the airport, abandoning any idea of a leisurely ferry ride back to Poole; she would be on a plane mid-morning, and in London by early afternoon. Any thoughts of staying in Guernsey for an extra week were abandoned. She wasn't even staying out her allotted month here, and there was no thought of letting anyone else know that she was leaving. She was needed at home.

Guilt was playing a very big part in her

mind now. Guilt at betraying Robert. Guilt at making love while her father was having a heart attack — in Margaret's mind it could be nothing less, of course. It was fate playing a cruel, ironic game with her. And by the time she reached her mother's house, she was in a complete state of nerves.

Her mother answered the door, looking as unperturbed as ever. Dumping her luggage, Margaret fell into her arms, and was rewarded by being briefly hugged and then held away and greeted with an impatient sigh.

'Darling, I told you this wasn't necessary; Keith should never have made such a fuss. Your father is perfectly all right, and when I phoned the hospital at lunchtime I was told they're almost certain now that it was an angina attack and nothing more. So you see, there was no need for you to come rushing home.'

At that moment, Margaret almost hated this self-sufficient woman who had no comprehension of how it had been for her own daughter, six months ago, when Robert had died in her arms. Metaphorically, anyway.

'What did you expect me to do? Carry on enjoying myself as if nothing had happened?' she said, enraged.

Carry on with Philip Lefarge?

Keith came out of the sitting-room then, and hugged her properly.

'Grannie Annie's right, Mum. Gramps is looking fine, and it was just a scare, that's all.'

She bit her lips, not sure whether to be relieved — well of *course* she was relieved — or angry at the lot of them for scaring *her* half to death. The others came out into the hall, and she was surrounded by her children, protective, nervous, not quite knowing what to say, and it was so much like an echo of that other time that it was fast knocking all the stuffing out of her. All the resolve she had built up over these last months was being stripped away — and she needed to see for herself that her strong, upright father was really going to be all right.

'When's visiting time? she asked tightly.

'We can go in any time,' her mother said and, at the look on Margaret's face, she sighed again. 'Now don't go reading anything into that, Margaret.'

He would be in a private room, of course, where visiting times were relaxed. She should try to do the same. It wouldn't help anybody if she went to pieces.

Her thoughts came and went in jerky little bursts. It occurred to her that in all her lifetime she had never seen her father ill. He had always been so robust, and it would be weird to see him in a hospital bed, surrounded by all the paraphernalia that went with heart patients. Her spirit balked, not sure whether she could take it.

'We can go as soon as you like, Mum,' she heard Jenny say. 'Best to get it over with.'

Her daughter looked at her with understanding eyes. Jenny hadn't been there when Robert died. Margaret would want to be there before — if — she took a deep breath, knowing she was letting the situation take over any logical thoughts.

'I'll put my stuff somewhere and have a cup of tea first,' she made herself say. 'It's the great panacea, isn't it?'

'Only if you stick a slug of brandy in it, Mum,' Ben advised, more worldly-wise than she had ever been at his age. Was she ever his age . . . ?

But the hospital visit wasn't as bad as she had feared, once she got beyond the familiar antiseptic smells that would always assault her senses. Her father was almost his usual self, brushing aside any fuss or threat of an emotional outburst. He was sitting up in bed, controlling the nursing staff and noisily comparing it all to Colditz, and demanding to know when they were going to let him out. Margaret began to breathe easier.

'You shouldn't have come rushing back

because of a bit of indigestion,' he stated, echoing everyone else's words, 'but I knew you would,' he added.

'It wasn't just indigestion though, was it, Dad?'

He shrugged. 'It's nothing that can't be dealt with, but the last thing I wanted was to cut short your holiday. You needed it, Margaret. So how was Guernsey? Did it live up to your expectations?'

She couldn't answer for a moment. How could she say what was instantly in her heart? That the island was as beautiful and tranquil as ever; that she felt she had gone some way towards laying to rest Robert's ghost? That she had discovered the twin pendants that had stirred up all her suspicions again? That she had met a marvellous man and almost fallen in love . . .

'Guernsey was fine,' she said woodenly.

'Then go back,' her father said. 'No need for all this fuss.'

She shook her head. 'No, I won't go back. I have things to do here, and I've decided I want you all to come down to Bournemouth for Christmas, providing you're OK to travel by then, Dad.'

She hadn't even thought of it until that minute, but now it seemed the right thing to do. Have a big family Christmas the way they always did, even if the main participant would be missing. But Robert would have wanted life to go on, and it would also give her plenty to do, and stop her thinking impossible dreams, and remembering them too well.

'Of course I'll be well enough. Your mother and I had already discussed you coming here, but if it's what you want — '

'I'm sure it's what we all want,' Keith said quickly.

Her children agreed, even though she guessed they'd much rather be revelling with their friends. And she must stop thinking of them as children, Margaret reminded herself. In reality, they didn't need her at all, but they continued to humour her as if she was the invalid and not her father.

They eventually left the hospital, with her father still complaining that the sooner he got out of there the sooner he'd be fit again. All crammed into Keith's car, Annie began to laugh, but there was a suspicious moisture in her eyes, too.

'Did you just hear him, ordering everybody about as usual!'

'He finds it hard to be ill, Gran,' Ben said. 'He doesn't like to feel he's out of control of his life. Like all of us, really.'

Annie looked at them all with fond affection. 'Well, you three are well in control of yours, aren't you? Your parents did a fine job with you.'

'Good Lord, is that a compliment?' Margaret said, managing a smile now that the atmosphere was lighter. And knowing that she truly had panicked on hearing that her father was in hospital — but with understandable reason.

'You've survived a bad time, Margaret, and we're all proud of you.'

I wonder if you'd be so proud if you knew how I spent last night. The realization that it was only last night — less than twenty-four hours ago when she had been so abandoned in Philip Lefarge's arms — made her shiver.

Keith said, 'Mum, I have to get back to Bournemouth in two days' time, and I can drive you back with me if you like. It'll be better than getting the train.'

'I'll have to see. It depends how your Gramps is by then.'

★ ★ ★

But going back to the hospital again later only confirmed that he certainly wasn't at death's door and couldn't wait to get home. Lying sleepless in her old bedroom that night brought back more childhood memories for Margaret, and with them, the knowledge that she had moved on, further than she had ever imagined.

The love of her life was no longer the only love in her life, and she was unable to ignore that fact. You couldn't change the past, and you couldn't bring back what you once had. But she wasn't ready yet to move on into those realms. Here, for a couple more days, she was able to cling on to the past, and refuse to think about a different kind of future.

It was foolishness, anyway. She had been wildly attracted to Philip, and the feeling was mutual, but she should have the sense to leave it at that. She wasn't looking for happy endings. She had done that once before, and it had all ended in tatters. Especially now, knowing what she knew.

But she didn't know it yet. Not for certain. Only in her heart.

'I will come back with you, Keith,' she told him, when her mother had assured her for the hundredth time that they could cope very well without her, and that her father wouldn't want any fussing when he came home.

'Good,' her son said. 'I'm sure you'll want to settle back into a routine, especially if you're planning to have us all there for Christmas.'

Settling back into a routine wasn't exactly what she had in mind, since it sounded so frumpish. She was more intent on dealing with the Sarah question, as she was now thinking of it. And on selling the house.

14

She wasn't sure where that thought came from. It simply seemed obvious. It was even more obvious when Keith left her at home, and she stood completely still inside the house for a few moments, feeling the emptiness where there had once been so much love and laughter. And sex. *Don't forget the sex.*

Where had Robert and Sarah done it? Or Robert and Emma. Or even Robert and John. Robert and anybody. Everybody.

She shivered, and then walked upstairs purposefully to unpack her things. The answering machine had been flashing, but she wasn't ready just yet to speak to Sarah or John or whoever else was calling to ask where she had been or how she was, or maybe to ask for Robert. There were still occasional calls for him from people who hadn't heard the news yet. Other Emmas.

But she couldn't stay upstairs for ever. There was laundry to push into the machine, and the familiar whirr of the motor pulsing around brought her back to normality. She went into the kitchen and put the kettle on for a quick fix of coffee, smiling at Mrs Ashley's various stick-up notes all over the place.

She was home. And once armed and revived with coffee and chocolate biscuits, and to hell with the effect on her hips, she went into the sitting-room and rewound the messages on the answer machine.

They were predictable. Her friends. Her bridge club secretary. The bank manager. The dentist's receptionist, reminding her of an appointment she had missed by going to Guernsey. A doubleglazing offer she really shouldn't miss. An offer of a one-week holiday in Spain in return for spending an hour looking around a brand-new time-share complex. Philip Lefarge.

Her heart leapt as she heard his voice. It was suddenly, vividly in her head, as close as if he was in the room standing next to her.

'Margaret, it's Philip. I was sorry to hear about your father, and I hope it's nothing serious. Please call me when you can to let me know how things go, and I do hope you'll come back to Guernsey soon. We have unfinished business to deal with. Take great care of yourself.'

The message ended and she switched it off quickly. Unfinished business indeed! What the hell did he mean by that! She rewound the tape and played it again. It wasn't romantic. There were no endearments. Nothing to say how they had writhed in one another's arms for one magical night, and even though love was never mentioned, love had been there all the same. Or so she believed.

Shocked, Margaret knew it was true. Like a wide-eyed schoolgirl she had imagined this was love. *Had* to be love because she wasn't the sort of person to go to bed with a man unless there was something more than mere lust. She wasn't that sort at all. Maybe Philip was. But if so, why had he bothered to call her? Why not leave it at that? And why hope she would go back to Guernsey soon? She never would, of course. And she wouldn't call him, either.

The sound of the front door opening made her physically jump. She turned to see Mrs Ashley's startled face, her arms loaded down with supermarket bags.

'My good Gawd, you gave me a fright! Whatcha doing back already?'

Of course she wouldn't know about her father's suspected heart attack-that-never-was, thought Margaret. And of course, she wasn't expected back for another week or even two. And of course, it was Mrs Ashley's day. Thoughts ran around her brain like wildfire, while she explained in a voice bordering on hysteria, preparing to put on the kettle again, as the whole drama overcame her again.

'You poor duck,' Mrs Ashley said sympathetically. 'Here, you just sit down and let me do that. I see you've already got stuck into the chocolate biscuits, so we'll have a good old natter and a cuppa and never mind the diet. But what a shame, spoiling your holiday and all. It probably did you good too, so I hope you managed to enjoy yourself before all this happened.'

She prattled on without pausing for breath, giving Margaret time to gather her senses, and agree weakly that yes, she had managed to enjoy herself before all this happened.

'Nice place, is it, Guernsey?' Mrs Ashley went on. 'Never been there myself. Did you meet any nice people?'

Nice was her favourite descriptive word. Oh yes, Margaret thought glibly. Guernsey's nice. I met a nice man. I had a nice night in bed with him.

'I stayed in a small hotel and did a lot of walking, which was what I intended doing,' she said instead.

'Oh well. To each his own,' she was told, which in translation meant that Mrs A couldn't think of anything more boring.

But God, was she glad of the woman's company! This house, that she had loved all these years, now seemed much too large, too empty, and too full of memories. They had always been good ones, but they seemed to mock her now. She felt restless inside these walls in a way she had never done before. And the thing that was doubly surprising was that she could view it all so dispassionately. Time and distance had done that for her.

Once the ritual coffe-drinking and biscuit-dunking were over and Mrs Ashley got on with her work, Margaret took stock. It was a beautiful place, but far too big for one person. It was a family home, and a family should be living here.

Robert had inevitably made the decisions. Her family always teased her that she never did anything without asking him first. But why not, she always replied airily, when they were so compatible that his choices were invariably hers anyway? Or had she just gone along like a wimp because it was an easy and cosy way to be? God, yes, she *was* a wimp. But he wasn't here to make any decisions now, and this time she was doing it her way.

The fact that he would never have considered selling this house was not a factor — except for the little devil of defiance at the back of her mind.

Once Mrs Ashley had gone, Margaret reached for the phone and dialled the number of a local estate agent, requesting a visit for a valuation of the house. She replaced the receiver carefully, aware that her heart was pounding. Aware of what a huge step this was, that she would face all kinds of arguments from her family. And that once it was a *fait accompli* she would have nowhere to live.

But that wouldn't be a problem, and of one thing she was very sure, two things, really: she wouldn't consider selling the house to any of her children, even if they could afford it or wanted it, because once she left it, she would never want to come back. And she would never consider moving in with any of them.

★ ★ ★

That afternoon, the estate agent sent round a dynamic young man, as eager as a young puppy to get his hands on dealing with this expensive and highly desirable property in such a prime position. His estate agent jargon spilled out of his mouth, and commission prospects flashed in his eyes like the dazzle of Las Vegas slot machines. Irrationally, Margaret hated him on sight, but as long as he did the business, as Robert would have said, who cared about personalities?

'There's one thing I must emphasize,' she told him, childishly refusing to suggest tea or coffee by the time he had looked the whole place over and was getting down to details on his clipboard. 'I do not want people inspecting the house while I'm here. It must be by appointment only, with you or one of your people in charge, and while I'm out.'

'No problem, Mrs Jarvis.' He made a note, probably glad of the fact that his client wouldn't be interrupting his flow of rhetoric.

'And the other thing is that I won't be selling until after Christmas.'

'No problem again.'

Were these people always so bloody amenable? Or perhaps it was only when they saw a big sale in the offing.

'I don't want the house advertised in local newspapers,' she pushed on, challenging him, 'nor in your office windows. And I wouldn't consider having a For Sale board in my garden. I want the sale to be discreet.'

He looked up from his clipboard now. 'We could get far more interest if we advertised in our usual way,' he said doubtfully.

'Those are my conditions,' Margaret said, smiling pleasantly. 'If you can't agree to them, then I'm sorry if I've wasted your time, and I will have no objection to taking my business elsewhere.'

'No *problem!*' he said at once, just as she knew he would. That fat commission was far too big an issue for him, and she really couldn't blame him for that, she thought, backtracking swiftly now that it all seemed to be going ahead with frightening speed.

Because this was only the first step. The next one would be to tell the family. And friends.

★ ★ ★

She called her mother that evening to check on her father's progress.

'He's practically ruling the hospital now,' Annie snorted. 'They'll be glad to see the back of him, I daresay.'

'And you'll be glad to have him home,' Margaret said softly. They were an odd couple really, her mother with her unfulfilled hippy ways, and her father with his stern military codes. But there was no doubting their love for one another.

'Well, of course,' Annie said, 'though I won't vouch for his temperament when he gets here. So are you regretting rushing back from Guernsey yet?'

'Of course not. You came rushing down

here after Robert died, didn't you?' But he had *died*, of course. She took a deep breath. 'Anyway, I've got something to tell you. I'm putting the house up for sale.'

She held the phone away from her ear, expecting to hear an explosion at the other end. But she should have known.

'Very good idea,' said her mother. 'You don't want that great albatross hanging around your neck any longer. Where will you go?'

'Go?' Margaret said faintly.

'Well, for heaven's sake, Margaret, the world doesn't start and end with Bournemouth. You're free to do whatever you like with your life, aren't you?'

'I haven't given it much thought yet. Maybe I'll live in Timbuctoo, or the wilds of Borneo, or go shooting the rapids,' she said sarcastically.

'You see?' her mother laughed, taking her seriously. 'You're more like me than you thought you were, and not so predictable, after all.'

'Thanks. I think that's a compliment. Anyway, you can tell Jenny and Ben, but be sure to say that none of it's going to happen yet. Christmas is still on.'

She hung up with something like relief, and an extraordinary sense of togetherness with her mother, and her globe-trotting sister Brenda, and Jenny, whom her father had always called her wild child. And Ben, who would be quite unconcerned, leading his own artistic life. But then there was Keith.

'You've done *what?*' he exploded. 'Are you quite mad, Mother? Why on earth didn't you consult me first?'

'Why the hell should I? You're not my keeper!'

'I'm your son, and I had a right to know what you were planning. This is completely out of character. You're just not thinking straight. Dad would be turning in his grave if he knew what you were doing.'

God, how she hated that expression. And if she had Keith there at that moment, she would probably have strangled him.

'You have no right to speak to me like that, Keith, or to try to dictate what I do with my life. I'm not a child, and you had better remember that. And it doesn't matter what your father would have thought about my plans, because this is my house now, and I'll do what I like with it.'

There was a stony silence at the other end of the phone.

'I'm coming round,' Keith said shortly.

He had hung up before she could tell him not to bother. He was taking on the pseudo role of his father, but in a far more aggressive way than even Robert had done. She didn't want it, she didn't need it, and she didn't like it.

The phone rang again and she snapped into it.

'Well, someone's got out of the bed the wrong side,' she heard Sarah say cheerfully. 'We weren't sure when you were due back, but how about a girls' get-together on Saturday night, then we can dish the dirt on what you got up to?'

'Saturday will be fine,' Margaret said, with admirable calm. 'Come round here and I'll rustle up a meal. And why don't you wear that pendant I haven't seen lately? You know, the one with the jagged edge that's half of a heart.'

For the second time that day there was a small silence at the other end.

'Well, if I can find it,' Sarah said cautiously. 'It was only a cheap thing.'

'Oh, I know that,' Margaret said. 'See you Saturday, then.'

The brief feeling of triumph vanished as quickly as it had come. She hardly knew why she had said it, except for the fact that her world was turning upside down for the second time in six months.

More than that. It was whirling, spinning

away from her, and she had to catch it quickly and make some sense of it.

She could have predicted that John Franklin would call her that evening. Whether or not Sarah had called him, she didn't know, and wouldn't ask. But it was no surprise when he called to check whether or not she was home, and asked her out for a drink.

'Great,' she said brightly. 'I wanted to talk to you anyway.'

She hung up carefully, with the strange feeling that for once she was pulling the strings. Manipulating her life. Her friends. Her family. It was an odd sensation, one that she hadn't felt before, nor expected to find quite so exhilarating. Manipulating — it wasn't a good word, but it was an intriguing one.

Keith and Laura arrived around six o'clock while she was soaking in the bath. Keith had his own key, and she could hear them muttering downstairs when she opened the bathroom door a chink, still swathed in towels.

'I'll be down soon,' she called out. 'Make some coffee or help yourselves to something stronger.'

She heard the phone ring, and she fumed, wondering if Jenny or Ben were about to have a go at her now.

'Answer that, will you Keith?' she called again. 'And whoever it is, tell them I'll call back later.'

She was humming by the time she went downstairs in a jeans and sweatshirt, intending to change properly when these two had gone. First, she had to deal with Keith's outrage at her daring to think of putting this house up for sale, and she almost relished the challenge, knowing she wasn't about to change her mind.

He and Laura sat at each end of the sofa like matching bookends, their mouths set in matching tight lines.

'Well?' she demanded, when neither of them spoke.

'Who the hell is Philip Lefarge?' Keith snapped.

Margaret felt her jaw drop. Just as the books described it . . .

'Where did you hear that name?' she said swiftly.

'I heard it about five minutes ago when he phoned, asking for you. When I asked if he was the estate agent, he laughed and said he was more of a close personal friend, and that he hoped to be hearing from you soon.'

Oh, for a camera at that moment, Margaret thought, to capture the Victorian melodrama of the moment, etched on her son's face.

Good God, what was the matter with him? Did he think she was never going to speak to a man again? Never going to be turned on by a man again, or fall in love with a man again?

'So who is he, Margaret?' Laura egged.

She turned her gaze to Laura, Keith's prim-faced screw, to use Sarah's words for her. Margaret had never really cared for her, and saw no reason to change that opinion. And she was still bristling over Keith's whole attitude.

'Philip is just who he says he is, a close personal friend,' she said coolly. 'So now that we've got that out of the way, what else did the two of you want to say? And don't make it too long, because I'm going out with John tonight.'

She knew that wouldn't please Keith either. She saw the glance that passed between them. It said that they thought she was going to the dogs, going senile, selling their heritage, going out with men they didn't know or didn't like . . . well, it was never going to be Laura's damn heritage, anyway, and she stuck her chin in the air, ready to do battle.

Seeing the glint in her eyes, Keith's aggression was less evident now. 'Mum, it's this house thing. I understand your feelings now that Dad's gone — '

'Actually, you don't, but we'll let that pass for the moment.'

'And although you know it's way out of my league, I'd try to get a mortgage on it if I possibly could, just to keep it in the family — '

'I wouldn't sell it to you, anyway,' Margaret said.

'Why on earth not?'

'I don't intend any of the family to have it. I want it to be sold to strangers, but don't worry, you'll all get your share of the proceeds, and it won't happen until after Christmas. So you'd better make the most of it, because this will be the last Christmas any of us will ever spend here.'

'You know damn well I'm not after your money, and I'm insulted by the thought,' Keith said angrily. 'But what do you intend doing, anyway? Where are you going to live?'

'I haven't decided yet. But as your grandmother reminded me, I have the whole world to choose from.'

'Oh well, she would,' Laura said.

'I beg your pardon?'

Laura went a dull red, knowing she had gone too far. 'I'm sorry, Margaret, but your mother is, well, rather eccentric, isn't she?'

Margaret mocked her. 'So you think making a new life for myself is being a bit

294

eccentric, do you? What a very insular life you lead, Laura.'

'There's no need to be rude, Mother,' Keith said.

'Then go home and leave me to get ready to go out with John. Or is spending an evening with another man considered far too eccentric for a widow woman now? I'm afraid I don't have any sackcloth and ashes handy to wear.'

Keith stood up, hauling Laura behind him. 'We're going, Mum. I think you should see the doctor and get some pills to calm you down.'

'Actually, darling, I never felt saner in my life.'

★ ★ ★

But after they had gone, she put a slug of brandy in her coffee, just to get pepped up for the evening ahead. It was true, though. She felt both sane and determined to live the rest of her life the way she wanted to. Like the song said — good old blue-eyes — she was going to do it her way.

When John Franklin arrived, she suggested that they stayed in as there was enough booze in the house to sink the *Titanic*, so why waste money going out? She also intended taking

295

the wind out of his sails before very long, and she preferred to do it without an audience.

By now, she was seeing all kinds of things she had never seen before. She could see that he was watching her warily, and she knew that Sarah had phoned him and mentioned that something was up. Otherwise, why would Margaret, dear dumb Margaret, have mentioned the jagged heart pendant?

The one Robert had given her to match his — or the other way around. With hindsight, she knew it was much more likely that Sarah had bought them both. It was her kind of tarty Christmas cracker jewellery.

'So what kind of a time did you have in Guernsey, Mags?' John said. 'I didn't think you were due back for a week or so.'

'I wasn't. In fact, I was going to stay on longer, but my father was taken ill, so I decided to come back.'

'Jeez, I'm sorry to hear that. It was nothing serious, I hope?'

Sarah obviously hadn't told him that bit. 'It might have been, but it wasn't. So why don't we cut out all this fencing around, John, and you can tell me all about Robert's infidelities instead.'

It was camera time again . . . maybe she should have installed hidden cameras all around the room, to catch the varying expressions of her family and friends whenever she dropped her bombshells.

'Are you crazy? You know Robert adored you, Margaret.'

'Yes, I do know that. We had a perfect marriage. Everybody said so, didn't they? But that doesn't mean he didn't like a bit on the side as well, does it?'

John looked mildly hunted. 'Look, I don't know what you're trying to do here, Margaret, but Robert was my best friend, and I don't like these implications you're making when he's not here to defend himself.'

'Well, Robert was my husband, and that gives me every right to say what I think about him. Even to thinking he's been a lying bastard all these years.'

She felt incredibly calm now, because she knew that her once perfect marriage had been taken away from her. She knew it as surely as she breathed. She hardly needed confirmation, except to make those who had betrayed her squirm.

She hadn't expected to want revenge, and she had never thought of herself as a revengeful person. But if revenge was what this was all about, then it was both sweet and sad, because she knew she risked losing her best friends. She also knew she had to do it if she was to survive.

'Margaret, it was all so long ago,' John muttered.

She blinked. 'Was it? Not all of it, surely. What about this Emma person from the Gladby Agency, who called here soon after he died?'

'Oh. I thought — I didn't think you meant — '

She heard him blustering, and felt icily cold. And very aware.

'What did you think I meant, John? You and Robert? Is that it? That it wasn't simply a schoolboy experimental thing after all? That it didn't end there? That you were doubly devastated when he died, because you didn't only lose an old friend, but someone far closer than that?'

God, she should take up quiz-mastering . . . or should that be mistressing? But that was someone else's role, not hers.

He wouldn't look at her now, but he became whiningly defensive. Funny how she had never noticed that about him before.

'It never did anything to harm your marriage, Margaret. Robert would never have wanted that, and nor would I. It was quite separate.'

She couldn't take any more of this. If he was about to confess what they did and where they did it, she was sure she would throw up.

298

And it would be a bloody shame to spoil the shag-pile carpet. She changed tactics.

'I see. Just like Robert's need to go to an escort agency from time to time was separate, and his sordid little affair with Sarah, my best friend, was separate?' she said, her voice a silky thread.

John sighed now, finally looking at her with sorrow in his eyes.

'I can't answer for Sarah, nor am I agreeing or disagreeing with it. I just want to know why you're doing this, Margaret. Why torture yourself like this?'

'Perhaps because I need to find out just how *imperfect* my perfect marriage really was,' Margaret said tightly. 'And I think I'd like you to go now.'

His good looks seemed to have lessened as they talked. He looked pinched, furtive, shamed. Maybe he had loved Robert as more than a friend, and that sickened her too. He would have done anything to save her from finding out the truth. Knowing it, she felt a brief pity for him, but she couldn't forgive him.

'So is this the end for us, Maggie? After all these years, when you know how much I valued your friendship?'

'Oh, I think that sharing my husband was more than enough for me, don't you?'

'It wasn't like that. It was never like that, and I can't bear it if we part like this. You know I've always loved you — '

'And now you disgust me. But one more thing before you leave, John: please don't speak to Sarah about any of this. I need to sort things out for myself and I don't need any go-betweens.'

He went without another word, and a part of her life went with him. All those years they had shared, years of friendship and laughter, the three of them as companionable as the three musketeers, seemed such a mockery to her now. But all the false dignity and bravado was fast leaving her, and without warning, she collapsed on the sofa and wept.

15

Philip called again a few evenings later. Although half prepared for the sound of his voice on the phone, it still made Margaret's heart leap.

'I take it that was the policeman son I spoke to before,' he began, without even announcing himself.

'It was. And he was none too pleased to hear a strange man asking for his mother,' she replied, registering the fact that they could slip so easily into conversation as if they had never been apart.

'Did he tell you not to speak to any more strange men?'

'If he had, I would have ignored it. I don't have to do what my children tell me,' she said, half nettled, half amused.

'I'm very glad to hear it. So how's your father, if that doesn't sound like a bad music-hall joke?'

With her heart settling down a little, Margaret found herself smiling. 'He's much better, thank goodness, and going home from hospital in a day or so to my mother's tender care. It was a touch of

301

angina, not a heart attack.'

'So when are you coming back?'

Margaret gazed unseeingly out of the window. In her mind was the instant memory of the walks they had shared along the warm sands; his crazy dog who was in love with her; the dinner Philip had cooked for her; the cartoony plastic apron that looked endearingly naff on his big macho frame; the night she had spent in his bed, in his arms . . .

'You know I only came for a holiday, Philip. It wasn't meant to be for ever.'

'Is there any reason why it shouldn't be?'

'You're bloody persistent, aren't you?' she said, but unable to resist laughing at the way he managed to bypass any problems and got straight to the point. 'I do have a life here, you know.'

'And I think you and I could have a life here.'

What was he suggesting? That she cut and run, and move in with him? A man she hardly knew? She drew in her breath. This had gone far enough. There was far too much crowding in on her right now to take any more of it. There was Christmas to get through. There was the house. There was Sarah. There was getting everything straightened out in her mind before thinking of anything else. And that didn't just mean him.

'Philip, you know how much I like Guernsey, and if I ever decide to go back there again for another holiday, I promise I'll look you up.'

She paused, hearing his answering snort.

'That's the kind of brush-off to flatten a man's ardour at once, if you see what I mean, Mrs Jarvis. But I don't accept it, of course. I think there was more between us than just a promise of looking me up again, one day, maybe, if ever!'

She felt her face go hot. 'All right, I really enjoyed meeting you, Philip.' *And being with you and sleeping with you, and making love with you.*

'But?'

'But that's it. I can't go any further than that right now.'

'Fair enough. Just let me know when you're ready.'

He hung up as abruptly as he had begun this conversation, leaving her frustrated and angry. He'd virtually brushed *her* off now. He was short on finesse and chat-up lines, and this was practically an ultimatum. If she didn't want him, then he wouldn't want her. Boom-boom!

The hell of it was, the more she thought about him, the more she knew she did want him. Every time she heard his voice, she wanted him more.

And every time she couldn't hear it any more, she wanted him back.

'Oh sod it,' she exclaimed out loud. 'Why did you have to go and complicate things, Philip Lefarge?'

But another part of her asked just how she would be coping with the other problem, the big question-mark over Robert, if she hadn't met Philip and heard his sane assessment of the situation. A marriage ended, for whatever reason, and there was still a lot of life ahead. If you were lucky. She shivered, knowing he was right, and knowing too, that he had also been through a hell of a time finding out that his wife had betrayed him. Maybe it was even worse for a man, with all the ego involved. He had shared the entire trauma of pain, hurt and disbelief that Margaret had. He'd gone to the brink of the abyss, and he had got through it. The same as she had to.

Oh yes, whatever else you did for me, Philip Lefarge, she said silently, you taught me that much.

★　★　★

She went shopping before Saturday, and when Sarah arrived before the others as always, Margaret was wearing a glamorous and sophisticated outfit of black silk shirt and matching trousers. Her high-heeled shoes were little more than glittery straps. Her hair had been highlighted to a perfect blonde frame for her face, and her lipstick was deep red to match her nail varnish. She knew she looked a million dollars, and she felt it.

By contrast, Sarah wore a pair of green trousers and a flashy shirt they had both seen before, tarty shoes, and the jagged heart pendant around her neck.

Her eyes opened wide when Margaret opened the door to her.

'I thought we were having a girls' night in,' she complained. 'You didn't tell me we were dressing up.'

'You never did like feeling inferior to anyone else, did you, darling?' Margaret said sweetly. 'Come and have a drink. I've ordered Chinese takeaways tonight, because I'm not ruining this expensive outfit in the kitchen.'

Sarah eyed her warily. Margaret knew she had never seen her quite like this before, not her attitude, nor her self-confidence. There was an edge to her that was quite un-Margaret-like. Personally, she *did* like it.

'So how was Guernsey really?' Sarah asked, when they were both settled with a drink in their hands.

'Just as I remembered it, except that

Robert wasn't there, of course.'

'But you enjoyed it.'

'Yes, I did. In fact, I'd virtually decided to stay on for an extra week, and I wouldn't have come back so soon if it hadn't been for my Dad's illness.'

Sarah put her glass on a side table, and clasped her hands together. Idiotically, Margaret noted her chipped nail varnish, and glanced at her own immaculate nails, courtesy of her manicurist.

'There's something different about you, Mags,' she said slowly. 'I can't really put my finger on it, unless you've got a new man. Is that it?'

She looked hopeful now, as if the unease inside her was starting to fade a little with this new thought. Letting her off the hook, even if she didn't yet know why, or how.

Margaret smiled. 'Actually, I rather liked the old one. I *loved* the old one. The thing is, Sarah' — she paused to take a long drink — 'I've only recently become aware that I wasn't the only one who loved him. Or should that be *lusted* for him?'

'You must be crazy,' Sarah said quickly. 'Mags, don't do this. You know how much Robert loved you — '

'That's just the kind of reaction I got from John. You and he are two of a kind, aren't you? Both lusting after my husband behind my back, and both getting your share of what should have been exclusively mine. Along with plenty of others, I daresay.'

It was the shock treatment the cops used in TV shows.

She tried very hard to keep her voice level, but she could feel it hardening and tightening as she looked unwaveringly at Sarah, her best friend. Her treacherous best friend. And if she had ever doubted that Sarah knew all about John and Robert, or the fact that Robert was a serial love-rat, she didn't doubt it now, because there was no hint of shock in Sarah's eyes on that score.

Only about herself. Margaret saw her fingers go to the jagged heart pendant around her neck. The tawdry jewellery, no better than Christmas cracker junk. 'Margaret — oh God, Margaret, I don't know what to say.'

'What is there to say? You had an affair with my husband. All those times when you flirted outrageously with him over the years, they were just a blind for what was really going on, weren't they? Are you going to insult me even more by denying it now?'

Slowly and deliberately, she put her fingers inside the neck of her blouse, and pulled out the other half of the heart pendant to lie against the shimmering silk fabric. She saw

Sarah swallow convulsively, and then she stood up clumsily, her eyes full of tears.

'I know it's useless to say I'm sorry, so I'd better go.'

Margaret unfastened the pendant from around her neck. She handed it to Sarah, who looked at it as if it was red hot, her face tortured now.

'Take it. I'm sure you earned it, along with Robert's other tarts,' Margaret told her. 'And I don't want you to go. Sit down, for God's sake. I've lost Robert, and probably John, but I've decided on reflection that I don't want to lose you. We have to get on with our lives. So I want to hear how June really is, and what you're all doing for Christmas. And by the way, I'm selling this house.'

Sarah's mouth fell open. 'You're selling this house?' she echoed, as if everything else Margaret had said was beyond her comprehension for the moment.

As it was to Margaret herself. Never in a million years had she imagined saying the things she had just said. She hadn't planned them. They had just come out, ready-formed, and perfectly logical. She had lost her husband and one long-time male friend. Why should she lose her women friends too? Things might never be the same between them, but it was history. The hurt had been

308

done, and now it was out in the open it could never hurt her quite so badly again. That was the theory, anyway. Philip Lefarge's theory.

'We're having a family Christmas here,' she went on, 'and then I shall find somewhere else to live. It's all arranged, but don't tell the others yet.'

Sarah looked bewildered as well as shocked. She gulped her drink, and before she could hold her glass out for another, Margaret had filled it.

'But leaving this house! Mags, I suddenly feel as if I don't know you any more. You've changed. You're so strong — and so decisive.'

'And I've always been so weak and so dumb, haven't I?'

'I didn't mean that. And if it's not a stupid thing to say, I'm so bloody, *bloody* sorry, about everything. And I never want to see this damn thing again.'

She wrenched the heart pendant from her neck, and threw the pair of them across the room. Margaret picked them up and held them aloft. They glittered in the lamplight for a moment, before she dropped them delicately into the bin.

'Neither do I,' she said quietly. 'Now bring me up to date on June before she and Fiona get here. Then we'll eat our Chinese when the guy arrives with the takeaways, and all get quietly pissed the way we always do.'

Although nothing would or could ever be quite the same again, and they both knew it. For one of them, especially, the knowledge that the friend she had betrayed knew all about it was humiliating and galling. For the other, it had a strange kind of healing, cathartic process that she hadn't quite expected.

★ ★ ★

Christmas cards began to arrive early in the month as they always did. There were a large number addressed to her and Robert from those who hadn't heard of his death, and Margaret had to steel her heart to open them. After a while though, she realized it was natural for this to happen, and that she would have to get down to sorting out the people she hadn't notified once Christmas was over. She thought she had done it all, but obviously she hadn't.

She had been in two minds about whether or not to decorate the tree and put up the usual trimmings, but in the end there was no question about it. This would be the last time. Robert would approve of her making an effort to give their children — who weren't children any more — the kind of festivities they had always had. She owed them that much. Jenny and Ben weren't too bothered about her selling up, but Keith was a different matter. Keith was still resentful, and egged on by Laura, he didn't mind showing it.

'You could still change your mind, Mum,' he told her one Sunday morning.

'I won't. I've made my decision, and I'm sticking to it.'

He hesitated. 'I've got something to tell you. Laura and I are considering getting married sometime next year. If you wanted to hang on to the house, we'd be happy to think about moving in with you.'

'Good God, why on earth would you think I'd ever want to do that?'

Share a house with Laura? She'd rather eat worms.

'We wondered if you were selling up because you were lonely here. It's far too big for one person, and you've got so many memories of Dad and all of us. We just thought it might be a nice idea.'

'Believe me, Keith, it has nothing to do with my being lonely. I want to make a new life for myself, and as you say, this house is too big for one person.'

'But the three of us — '

'Would be two people too many,' Margaret said firmly. 'I'm sure you mean to be helpful,

311

Keith, but I shan't change my mind.'

'Is it Laura?' he persisted. 'I know you don't always see eye to eye, but I know she'd make an effort.'

'Well, I won't, so forget it. For pity's sake, darling, do you think I'd be content to be put on the sidelines and sit around knitting or something, while you and Laura lord it in my home? I'm forty-two, Keith, not an ancient monument who needs looking after.'

He went off in a huff as usual, and for once she didn't call him later to placate him. In her mind, the very idea of living with Laura was enough to put her off her lunch. And the fact that they were *considering* getting married, which were his calculating words, seemed to sum up the difference in their relationship and hers and Robert's.

Robert had simply swept her off her feet, married her and filled her belly with babies at the first chance, with the promise of all of them living happily ever after. The sweet ache in her heart reminded her of all those magical times when she had truly believed it would last for ever.

Nothing could take those memories away. They were still there, intact, and unquenchable. It was the one final thing that had dawned on her while she had wrestled with how to get the full measure of her revenge on

Sarah. But then she saw that keeping their friendship was the way to prove herself stronger than they were, and that their little fling meant nothing in the great scheme of things.

Because Robert hadn't left her. Robert had always loved her and their children, and made a wonderful home for all of them. It was the thought she had clung to in the long, sleepless hours after Sarah and June and Fiona had gone home that night, when they were all so drunk on wine and laughter that Margaret was only a hair's-breadth away from breaking down completely.

But she hadn't done so. She had come through it, and now there was only Christmas to get through before she started on the next big adventure of her life. Only this time it would be very different, because this time there was nobody to do it with her. No Robert to rely on and take all the business-side of things off her shoulders. She had relied on him far too much over the years, content to be the wonderful hostess, the beautiful company wife, the woman most of her contemporaries envied.

And she'd see hell freeze first, she vowed, remembering Keith's tentative suggestion, before she allowed him and Laura to move into this house and take it over, making memories of their own. At least those were exclusively hers.

★   ★   ★

But if she had expected everything to be the same between herself and Sarah from now on, Margaret knew she was asking far too much. The four of them still met for their weekly dates, they went clubbing, they had meals at one another's houses, but June and Fiona would have to be wearing blinkers, not to see that something had changed.

'You aren't being funny lately because of my op, are you, Mags?' June asked her at last.

'Funny? That's hardly the word I'd have used about a serious operation,' she said, genuinely puzzled by the question.

June shrugged. 'Some people seem to think it's catching. That if I breathe over them they'll catch it. Stuff like that.'

'Well, I'm not *some people*, and I didn't know I was being funny lately.'

'Well, not funny, exactly, but you and Sarah don't seem to be on the same wavelength any more, and it's rubbing off.'

Margaret sighed. 'I suppose you might as well know. I knew I'd have to tell you sometime, and I can't keep it a secret for ever.'

She saw Sarah draw in her breath, and went on quickly, 'I've decided to sell up after Christmas and I'll probably move away from here. I made the mistake of letting Sarah in on it, and I know she's had a hard job not to tell you.'

It covered the moment, and she smiled at Sarah more naturally than at any time since that awful night. It sent a mutual vow of silence between them, about the one topic that both united and divided them. It was the weirdest bond, but it was a bond, nonetheless.

And once they discovered there was no way she was going back on her idea, it inevitably started speculation about what Margaret was going to do.

'No idea,' she said airily. 'I might even go and live in Guernsey.'

Immediately she said it, she wished she hadn't, because she had no intention of doing any such thing. But Fiona sussed it out at once.

'I bet you met a man there. Come clean now, Mags. Is that it?'

'Of course not. Well, of course I met people, but no one in particular.'

And if *that* wasn't a complete denial of the something very particular she and Philip Lefarge had shared together, she didn't know what was. But she wasn't prepared to let anyone know about it yet. There was really nothing to know.

★   ★   ★

Her parents arrived two days before Christmas, ostensibly so that Annie could help Margaret with the preparations, but also to give her father a breathing space before the big day. They all knew it, but nobody referred to it. Jenny and Ben came down together on Christmas Eve, and Margaret began to feel the old excitement of a family Christmas, even though Robert wouldn't be with them this year. But it would be the last one in this house, and it had to be a good one for all their sakes.

Keith brought round the turkey during the evening, when the whole family was together, with Laura tagging along as usual, Margaret thought uncharitably. Keith was still a little distant with her because of her refusal to consider letting him try for a mortgage and move in, but neither of them had told any of the others about it, and they had called a mutual truce.

'We must drink a toast to absent friends,' Annie said suddenly, when the general gossiping had briefly died down. 'To Robert,

316

of course, and also Brenda and her new husband — whose name I can never remember — '

'Oh Mum, honestly!' Margaret said with a laugh. 'It's Greg, as you know perfectly well.'

'Oh yes, I remember. I wonder if he goes around wearing one of those hats with corks all around the edge and playing a didgeridoo.'

Jenny shrieked. 'He's American, Gran. Just because they're living in Australia right now doesn't mean he's gone native. I wouldn't mind going to Australia sometime. I wonder if I could swing it with my company.'

Her grandmother looked at her fondly. If she'd said she was flying to the moon, Annie Vernon wouldn't have been at all fazed. And if Margaret said she was going to live in Guernsey, neither of them would turn a hair.

Not that they didn't love her. They had always protected her in their various ways, especially Keith, whose love could be in danger of smothering her — but she was also aware that lately they had come to respect her strike for independence. They didn't even know how much of a strike that was, but they recognized it in her all the same. In fact, if any of them bothered to analyse it properly, Margaret guessed they were thankful she hadn't totally fallen apart after Robert died. She hadn't clung to any one of them.

'I've got mince pies and sausage rolls in the oven,' she announced, having had enough of this introspection for one evening. 'How about having some of them now, before we go to church for the midnight carols?'

'Must we, Mum?' Ben groaned.

'What, the food or the carols? And before you answer that, it's both, of course. We're not going to break one of the last traditions we'll have here,' she said. 'Your father wouldn't like it.'

She deliberately said it in the present tense, because she was very aware that Robert's presence was still here tonight. Christmas had always been such a happy time for all of them.

The doorbell sounded at that precise moment as they all fussed about being busy, and not quite knowing how to answer this statement. Why the hell did bereavement always cause such embarrassment, such awkwardness, Margaret thought, when they should all have got through this stage of things months ago.

She was fetching the snacks out of the oven, which were by now filling the house with the mouth-watering smells of pastry and mincemeat and sausages, when Keith came to the door of the kitchen.

'It's someone for you, Mum,' he said

stonily. 'Or rather, some*thing*.'

She looked up, her face flushed from the oven, and then gaped. In Keith's arms was the most enormous basket arrangement of flowers she had ever seen.

'Good Lord. Who on earth — ?'

'There's an envelope attached. I daresay it's from that slime-ball Franklin.'

His resentment was childish, Margaret thought mildly — and so unnecessary.

'Actually, I doubt that. He was going away for Christmas, and he's already sent me a card. And for another thing, we had a few words recently,' she added for good measure. Though why she should even try to quell Keith's darkening suspicions, she couldn't think.

But she knew there was only one other person who would have thought to send her such a lavish arrangement of flowers, even if they hadn't come from his own establishment in Guernsey and were ordered through a local florist . . .

She went back to the sitting-room to take the envelope from the basket. By now everyone was waiting expectantly for her to say who these flowers were from. If only she could have handled this alone.

'Come on then, Mum. Who's this secret admirer who's spending a pot of money on you?' Jenny said mischievously, not really believing it.

'Don't be ridiculous, Jen,' Laura said. 'Your mother wouldn't have any such thing, and you shouldn't embarrass her like that.'

'Oh, don't be such a stuffed shirt, Laura,' Jenny snapped, as contrary as ever. 'Why wouldn't Mum have an admirer? She's not dead yet.'

She clapped her hands over her mouth the minute she said it.

'Well, neither are we,' Ben said, covering the moment. 'But we're all going to die of curiosity if you don't open that card and let us in on it, Mum.'

'I expect it's from my Ladies' Luncheon Club,' Margaret said desperately. 'They always choose one member at Christmastime to send a special gift to, and it's probably my turn.'

'You'll never know until you open the envelope, will you, darling?' her father put in.

And the winner is . . .

She felt as if the envelope was red hot as she slit it open and pulled out the card inside. It couldn't have been a tiny card with a printed message on it, leaving room for just a signature, of course. It had to be large enough for him to dictate far too many emotive words. Which would have been lovely, if she had been reading them privately.

Before she could do a thing, Jenny had snatched it from her hands playfully and held it aloft. They were all laughing at her teasing now, but Margaret could already feel her face going red, anticipating the moment.

'Let's see what lost cause is chatting up my mother!' Jenny screeched, and then stopped, as her eyes took in the message on the card.

'Grow up, Jenny, and please give it to me,' Margaret snapped.

Her daughter's sudden silence as she handed it over said more than words. But they all knew Jenny wasn't someone who could be silent for more than seconds.

'Who the hell is this Philip, and why is he sending you lots of love, and asking when you're coming back to take up where you left off, because he's missing you so much?' she yelled, hardly pausing for breath.

16

'Is that the bloke who phoned the other day, Mum?' Keith said sharply.

'You know very well it is. You took the call, didn't you?'

'So what's going on?' he said, his voice full of accusation.

Jenny suddenly looked as frantic as a little girl in danger of having a favourite toy taken away. 'You aren't really seeing somebody else, are you, Mum? You couldn't be, so soon after Dad! How *could* you?'

'Actually, he's been gone for nearly nine months, darling,' Margaret said delicately, 'and not that it's any of your business, but I have not been seeing somebody else, as you put it. Though with your usual finesse, I'm surprised you didn't put it far more crudely. Philip is just someone I met in Guernsey.'

And there was no bloody reason why she had to explain it all to them either, she thought resentfully. They didn't own her.

Jenny's temper was always on a short leash, and right now it was ready to explode. 'Well, that's it then, isn't it? So much for loyalty. Everybody said you and Dad had a perfect marriage, but it didn't take you long to forget him, did it?'

Oh, if you only knew, my darling . . . if you only knew the half of it. The irony of it all nearly took Margaret's breath away.

Ben's voice was just as harsh. 'And I suppose you haven't forgotten that you were going there because it was your silver wedding anniversary, and you wanted to be where you and Dad had spent your honeymoon?'

'Absolutely right,' Margaret said, as calm as the others were tense. Though Keith and Laura were sitting back with what practically amounted to self-satisfied looks on their faces, Margaret noted. As if to say they had seen this coming all along, and were content now to let the others do the ranting and accusing.

But Margaret's father was starting to look distressed, and her mother obviously decided it was time to pour oil on troubled waters as quickly as possible. 'I think you children are getting all this out of proportion. So your mother met a nice man on Guernsey and he sent her some flowers at Christmas. There's nothing wrong in that, and those who think so are just being ridiculous. Now why don't we all eat some of those delicious sausage rolls and mince pies that Margaret's made and think about getting ready to go to church? This is supposed to be the season of goodwill, after all.'

'To all men, apparently,' Jenny muttered.

'*What* did you say?' Margaret snapped.

'Well, Grannie Annie might be able to forget it, but we can't.' She spoke collectively. 'Whoever this Philip is, he shouldn't have sent you lots of love and said he was missing you and when were you coming back?'

The words were clearly imprinted in her brain now. Angrily, and before she had time to think about it, Margaret tore the gift card into pieces and dropped them on the carpet as if they meant less than nothing to her.

'Well, now the card doesn't exist any more, so let's do as your grandmother said and try to enjoy Christmas, shall we? I don't know what's got into you all, making such a fuss over nothing. I suppose if the flowers had come from John, you wouldn't have thought it odd at all.'

'Not much,' Keith sneered. 'But at least we knew where we stood with him.'

And that's all you know, too.

But even as they all coped with this new intrusion into family harmony and Annie tried to pretend none of it happened, and insisted on passing round the plates of food and ordering Keith to top up their drinks, something else was coming very forcefully into Margaret's mind.

Robert had betrayed her, and she had to cope with it. *Was* coping with it, and she considered she was doing pretty well now, give or take the dark moods that could still sweep over her when she was least expecting them. But there was no reason for his children to know. She couldn't bear to taint his image by letting him down. Two wrongs didn't make a right, and they had always adored him, and must continue to do so. It would be cruel to lash out and defend herself, and it would serve no purpose.

She knew she wasn't being totally saint-like. There was also an element of self-pride in her thinking. She simply couldn't bear to face her children's anger and disbelief, and then the natural sense of betrayal of themselves, and finally pity for her. Nor for them to be aware that their parents hadn't always had the perfect marriage everybody thought they had.

Because once they had got over the shock — if they even believed it at all — she knew they would rally round her the way they had always done. She would once again be the martyr, bearing up admirably. And she couldn't take that.

In any case, the greatest irony of all was

that their marriage *had* been perfect, both for her and for the outside world. She had known nothing of Robert's infidelities, and right until the time of his death, she had believed in their love totally, and to besmirch it now would be to destroy something very precious. She couldn't do that to him, and she wouldn't do it.

'I've got a very special Christmas present for you all,' she said a little while later, when tempers had cooled.

By then the basket of flowers stood in pride of place on the sideboard, because she saw no reason not to enjoy it. 'You know Keith has seen to the sale of the boat and your father's cars, and the proceeds are going to be shared between the three of you. You'll have the cheques in the morning.'

Ben gasped. 'Good God, Mum, that's far too much!'

'Of course it's not,' she said, smiling, his face so like Robert's at that moment as he tried hard not to look too pleased, and failed completely. 'It's a Christmas present from your father and me and I know it's what he would have wanted. Jenny's already had part of her share in buying her flat, but there's still a nice little sum left. Enough to take you off on holiday to Australia, for instance, Jen,' she added, knowing her daughter. She was rewarded by a flushed face.

'I don't know what to say now,' Jenny said, with a convulsive swallow.

'Well, that's a first,' Keith put in drily.

The next minute Jenny put her arms around her mother and hugged her.

'Thanks, Mum. And I'm sorry for being so bitchy just now,' she choked.

'Forgotten and forgiven, so let's put on our coats and boots and go to church, shall we, and remember what Christmas is all about.'

★ ★ ★

They had always loved walking to the midnight service at their local church; it had been a ritual ever since the children were small. They saw the same friends and acquaintances every year, and there was a lovely sense of continuity and tradition in singing the same old carols and Christmas hymns.

This year, her father had almost decided to stay behind in the house, but at the last minute he accompanied them on the short walk to the church, and they were as solid a unit as they had always been. Minus one.

A light dusting of snow was falling when they came outside, but it melted as soon as it hit the ground. There were a myriad stars in the sky, and the faint sound of carollers and revellers in the distance. A great feeling of peace came over Margaret. She had dealt with some difficult problems in the last months and days, and now there was only the way ahead, wherever it took her. She gave a small shiver, and felt her father tuck her hand in the crook of his arm.

'You know I'm not a religious man, Maggie,' he said, 'but I reckon Robert's been looking after you all this time, and he'd give you his blessing on whatever you want to do. And if you think it's right to sell your house and make a new life, that would be all right by him, too. He was never one for standing still and letting things pass him by.'

'You're a wise old bird, aren't you, Dad?' she said softly, hugging his arm and knowing it wasn't only Robert who was giving her his blessing.

But his blessing for what? You didn't throw away twenty-five years of memories because you had spent one wild, magical night with a man who made you feel seventeen again . . . she wouldn't let herself think along those lines.

'Laying ghosts, darling?' her father said, as she shivered again.

'Trying to decide what to do about them, actually,' she admitted. She didn't expect him to understand, because she didn't really understand why she had said it herself, but he gave her arm an extra squeeze.

'You'll know when the time comes,' he said enigmatically.

'What would you do if you didn't have Mum around?' she said, without thinking.

'It was more a question of what she would do without me a few weeks ago, wasn't it? But everything came good in the end, and so it will for you, my love.'

It hadn't come good for Robert, but she just managed not to say it, because for a frantic time she had thought she was going to go through the same trauma again on her father's account. But it made her wonder just what either of her parents would do without the other. It was something you never thought about as you went about your everyday life, but it was something that everyone had to face eventually — unless it happened the wrong way around, and a younger one went first, like Robert.

Her parents were devoted to one another, but they were also completely self-sufficient. Annie had had to be, all the times when her husband had been away on military service, and she had virtually brought up two daughters alone, when she wasn't traipsing around the word after him. Many couples wouldn't have survived it — many nowadays gave up at the first hurdle — but these two had always been strong, and Margaret knew there was more of that strength in herself than she would have believed.

'Hurry up, you two,' her mother called back to them now, as they dawdled companionably behind the others. 'Keith and Laura are on their way home, and I want to get my feet up and have a good hot drink after all that singing.'

'She means one that's well laced with brandy to knock her out before the rigours of Christmas Day,' her husband said in an aside, which set Margaret laughing again. Oh yes, some rituals would never change.

★   ★   ★

This particular Christmas Day might have been an ordeal, but in the end, it wasn't. Individually, it was as if everyone had made a personal vow to keep up their spirits for each other, to have a good time, to eat until they dropped, to drink a toast to Robert, and to swap stories about Christmases past.

During the morning, Sarah, Fiona and June had called round on their way out for a pre-lunch drink, though no amount of persuasion would make Margaret agree to join them. This was a family day, and she intended keeping it that way. There was a phone call from John, who kept telling her he was somewhere hot, and missed her like hell, and wishing her and the family a lovely day. He was so like his old self, she couldn't be stand-offish with him, and she said they must get together sometime when he got back to England.

And she didn't need Keith's raised eyebrows to know that he was mentally adding 'and don't make it too soon.'

'That was John,' she told him. And some devil made her add, 'And if you thought it was going to be Philip Lefarge I'm sure he has better things to do on Christmas Day than make phone calls to someone he hardly knows.'

'It's an unusual name, isn't it? Is he French?' her mother said, as Keith turned away to mutter to Laura.

'I don't think so,' Margaret said, 'though many old Guernsey families have French surnames, like all the Channel Islanders.'

'What does he do there?' Ben asked, not really caring, but clearly assuming that someone in the family should show an interest.

'He has a very successful market garden,' Margaret told him.

'Oh, so he's just a gardener, is he?' Laura said, poker-faced.

God, she was a pain.

'Hardly. If Keith had taken more than a second's notice of the card that came with the flower arrangement, he'd have seen that Philip supplies Guernsey flowers to a variety of mainland shops, and that these had his endorsement on the card.'

She wouldn't have realized it herself if she hadn't rescued the pieces of the card when they had all gone to bed, and reread it a dozen times, and that the fact had charmed her all over again. But that was something they didn't need to know.

'It's quite a big concern then, is it?' Ben asked.

Margaret could almost see the wheels turning in his head. If his mother had to take up with somebody, then at least it wasn't some wastrel who was cashing in on his inheritance. Or maybe she was doing her son an injustice. When had Ben ever been acquisitive? He was the least materialistic of any of them.

'It's a very big concern,' Margaret said coolly. 'But I'm sure you've heard enough about someone I met so briefly, so why don't we just get on with enjoying Christmas Day?'

She began to realize she would be glad

when this day was over . . . and tomorrow
. . . and then they would all go away and leave
her alone, and she could begin to take stock
of the future properly. It gave her a mild
shock to know that she was tiring of their
company so soon, and she felt a stab of guilt
that she did so.

She had always been an honest person,
never having the need to be anything else.
She was also in the habit of facing truths, and
not flinching away from them. And although
she loved them all, she was keeping secrets
from them now. There was the secret
awareness that, even though she had always
believed Robert to be the love of her life, she
could fall in love again, and so soon — if it
was, indeed love that she had felt so briefly
and spectactularly for Philip Lefarge.

And there was the bigger, uglier secret
about Robert, and she had vowed never to
inflict the pain of that on his children.

So it was a tremendous relief when Boxing
Day came and went, after the traditional
family walk along the beach, supposedly to
work off the extra Christmas calories, before
a huge brunch which threatened to undo it
all. Keith and Laura hadn't joined them for
once, having arranged to meet friends
instead, and Margaret wasn't altogether sorry.
She felt less than easy with Keith lately, as if

he had X-ray eyes that could see right through her and the secrets she was keeping. It wasn't a comfortable feeling.

But now that the festivities were over, she had no intention of leaving the tree and trimmings up until Twelfth Night, as they had always done, taking them all down with much laughter and plenty of mulled wine and snacks to bid goodbye formally to another year. New Year's Eve would also pass unnoticed, she vowed, because she wasn't going to live it up, despite her friends trying to coax her into it. All except Sarah, she noted, who habitually said she was going to get rat-arsed, and find herself a new man, if only for one night.

She had obviously had Robert for much longer than that, Margaret thought bitterly, and although she didn't quite know what she was going to do with New Year's Eve, she wasn't going to be having a wild time.

John Franklin called her two days before then. 'I'm back from Tenerife, and I don't know if you've got any plans for New Year's Eve, but if you want a quiet night in, I'm your man,' he said cautiously. 'Absolutely no strings, no dragged-up memories, just two old friends having a quiet drink together. What do you say?'

'In other words, you're at a loose end and

have nowhere else to go, right?'

But her mouth was curling into a small smile, because he *had* always been a friend, a very good friend, an old friend. And the past was dead and buried.

'You know me too well. But if it's a bad idea, I'll quite understand.'

'No, it's not a bad idea. I'll cook something special if you like, and we'll get quietly smashed together. I've got things to tell you, anyway.'

Why not? He might as well know she was selling this house and probably quitting Bournemouth altogether. Not that she knew where she was going yet. Maybe to London to be near her parents and her younger children. But from undeniably feeling a bit in limbo now that Christmas was over, sharing New Year's Eve with John was something positive to look forward to.

And because she *did* know him so well, there was one sure thing: he would be very careful not to rake up anything she didn't want to know, and he wouldn't be getting smashed, either, in case he let anything slip that he shouldn't. It gave her an unexpected sense of power, knowing she was in control of things.

★　★　★

Once they were over the first few awkward moments, they settled back into the old routine of banter, with John sniffing the air and appreciating the fact that she had prepared a succulent meal of pork in apple and cider. He told her about his trip to Tenerife, and eventually the questions began.

'So what have you got to tell me then?'

She took a deep breath. She wouldn't have been human if now and then she didn't feel a pang about what she was planning, but every time she said it, it became more real, and in her heart she was certain it was the right thing, and that there could be no turning back.

'I'm selling the house,' she said flatly.

His good-looking face was almost comical. He said nothing for a few minutes, and then the words almost leapt out of him.

'You must be joking! You and Robert were always so happy here. And your family, too, the children, all those wonderful times they had — we *all* had here. Tell me I'm not hearing this!'

'For heaven's sake, John, it's only a house,' she said, as if she didn't know and appreciate everything he was saying. But she had to bring it down to size, to reduce it to what it was, a place that had known enormous happiness and love, but from which she now had to move on. Because eventually it had shown her the meaning of heartbreak too.

'How can you say that!'

'I say it because it's true. And you yourself said it's been a lovely family home, but I no longer have any family around me, and I want to move on. I have to, John.'

Her eyes were steady as she looked at him, her old friend, one-time lover of her husband and his treacherous ally. But she wouldn't allow any of that bitterness into her heart right now. All she wanted to see was the friend, and not the enemy.

'Have you really thought this through? What do the family think? I can't imagine Keith being too happy about it.'

'Keith has Laura, and if you want a laugh, he offered to try to get a mortgage and for them to move in with me.'

'Good God!' For the first time, he broke into a laugh. 'I would have said it's a fate worse than death, but you wouldn't like me saying such things.'

'Why not? It's exactly what I thought,' Margaret said drily. 'As for the rest of them, they're fine about it. In any case, it's not really any of their business, is it?'

Nor yours, she added silently.

'Well, I wish you luck. What are you going to do — buy a granny flat or something? I

337

can't see it, after having so much space here.'

'Hardly. And I'm not a granny, either. I haven't made up my mind yet, but one thing's certain — I've got the entire world at my disposal, haven't I?'

He trailed to the kitchen after her as she went to check on the pork.

'Have I ever told you how much I admire you, Margaret? I probably have, but sometimes I don't think any of us says it often enough. You're much stronger than any of us ever gave you credit for.'

'Well, thank you for that,' she said, touched. 'I know I was happy enough to rely on Robert for everything for all those years, but I guess we all have a certain amount of strength and resilience inside us for when we need it.'

And you can make of that what you will, dear John.

But after all, they had a good evening together, and celebrated midnight by toasting each other and absent friends, and tuning in to some inane New Year's Eve rantings on TV, which was about all they could cope with before bedtime. It was no problem for John to stay the night, rather than drive home in his over-the-limit state, and Margaret found herself thankful that some of her life was at last slotting back into place.

She had lost her husband, but she hadn't lost her friends, and in keeping their friendship, even while they knew she was aware of their betrayal, she believed she was stronger than any of them. It was what American TV shows would call closure.

It was only when John left the next day that she allowed herself to think about Philip Lefarge. The huge basket of flowers was still in perfect condition, and she couldn't fail to see it whenever she went into the sitting-room. She hadn't called him to thank him, as she knew she should have done. But nor had he called to wish her a happy New Year, as she had certainly expected. She shouldn't feel piqued about it, but she did.

It was ridiculous, of course. He would have been sharing the evening with friends, and there was no earthly reason why he would have called at precisely midnight. She knew the onus was really on her, to call and thank him. And the words on the florist's card which she had carefully pieced together and stuck down with sellotape to resurrect it, were hardly the words of someone who never wanted to see her again.

'I'm being stupid,' she muttered out loud, as she tweaked some of the foliage in the flower arrangement into a better position. 'Why would he bother with someone who rejects him at every turn?'

Well, except for sleeping with him, and sharing a night of love and lust, which was hardly the act of rejection!

Two weeks into January, she still hadn't heard from him, and she was still dithering over what to do, when the phone rang late one afternoon. She snatched it up quickly, and when she heard the estate agent's smooth voice at the other end she smothered her disappointment.

'Good day to you, Mrs Jarvis, and a Happy New Year,' he said formally. 'I'm just calling to let you know that we have several clients interested in looking at the house and I wanted to arrange a convenient time for you. I believe you said you didn't want to be involved?'

'That's right.'

So he wanted her out of the house. And quickly, if he was in line for a big fat bonus from this Very Desirable Property in Prime Position.

'So when would be convenient?' he repeated, when she remained dumb with shock for a few moments. She couldn't help it. Because now it seemed inevitable. The house would be sold, and other people would be living in it. Using her kitchen. Sleeping in her bedroom. Swimming in her pool.

Covering up the faint patches on the walls where her pictures had been and making the house their own. It was what she wanted, but it also filled her with an intense feeling of sadness. It was the end of an era.

'Are you still there, Mrs Jarvis?' He was impatient now, businesslike while she was dreaming of things that could never come again.

'I'm sorry, I was just trying to think which days would be best. How about Thursday and Friday of this week, in the afternoons? I shall be out then.'

She didn't know where, but she would definitely be out.

'That will be fine. I'll speak to my clients and arrange for them to view at three o'clock each afternoon.'

He hung up, and Margaret replaced the phone slowly. Now wasn't the time to start having second thoughts. Now was the time to start planning for the future and decide where she was going to live once this house no longer belonged to her. The magnitude of it all suddenly overwhelmed her, and her legs began to shake. This time last year she and Robert would never have given a thought to leaving this house. It was where they had brought up their children, and where they had assumed they would grow old together.

The sound of the doorbell jarred through her thoughts. She wasn't expecting anybody, and she was far too jittery for company, and if it was a couple of black-suited Mormons or Jehovah's Witnesses, she would find it hard to be civil to them right now. She threw open the door in annoyance.

'I know you weren't expecting me to turn up like this,' said a well-remembered voice, 'but I decided that surprise was the best form of attack, so are you going to let me in, or do I have to stand here and freeze?'

17

'How did you get here?' she said stupidly.

'Can I come inside?' Philip repeated, when she seemed incapable of moving. 'The neighbours will be getting restless.'

They didn't have any neighbours, at least none that could see into the property. It was one of the things she and Robert had liked when they had first seen the house. And why should she think of that at this precise moment? She stood aside, and Philip Lefarge stepped inside, dumping his holdall and garment bag on the floor, and taking her in his arms. She reacted by stiffening slightly.

'Don't I get a kiss? A friendly one, at least,' he teased her. 'I've clearly shocked you by my sudden appearance, but I hoped I would be welcome.'

She wilted against him. 'And so you are, but you're right, it is a shock, and you had better explain just what you're doing here.'

'I came to see you, of course, among other things.'

'What other things?'

He gave an elaborate sigh. 'You may not have noticed, Mrs Jarvis, but I am a

343

businessman, and I do have links with the outside world, especially in this part of it. At this time of year I always come to the mainland make a personal visit to the outlets that take our produce.'

Margaret moved out of his arms, feeling slightly ridiculous to be held so closely all this time, before he had even taken off his outdoor coat.

'It wasn't just to see me, then,' she said. She didn't want to dwell on whether or not that was a disappointment. Her thoughts raced on. He would obviously be booked into a hotel for however long he was staying. It was a minor relief. She could just imagine Keith's reaction if he had wanted to stay here. But then again, why not?

'Are you disappointed?' he said, in answer to her statement.

She ignored that and decided that this fencing had gone on long enough. 'Would you like some tea or coffee? You must be frozen, and I'm not being much of a hostess, letting you stand here on the doorstep.'

He followed her properly inside, his eyes laughing at her, just as she remembered them.

'I didn't come here looking for a hostess, darling.'

The endearment took her by surprise. It

344

occurred to her that he didn't use them often, at least, not to her. Which led her to wonder just what kind of Christmas he had had, and with whom.

She did the domestic things that kept her hands busy and took her mind off the suddenness of his appearance. Ten minutes later, over coffee and biscuits, she realized how awkward she felt with him. They were out of his environment, where she had felt defensive and yet reasonably secure, perhaps even *because* of that sense of putting a barrier around herself. Until he had broken it down . . .

They had once been so close, however briefly, yet here in her own home, where he looked at ease already, she was the one who was fidgety, as if seeing it all through his eyes, the suburban housewife who had fallen for his charms. It was the element of surprise, of course. Turning up like this, without warning.

'You really should have let me know you were coming,' she accused.

'Should I? But then I would have missed that look in your eyes that told me you were glad to see me. You might have sounded shocked, but you couldn't hide that look, Margaret.'

'It was probably guilt, because I hadn't thanked you for the lovely basket of flowers you sent me,' she prevaricated.

'It wasn't guilt. You and I have nothing to feel guilty about, do we? Or did it cause a few problems with the family that you're not telling me about?'

'What do you think!'

He didn't say anything for a few moments, and the only sounds in the room were the ticking of the clock and her own heartbeats. Oh *please*, Margaret thought, *how melodramatic can you get!*

'I thought we had something very special, Margaret, and I don't want to let that go. But I find it difficult to conduct a relationship with so many miles of water between us.'

'We don't have a relationship,' she said, in a cracked voice.

He stood up and pulled her to her feet. Two sets of heartbeats were so loud and so close now they were merging into one . . . and Margaret desperately wished these romantic schoolgirl phrases would go away. She was practically writing a eulogy in her head.

'You know that we do,' Philip said. 'But I won't pursue it right now. Will you have dinner with me tonight? I haven't checked into my hotel yet, but I'll pick you up around eight o'clock.'

It was the middle of the afternoon, and

nice suburban women didn't do what she was about to do now. Or maybe they did, if they didn't stop to think any more than she did at that moment.

'You could stay here. There's plenty of room.'

And it would prove once and for all if there really was anything between us. Or if it was just sex. Or lust. Not love. Not anything with a future.

'I was hoping you'd say that, but I wasn't asking.'

He never did, at least, not more than once. She remembered that about him. He left it to her to make the final decisions. He wasn't Robert, who had always bombarded her with words, wearing her down until she gave in to whatever he wanted because it was simply easier to agree than to argue. Philip had made a couple of phone calls, sent one basket of flowers, told her he was missing her, and asked when she was coming back to his island. The rest was up to her. Except that he was here now. That had to mean something.

She moved out of his arms, because this closeness was making her feel weirdly claustrophobic in a way she couldn't explain.

'Do you know how mixed up I'm feeling right now?' she asked slowly. 'Less than a year ago I thought my life was mapped out in front of me. Everything was taken care of. I was loved and cherished, however old-fashioned you might think that sounds. I was blissfully happy. And then everything changed. In a split second, it changed from happy to sad — and that's the feeblest word in the dictionary to describe the way I felt when Robert died. I was totally devastated.'

'I know. I've been there — remember?'

'You were divorced. It's not the same,' she said, as if he had no right to share any of the ragged pain that was surging inside her all over again.

'When you lose someone you love, for whatever reason, it's exactly the same. Anyway, does all this analysing mean you've changed your mind about my staying here? I've still got a hotel booking for four days, and I've arranged to see one of my clients in half an hour, so the decision is yours, Margaret.'

And she had the feeling that she would be turning down more than a few days of his company. He was very calm, but she could see that his jaw was tight. He was testing her. Oh, to hell with it. She really didn't want to deal with all this now, especially with the estate agent bringing people to see the house on Thursday and Friday afternoon. She felt jittery all over again at the thought.

'Of course you can stay here. I'm rattling around in this big house on my own, so I'll be glad of the company.'

She was gracious. The perfect hostess. And she hated herself for being so bloody pompous.

'Right. Where do you want me to put my stuff?'

'Just leave it, and we'll sort things out when you get back from your meeting. And Philip — I really am glad to see you.'

'Good. I was beginning to wonder about that. I'll see you later then, probably around six, and I'll book us in for that dinner,' he said with a smile.

She watched him go, and heard his car start up outside. He'd obviously brought it over on the ferry. He was so self-contained, but there had been a moment when he had looked almost vulnerable. Then a thought struck her: if he was booked into a hotel and had his car with him, why would he have brought his holdall and garment bag into the house, unless he was very certain that she would be asking him to stay? So certain of *her*.

She had intended putting his stuff in one of the guest bedrooms, at least as a gesture — and she wasn't thinking any further ahead than that right now — but now she left it all exactly where it was, in the middle of the sitting-room floor.

It was still sitting there, like a reproach, when she heard the front door slam a while later, while she was upstairs checking the guest bedroom.

Too late, she heard Keith's voice a few seconds later. She had completely forgotten his occasional habit of calling in on his way home from work.

'I'm coming down,' she said, as flustered as a bride, and knowing exactly what his reaction was going to be.

He was staring at the holdall and garment bag that had Philip's name plastered all over them. He couldn't have travelled incognito, of course, Margaret thought in annoyance, so she could have passed him off as a woman friend staying overnight . . . the thought of it made her smile, and Keith misinterpreted it at once.

'So he's moving in, is he? You seem to have forgotten Dad pretty quickly, haven't you?' he snapped.

Her temper flared. 'Keith, he is not moving in, as you call it, and you really are turning into the most pompous pig of a man.'

His handsome face went a furious dark red. He was an imposing figure, who could quell any miscreants with a glance, but he was still her son, and she wasn't going to be dictated to by him or anyone.

'What's all this then, Scotch mist?' he said sarcastically.

'If you must know, Philip is over here for a few days visiting clients as he always does at this time of year. He is booked into a hotel, but he dropped in to see me first and left his things here while he goes to his first meeting. Is that any big deal?' She neatly wove her way around the truth of it, since the part about him being booked into a hotel *was* true. The fact that he was going to cancel the booking was no business of Keith's, or anybody else's.

'Be careful, Mum,' he said at last. 'You don't know anything about this man, and you're still vulnerable.'

It was odd that he used the same word she had thought about in regard to Philip not long ago. And although she knew he cared about her, it didn't endear her to him.

'I'm not a child, and I'm perfectly capable of looking after myself. I know you mean well, but please don't smother me. Philip's only here for a short time, and then I'll probably never see him again. Would you have me be so rude as to turn away someone who was kind to me when I went to Guernsey?'

She prayed he wouldn't remember the

words on the card that came with the basket of flowers, the way Jenny had.

Taking-up where we left off . . . sending you lots of love . . . missing you so much . . . and when are you coming back to my island.

'Kind, was he? And that was all?'

Without warning, Margaret began to laugh. It was so ludicrous for them to be standing here like virtual combatants in a duel, hands clenched at their sides, ready to do battle.

'Darling, go home. I promise you Philip is just a very nice man I met on holiday, and he just thought he'd look me up while he was here on business.'

After a moment, he said, 'All right. I'm sorry.'

She thanked God as he capitulated. If he'd hung around long enough for Philip to come back he would have sensed the unmistakable charge of electricity between them in an instant. He wasn't nicknamed by some of his colleagues as hawk-eye for nothing.

Anyway, she wasn't going to waste time worrying about what Keith thought. Once he had gone, her thoughts returned to the fact that the most dynamic man she had met, since Robert, had swept back into her life and was going to stay for four days. She had told

Keith she wasn't a child, and she could have added to that, because the excitement growing inside her now was of a far more adult and sophisticated kind.

★ ★ ★

When Philip returned around six o'clock his belongings were in the guest bedroom. It was a strangely surreal moment, because although he didn't have a key to the house and she had to let him in, it was almost like a wife welcoming her husband home from work, ready to offer him a drink of whatever variety he chose.

'I'd like to take a shower and change first,' he told her, 'then I'll have some coffee. So if you'll point me in the right direction — '

'Follow me,' Margaret said, her heart thumping. 'You're in one of the guest bedrooms overlooking the sea. I thought you'd like to feel at home.'

'I already feel at home.' He caught at her hand. 'Do I make you feel uncomfortable, Margaret?'

'No, of course not.'

'But I'm in one of the guest bedrooms.'

She felt a stab of anger. 'What did you expect? That because we had spent one night together, I was going to take you straight to my bedroom? You are an uninvited guest, after all!'

She didn't add that it was the bedroom she and Robert had shared for almost twenty-five years, but he got the message.

'I didn't actually think that, nor that you would have put it so blatantly. But I'd like to think you considered that one night as unforgettable as I did.'

She wouldn't deny that. She had relived it often enough in waking and sleeping dreams. 'Let's just say that we agree on that, then.'

'Thank God we agree on something,' he said, the smile back in his voice.

By now they had reached the top of the stairs and she threw open one of the front bedrooms with its fabulous view over the swimming-pool, the rear gardens and lawns sloping down towards the sea, with the glittering view beyond. It was the wrong time of year for the many small sailing boats and other craft that were usually bobbing about in the Channel, creating an ever-changing view, but there were still others to be seen, majestic larger vessels on the horizon, and a ferry buzzing its way across towards Poole harbour. Philip went straight to the window, and then nodded slowly.

'I can quite see why someone would never want to leave all this,' he said, after a moment. 'It puts Guernsey into quite a different perspective, doesn't it?'

It was on the tip of her tongue to tell him she was leaving this house just as soon as the estate agent could find her a suitable buyer, but she managed to resist it. She wasn't looking for the extra pressure such a disclosure would produce. It might be subtle, but it would be there, all the same.

Who was she kidding? It would be more than subtle. He would instantly want to know where she was going to live, and if she didn't have anything in mind, what was wrong with Guernsey? She could hear it as clearly as if he was saying it right now.

And then Keith's cautionary words were in her head too. How well did she really know this man? A few walks along sun-drenched beaches and one magical night couldn't compare with a lifetime.

'There's an *en suite* bathroom through that door, Philip,' she said quickly. 'And I'll have the coffee ready by the time you come downstairs.'

She was all fingers and thumbs, and excitement kept surging and retreating in waves. Sarah would have handled this so much better than she did, she thought resentfully. Sarah would be all cool flirtation, and to hell with the consequences. But the upside was that Philip would never have fancied Sarah in a million years. She was too brash, too everything, too much Robert's over-the-top style, and not his. It made her wonder, now that she knew it all, why the hell she had never seen it before — and why Robert had ever fancied herself in the first place.

The phone was ringing when she got downstairs. It was Keith. Checking up on her already. She was ready to flare up at once when he stopped her.

'Just listen to me for a minute, Mum. After I left you I went back to the nick and got one of our computer nerds to run a check on your Philip Lefarge.'

'You did *what?*' Margaret said, almost too incensed to believe what she was hearing.

'I know you think I'm interfering, but it's only because I care about you, and I don't want to see some jerk cashing in on you because you're lonely. You're still in shock over Dad, whether you know it or not.'

Well, thanks for the psycho-analysis . . .

'He's exactly what you said he is, Mum, owns a market garden in Guernsey and is pretty well-heeled by all accounts, but that doesn't mean he wouldn't like a share of your assets.'

'Really?' Margaret said acidly.

'Really. But that's not the thing that concerns me. This may come as a shock to you, but there's also a wife. Her name's Angela.'

'I know,' she said.

After a moment's complete silence, he spoke more sharply. 'You *know*?'

'I know. So that if that's the end of your nasty little snooping, perhaps you'd leave me to get on with my life, and get back to yours, Keith.'

Her hands were shaking when she put down the phone, but predictably, ten minutes later it rang again. Keith wouldn't have thought twice.

'What are you getting yourself into, darling?' her mother said.

She sighed. 'I suppose Keith has been reporting in?'

'He has. Now, much as I adore your father, you know I've always said there's more than one person in this world for everybody. So as far as I'm concerned, I think the best thing you could do is find someone to share your life with instead of turning into a lonely old bat.'

'You have a very colourful turn of phrase,' Margaret said, forced into a smile, despite herself.

'Never mind that. If this man is married, watch out for yourself, darling, that's all I'm saying. It'll only end in heartbreak, because married men rarely leave their wives, you know. It's the nature of the beasts.'

Oh Mum, if you only knew how right you are!

'If Keith had done his homework properly, he might have learned the rest of it, Mum,' she said quietly, because she didn't know how near Philip was to coming downstairs. 'He's divorced, and before you ask, I'm quite sure about it.'

'Oh well, that's all right then!'

'So you don't think it's too soon?' she heard herself asking, though she had never imagined herself asking Annie for such advice — or approval.

'I do not. You gave Robert twenty-five years of your life, and you don't think he's up there on his cloud expecting you to be faithful to a memory, do you?'

This was the most extraordinary conversation she had ever had with her unconventional mother, Margaret found herself thinking. She was as good as giving her blessing to Margaret having a relationship with the most gorgeous man, who at this moment was taking a shower in her house. But hadn't her father also given her his blessing in his own restricted way on Christmas Eve?

'Thanks, Mum,' she said.

'And don't forget to report progress,' Annie said with a laugh, before she put down the phone.

Margaret turned with a start as she heard Philip coming downstairs, frantically hoping he hadn't overheard any of the conversation. He looked marvellous, she thought automatically, his hair still damp and slicked down, his skin smooth and fragrant from shaving, wearing a pair of dark slacks and white shirt, the neck still open until he added a tie for dinner later.

'Will I do?' he asked.

'Of course. Now, how about that coffee?' she added, before he could put any other interpretation on her words.

But who the hell was she kidding now? Wasn't she thrilled and excited that he was here, staying in her house, and undoubtedly in her bed? But not quite. It was the single, most important reason she had given him the best guest bedroom. Because although she had made it plain he wasn't going to sleep with her in what was her and Robert's old bedroom, there was nothing in the rules to prevent her moving in with him. But he wasn't aware of that yet.

She gave a mischievous smile. 'In case you heard me talking to someone just now, it was my mother on the phone, checking up on me.'

'Oh? And what did you tell her? Let me guess. I don't imagine it was that you had your lover staying for a few days — '

'Is that what you are?'

'Isn't it? What else would you call it? I don't really care to be thought of as your fancy-man, and definitely not toy-boy, since I'm older than you are. So let's settle for lover, shall we?'

'Why not?' Margaret said softly, realizing they had fallen into a more natural way of talking to one another now.

Except for the surroundings, they might still have been in Guernsey, with that heady first awareness of one another that had merged so swiftly into an easy companion-ship. She had liked him then and she liked him now, and if liking could some day move towards something deeper than friendship — if it hadn't been halfway there already — then, why not? She certainly wasn't going to defend herself to any of her children.

'If we're going out for dinner this evening,' she went on huskily a little while later, 'you'll have to amuse yourself while I get ready. Turn on the TV or the CD player or read the newspapers — whatever — just make yourself at home — '

'Margaret,' he said gently, 'don't fuss. Just be yourself, and stop thinking of me as an honoured guest. This is me, Philip, remember? The man you're going to marry.'

Her heart stopped for a moment, wondering if he really had said those words. 'If that was a proposal, it was a very odd way of asking, and if it wasn't, then you've got a bloody nerve in presuming that I've even thought about such a thing, and taking my answer for granted.'

'All right, so it came out clumsily, and maybe it was a bit presumptuous. It was a proposal, but you know me well enough by now to know that when I feel strongly enough about anything, I see no point in wasting time — and that I rarely ask twice. So rather than embarrass both of us, let's leave it at that, and when you've made up your mind to say yes, you can just let me know.'

He was impossible! But he made her heart race faster than anyone had ever done before — except Robert, and that was a long time ago.

'I'm going to take a bath,' she said abruptly. 'If you want something stronger than coffee, help yourself from the sideboard.'

She fled upstairs, as gauche as a schoolgirl on her first date. Her heart was positively fluttering . . . either that, or she was about to have a heart attack, and she wasn't going there, thank you very much.

Instead she shut the door very firmly on her own bathroom and wallowed in a scented bath for longer than usual while she thought over what he had said. He was irritating enough *not* to propose to her again, ever, but also persistent enough to persuade her with phone calls and flowers and occasional visits like this. Or to do none of those things, and decide that she was still too caught up in the past to think of marrying again, now or ever.

She shivered, despite the warmth of the bath water, but it was an endearing thought that he didn't want to be simply her occasional lover, and nor had he asked her to move in with him. He had asked her to marry him — well, in a roundabout way. He was conventional and old-fashioned enough to do that, but certainly not staid enough for the old bended knee routine, thank God.

She wasn't considering it, of course. Not for a moment. Not at *this* moment, anyway. At this moment, she was getting out of the bath, swathing herself in a bath towel and thinking about what she was going to wear that evening. And that was as far as her thoughts were going for now.

★ ★ ★

When she emerged some time later, Philip looked up as he heard her heels on the stairs, and gave a low whistle as he took in the scarlet cocktail dress and gold necklace and ear-rings.

'I'm glad I came,' was all he said, but his eyes said a whole lot more.

They went to an intimate little restaurant that Philip knew where the food and wine were excellent. Despite not living in Bournemouth he had been here many times, but he only knew the town through business contacts, hotels and restaurants. Towards the end of the evening, he told her teasingly that all this time he hadn't even known that Margaret Jarvis had been living a stone's throw from one of the elegant little florist shops selling his flowers all year round. He said it with an artlessness that made her laugh.

'And what if you had known? I don't recall using that particular shop. But if I had, I'd have been just one more person buying wedding buttonholes when friends got married, or sending flowers to sick relatives and so on.'

'It would just have been nice to know, that's all.'

And last year — it *was* last year now, Margaret thought, almost in surprise, it had been floral tributes to her husband. Time changed everything.

He looked at her as if he understood the small clouding in her eyes that quickly passed. By now the meal was over, the liqueurs finished, the bill paid.

'Time to go?' he asked quietly.

★   ★   ★

When they returned to the house, it was bathed in the subtle lighting that supposedly kept burglars at bay, according to Keith. It looked as lovely as it always did, and yet, to Margaret's mind at that moment, came the words she had used to her family. It was just a house, no more. It was no longer the home it had once been without the family that had made it so. But she still hadn't mentioned to Philip her intention of selling it. She didn't really know why, unless it was for the fear that he would put pressure on her to go back to Guernsey with him. And she wasn't going to be pushed into anything, not even by him.

'Do you want a nightcap?' she asked him, to cover the tiny awkwardness she felt now. 'Or more coffee?'

'I don't think so. I shall have coffee coming out of my ears if I'm not careful. I just want my bed.'

'Right. I just have a few things to see to before I do the same.'

Margaret didn't look at him as he went upstairs. She went around the house, doing the familiar routine of checking the security system and putting out the lights. For a few moments she lingered by the wide French windows leading out to the patio and the garden. The swimming-pool was faintly lit by the underwater lighting, and the moon and stars lit the night sky. Away in the distance the moonlit sea was a glassy sheet of dark perfection. She and Robert had stood here so often like this in days gone by, loving the silence when all the children were in bed, and feeling as if they owned the world.

She became aware of small sounds from upstairs, footsteps moving about, a creaking of floorboards, the soft click of a bedroom door opening, and she gave a deep, reflective sigh. She had been alone for so long in this house now, alone where she had once been the hub of a loving family, the way a woman always was. But tonight she was no longer alone.

She turned and went up the stairs and along the landing to where the door of the main guest bedroom was partly open. She hesitated for no longer than a heartbeat, then pushed it fully open as Philip came out of the *en suite* bathroom wearing a bathrobe, his long legs visible beneath it.

'I take it this belongs to you, ma'am,' he said, pointing to the silky nightgown she had placed on one of the pillows. 'Either that, or you're trying to tell me something about myself!'

His teasing broke the small tension of the moment, and she laughed, crossing the divide between them as if it didn't exist, and being caught up in his arms. His desire for her was unmistakable, and his kiss was warm on her mouth, as hungry for her as she was for him.

'I didn't think you'd be the one wearing it,' she said huskily against his lips.

'That's funny,' he said, still teasing, but with a deeper tone to his voice, his mouth still a fraction away from hers. 'I didn't think you'd be wearing it, either.'

18

The morning after the night before took on a whole new meaning for Margaret. She was awoken with a kiss, and a feeling of deep contentment. A very caring voice told her to just lie there and relax, and breakfast would be served imminently. She smiled lazily, halfway between sleeping and waking and dreaming. But it hadn't been a dream; it had been spectacularly real. And last night had been so good . . . so very good . . . so full of love.

The sound of a scream jolted her into full consciousness. She sat up in bed so fast that her head spun. She snatched up her nightie from the floor, slid it over her head and rushed downstairs. She reacted so much like an automaton that the whole thing had taken seconds, and by the time she reached the kitchen, Philip was still trying to placate a bug-eyed Mrs Ashley.

Margaret groaned, having completely forgotten she was due that morning, and she was acutely aware that the flimsy nightie she was wearing did little to hide the body beneath. Philip looked at her desperately, kettle in hand, tea-bags spilled all over the floor.

'Will you please explain to this lady that I'm not here to burgle the house, Margaret?' he pleaded.

The whole scene was so comical, and so awful, that Margaret could do nothing but laugh, even as Mrs Ashley pulled off her thick woollen coat and thrust it at Margaret, muttering that she'd catch her death of cold if she wasn't careful.

'Mrs Ashley, I'm so sorry,' she said in a tortured voice. 'This is Philip, a friend of mine. He's from Guernsey,' she added, as if that explained everything. 'You must have had a shock finding a strange man in my kitchen.'

That much was obvious, but Philip was the one who recovered first.

'Why don't you both go and sit down, and I'll bring you a cup of tea as soon as the kettle boils?' he said kindly.

'Yes, let's do that, Mrs Ashley,' Margaret said, steering her away from the incongruous sight of Philip's bare legs and feet beneath his dressing-gown. 'You sit down and I'll run upstairs and put some clothes on.'

She didn't wait for an answer. In less than five minutes she was downstairs again, wearing a high-necked sweater and jeans. A shower could wait. It was far more important to calm down her cleaning lady.

'You might have warned me, Mrs J,' Mrs Ashley hissed at her. 'I didn't know where to look!'

Margaret smothered an unbecoming urge to giggle. 'It was an unexpected visit, and he'll just be here for a few days. And he's very nice.'

God, what an understatement, but she could hardly say 'he's my lover, and I'm definitely falling in love with him'. Anyway, even that was wrong. She *was* in love with him. She had no doubts about that now. Her head jerked up as Philip brought in a tray of tea and biscuits; she had to admire his panache.

Even in his dressing-gown, padding about on bare feet, and having been startled by Mrs Ashley's appearance as much as she had been startled by him, he was superbly in control now.

'Here you are, ladies, and once I've made myself respectable, I'll make you some breakfast as promised, Margaret.'

He didn't turn a hair, and neither did she, even though she guessed they were both thinking how different — and how delicious — breakfast in bed would have been, had she not forgotten that this was one of Mrs Ashley's days.

She spoke quickly. 'No, I'll just make myself some toast. You mustn't be late for your business appointment.'

Please catch on, she begged mutely, to make this visit seem more official, and less clandestine that it looks. Not that it mattered . . . but somehow it did.

'You're right; I'd better get a move on.'

They both watched him retreat upstairs, and Mrs Ashley took a long drink of tea before nodding approvingly.

'I'll say this for you, Mrs J. You certainly know how to pick them.'

'He's just a friend, and since he's here on business it seemed mean not to offer him a roof for a few nights.'

She nearly said bed, but just managed to change her mind at the last instant. To her surprise, Mrs Ashley patted her hand.

'I'm not as narrow-minded as you might think, dearie. It's good for you to have friends, including men friends. Is he the one who sent you the flowers?'

'He is,' Margaret said, wondering if everything there was to know was transparently obvious in her face now.

'Oh well, I'd better get on. I'll leave upstairs until later, shall I?'

Well, yes until I've had a chance to make it look as if I slept in my own bed last night,

370

Margaret thought . . . which was ridiculous, since she was answerable to nobody but herself.

'Just until Philip's gone,' she agreed weakly.

★ ★ ★

They had a good laugh about it later that afternoon. She hadn't known whether or not to expect him for lunch, and it was nearer four o'clock by the time he returned.

'You realize I'll be a scarlet woman now, don't you? Although I think I also gained a few points from Mrs Ashley for not being such a stick-in-the-mud as some people might think.'

'I'm damn sure nobody ever thought that about you. So what shall we do this evening? Any ideas?'

'Yes. It's my turn to cook for you. I thought we'd stay in and have a lazy evening watching TV, or does that sound too boring?'

'It sounds beautifully domesticated. What have you been doing all day?'

'Oh, this and that.'

Turning out the attic and other rooms, actually, and packing up things in boxes that would need to be disposed of before I move out . . .

'Are you busy on Thursday and Friday,

Philip? If not, I thought we might take a couple of trips. See the local sights — or something.'

'Great. I'd planned on not leaving before Saturday, anyway. So where do you suggest?'

She breathed more easily. She didn't want to tell him the reason for being out of the house on those two days until she had time to think about things, and she couldn't really do that while he was around. He was upstairs changing into casual clothes, and she had started cooking their evening meal, when Keith and Laura arrived in force.

'Has he gone?' Keith said.

'If you mean Philip, you know he hasn't, since I told you he was here for a few days, so sit down and have a glass of wine and say hello,' she said graciously, refusing to show how she was seething at this intrusion.

'Is he staying here?' Laura asked.

'Yes, Laura dear, I always offer hospitality to out-of-town friends.'

Laura's lips clamped together, but Margaret had a feeling they wouldn't stay that way for long. Sure enough, when Philip came downstairs, dressed casually, she and Keith exchanged meaningful glances. The introductions were cool, and Margaret gave an inward sigh, knowing that there was no one Keith would give his approval to after Robert.

In his eyes, his father was a hero and always had been, which only strengthened her resolve of never letting him down by revealing to his children what a rat he had really been. It was a secret known only to her and those involved — and Philip. And it was going to stay that way.

'It's an odd time of year to be leaving home, even on business,' Laura said pointedly. 'Doesn't your wife object?'

Laura could be a real bitch, Margaret fumed . . . and the only saving grace was that she presumably thought she was doing it for Margaret's sake.

Philip laughed. 'My wife and I were divorced five years ago. She's somewhere with her new man now, so I hardly think she gives a damn where I am,' he replied.

He looked Laura squarely in the eyes, and Margaret saw her blush. She was so bloody transparent that she was almost sorry for her at that moment.

'My father died less than a year ago,' Keith said, just as pointedly, 'and I believe you and my mother only met a couple of months ago.'

'Quite right. That's why I'm so glad to meet some of her family. On Thursday and Friday we're taking a trip to London to meet the rest of them.'

Margaret drew in her breath. This was

news to her, and if it was said on the spur of the moment, it was inspirational, since it completely took the wind out of Keith's sails.

Besides which, it was absolutely the right thing to do — if there was ever to be a future for her and Philip.

'Oh well, I suppose that's convenient,' Keith went on. 'I know Mum wanted to be out of the way when the estate agent brings the prospective buyers to view the house on Thursday and Friday.'

Too late, she knew now that she should have forewarned Philip about this. Which she might have done if Keith hadn't managed to let it slip. Or not.

'Are you sure you don't want either of us here, Margaret?' Laura added. 'You can never be sure who you're letting into your house.'

'The estate agent is seeing to it all. And I'd ask you to stay for dinner, but I'm afraid I've only prepared enough for two.'

The hint was broad enough, and when they had gone, Margaret relaxed, but only until Philip took up where they had left off, exactly as she expected.

'Why didn't you tell me you were selling this house?'

'I'm sorry,' she said edgily. 'I didn't want to complicate things. I wish to God I hadn't told Keith, either. He's a champion at interfering, and I'm sorry if Laura embarrassed you.'

'It takes more than that to embarrass me, as you should know by now. I think those two deserve one another. I meant what I said, though.'

'About what?'

'Going to London to see your family. I'd like to meet the rest of them, and we can stay in an hotel if you prefer. What do you say?'

She didn't really know what to say. She wasn't sure if the whole situation was running away with her, running too fast, leaving her breathless.

'Are you serious?' she said, avoiding any more objections.

'I was never more serious about anything, or anyone.'

'I think I can smell something burning,' Margaret said, and fled to the kitchen before he could ask the next obvious question, which was where she was going to spend the rest of her life, if it wasn't in this house. And since she didn't know the answer to that one herself, there was nothing to tell.

But once they had eaten, she had to telephone her mother and tell her of their impending visit, and to make sure Jenny and Ben would be there. The whole thing was making her nervous and excited, like a girl on a first date, taking her boyfriend home to meet the parents for their approval.

'What's so funny?' Philip said, seeing her smile as they loaded the dishwasher together after the meal.

'I just wish I could see my mother's reaction when I tell her I'm bringing a friend to see her.'

'Will she object?'

'She'll be vetting you like mad, and my father will give you the third degree,' Margaret said with a grin. 'But I think they'll approve. I know Jenny will. One of Robert's old school friends used to come here on a regular basis, and the kids always thought he'd be after me like a shot after Robert died. Ben couldn't have cared less about him, but Jenny and Keith more than disliked him.'

'I begin to have a little more respect for Keith's taste then.'

It wasn't until the visit had been OK'd by her mother and they were listening to music, that he came up with the sixty-four-thousand-dollar question she was expecting.

'So this decision to sell the house. Was that a sudden idea, or had you been planning it for some time?'

'It wasn't planned at all. When I thought about how silly it was for me to keep it on alone, it just seemed the right thing to do. Keith and Laura offered to try to get a mortgage for it, but I wasn't having any of that, especially when they told me I could live here with them for as long as I liked.'

'Having met them, I can just see your reaction to that! So where will you go? Have you got something in mind?'

'Not yet. I don't anticipate anything will go through in a great hurry. It's an expensive property, and although the estate agent already has a couple of people interested, I imagine it will take time.'

'But then you'll have to decide.'

'I know. And I will.' And they both knew she was talking about something other than just selling the house.

'Meanwhile,' she went on, 'let's just leave it. You'll be the first to know my decision when the time comes.'

'That's good enough for me,' he said lazily. 'And *meanwhile*, why don't we have an early night?'

★ ★ ★

It was so easy to fall into a pattern of doing things. Breakfast in bed the following morning wasn't interrupted by Mrs Ashley, because it wasn't her day, so it was a leisurely, sensual occasion, and seeing Philip off to the last of his calls meant that she had the rest of

377

the day to prepare for their visit to London, and to book a table at a good restaurant for dinner that evening. He was definitely spoiling her, and she knew it was a spoiling she could very soon get used to.

Her mother was delighted she was coming to visit, and promised to get Jenny and Ben there, saying she would cook them a meal each evening, so she wasn't to think of eating hotel meals — as if it was the worse fate in the world. If they had the room, she said she would put them up at the flat, but she wasn't sure Margaret's father was quite ready for that, she added darkly and expectantly.

Margaret laughed. 'You're not getting anything out of me, Mum, so don't even hint. But I know you'll like Philip. We'll see you tomorrow.'

It would be so different from the last time she had gone to London, flying in a panic from Guernsey to be at her father's hospital bedside, she remembered. It would be so good to be there in happier times.

★   ★   ★

But first there was dinner that evening, and to Margaret's chagrin, she saw a familiar face across the restaurant, her eyes widening at this unexpected *tête-à-tête*.

'Someone you know?' Philip asked.

'Oh yes.'

And even though she was with a group of people, she knew there was no way Sarah would let this opportunity go by. Margaret watched her weave her sinuous way between the tables until she reached them.

'Mags, how lovely to see you. I was going to call you tomorrow — '

'What a shame. I won't be here. I'm going to visit my parents.'

'Really?'

Margaret could almost see the wheels turning. Whoever this dishy guy was, if Margaret wasn't going to be around there was no reason why she shouldn't dig her claws in . . . annoyed at her own thoughts, Margaret introduced him quickly.

'Sarah, meet Philip. Philip — Sarah.'

Her eyes widened even more. 'The man from Guernsey?' she said, in the same tone as she might have said *the man from Del Monte*.

'The very same,' Philip said with a smile.

'How nice. Are you staying long?'

As if she was the silent prompt in a play, Margaret listened to the interaction, willing Philip not to respond to the unmistakable interest oozing from Sarah now. Especially since she would now be assuming that

Margaret would be well out of the way tomorrow.

'Afraid not. Margaret and I will be spending a few days in London, and then I go home on Saturday.'

Oh yes, there is a God, Margaret thought, and Sarah's face was a joy to behold. She gave her a brilliant smile.

Yes, my fairweather friend, she wanted to shout. *We are going to visit my parents and you can make what you like of that!*

'I'll call you next week then, Mags,' Sarah said at last.

'Yes, why don't you do that?' she said, and turned at once to Philip, feeling as if it was the first time she had ever felt really on top as far as any interchange with Sarah was concerned.

Later, when she and Philip were in bed together — and it really was much, much later — he said, 'Don't tell me if you'd rather not, but was she the one?'

Margaret laughed self-consciously. 'Oh Lord, was I that obvious? I thought I was over it.'

'You are. Aren't you?'

'Yes,' she said slowly. 'I do believe I am.'

'Good. Because there are far more important things to do than to waste time thinking about other people right now.'

The London visit was a wild success. After the first few awkward moments, Jenny was cautiously ready to accept him; Ben was sociable, and her parents were definitely approving. All through the family dinner and afterwards, her mother kept giving her sly winks, until finally, Margaret could stand it no more, and told her so when it was time to go back to the hotel on their last night.

'For pity's sake, stop it, Mum. You look like as if you've got a squint half the time. Philip will think you're peculiar.'

'I'm only trying to let you know I approve, and that if you've got any doubts, or any thoughts of disloyalty to Robert, then you shouldn't have. You've only got yourself to think about now, so go wherever your heart leads you.'

'I'm not thinking of marrying him,' she said, in answer to this flowery speech, and hoping Philip couldn't overhear as he said goodnight to her father.

'Why on earth not? If I was twenty years younger and not still in love with your father, I'd give you a run for your money. And if Philip's not a passionate man, then I'm a Dutchman, so if you're in separate rooms at your hotel, then you're not the daughter I thought you were,' she added for good measure.

Margaret laughed. Her mother was as outrageous as ever, but she had never been one for making snap decisions, and she wasn't going to start now. There was far too much to consider. And before she thought about anything at all, she had to sell her house. Prosaically, she knew that had to be her first priority.

And true to his word, Philip made no further demands on her. He had asked her once to marry him, and it was up to her to give him her answer. He wasn't like Robert, who would have overwhelmed her, smothered her, out-willed her.

But she missed him so much when he left for home, promising to keep in touch, and having to put up with Sarah and the others coming round and demanding to know everything about this man she had been seen out with in one of Bournemouth's swishest restaurants.

'I told you. His name's Philip and I met him when I went to Guernsey,' she told them, oddly flat, because phone calls weren't the same as being with him, able to touch him and breathe him.

'*And?*' June said. 'Are you going to see him again?'

'Perhaps. I'm not thinking about anything else until I've sold the house. That's a big enough upheaval for now.'

'Won't you miss it, Mags?' June asked.

'Of course I will, but life goes on, doesn't it? And I have to go on as well.'

'You won't have any trouble selling it anyway. It'll go like a shot.'

But that was another of life's little surprises, Margaret thought, three months later, when there had still been no definite buyer for the property. Keith was still urging her to think over his and Laura's offer, and she was still obstinately refusing to even consider it.

'You know what I think, don't you?' Mrs Ashley said, conversationally, over the tea-cups on one of her 'days'. 'I think you should go and marry that nice Guernsey chap of yours.'

'Do you?'

'Well, it stands to reason you were made for each other. I could see that the minute I set eyes on him. And you don't want to think badly of yourself, neither. You and Mr Jarvis had a good innings, God rest his soul, but you're still a young woman, and he wouldn't want to think of you pining away for the rest of your life. Anyway, I doubt if it would be that way if the shoe was on the other foot.'

Margaret's senses were suddenly alert. There was something in the way she said it. Some tiny nuance. A quickening of her voice. A knowing. A sureness in the way she put her cup down hurriedly and busied herself with picking up her duster again and doing the silver, as she called it. As if she had said something she hadn't really meant to say. It was nothing really. And yet it was everything.

'You don't think my husband would have stayed faithful to me for the rest of his life if I'd been the one to die then, Mrs Ashley?' she said lightly.

It took a fraction too long before she got an answer. Just long enough for Margaret to put the words in her mouth that she didn't say:

Why would he? He never stayed faithful to you before . . .

They always said other people saw the things you never saw yourself. John knew about Sarah and Robert — and about the escort agency. Sarah quite possibly knew about John and Robert. Keith and Jenny had always been wary and suspicious of John and his motives towards herself, but thankfully, had never suspected anything about their father. They had been as blinkered about him as she had been. But Mrs Ashley . . .

'I just think that when people pass on, the one that's left has to make the best of things, and if somebody else comes into their lives, then that's the way it was probably meant to be,' the woman said, neatly dodging the question.

'You could be right,' Margaret said.

'Anyway' — Mrs Ashley gave Robert's silver tankard a final flourish — 'I always think things go full circle, and since Mr Jarvis will have been gone for a year in a few weeks, you mark my words, that's when you'll get a buyer for the house. It'll be a sign, see? Time to move on in every respect.'

Although her logic gave her a kind of comforting feeling, Margaret didn't really believe it for a minute. And although she had dreaded the anniversary of the day Robert died, it came and went, with calls from her children and parents, a visit from Keith, and then John.

None of them really knew what to say, and in the end she felt frustrated by the way they were all pussy-footing around her as if she was an invalid, throwing her right back to that awful day a year ago, when so much had happened since then, and she had survived it all. She was still here. Still intact and alive.

'How's the house selling going?' John said cautiously. 'Any luck yet?'

'I think there might be. We're having another viewing next week. This time the estate agent sounded more definite and said the people seemed pretty keen to buy the place.'

'What will you do then? You can't go on being in limbo, Maggie. You really should have some plan for the future.'

'I know. Tell me, John, do you believe in fate?'

'Sometimes. But I also think you can give fate a pretty good helping hand.'

'That's what I think. But it will be something of a coincidence if I sell the house so soon after Robert's anniversary, don't you think? As if it — or he — was telling me something. Time to move on, and all that stuff. Or am I just being bloody silly and talking through the bottom of a wine glass?'

'Well, you have had quite a few tonight,' he said uneasily. 'And you know all that afterlife talk makes me uncomfortable, Mags.'

'All right. Sorry. Anyway, I've probably made up my mind what I'm going to do, but I'll tell you definitely when the time comes. It all depends on these people viewing the house.'

And if she was using that as a kind of yardstick, she wasn't telling him, or anyone about her plans. People would start to think she was going crazy, when in reality she was starting to see things more clearly than anything in her life before. Except for marrying Robert in the first place. Because it *had* been a perfect marriage for all those years, and nobody could ever take that away from her.

Ten days later, the estate agent called round. There had been an offer on the house for the full asking price, which she accepted at once. The couple wanted to move in within a month if possible, and he hoped that it would be convenient. The fat commission involved clearly loomed large in his mind, but she couldn't blame him for that. Margaret had already negotiated to sell most of the carpets and furniture with the house, except for the things her family had already chosen, and a few pieces that had specially sentimental value for herself, so there was going to be little delay in getting it all sewn up, the estate agent went on jubilantly.

So now there was only one more thing left to do. But before she did it, she took a very long walk around the grounds, and then through every room in the house, pausing to remember so many things, so much of the last twenty-five years of her life, the love and the laughter, the children, and all the rich, sweet memories of what she was still adamant in thinking a perfect marriage. Which it had been, in her eyes, right up until the day Robert died.

But she was finally able to lock the memories away inside her heart, knowing it was truly time to move on. And with a quickening heartbeat, she marvelled anew that out of all the world she had found something else that was equally precious. Far too precious to be thrown away.

And then she dialled Philip's number.

THE END

We do hope that you have enjoyed reading this large print book.

Did you know that all of our titles are available for purchase?

We publish a wide range of high quality large print books including:
Romances, Mysteries, Classics
General Fiction
Non Fiction and Westerns

Special interest titles available in large print are:
The Little Oxford Dictionary
Music Book
Song Book
Hymn Book
Service Book

Also available from us courtesy of Oxford University Press:
Young Readers' Dictionary
(large print edition)
Young Readers' Thesaurus
(large print edition)

For further information or a free brochure, please contact us at:
Ulverscroft Large Print Books Ltd.,
The Green, Bradgate Road, Anstey,
Leicester, LE7 7FU, England.
Tel: (00 44) 0116 236 4325
Fax: (00 44) 0116 234 0205

Other titles in the
Ulverscroft Large Print Series:

DEAD FISH

Ruth Carrington

Dr Geoffrey Quinn arrives home to find his children missing, the charred remains of his wife's body in the boiler and Chief Superintendent Manning waiting to arrest him for her murder. Alison Hope, attractive and determined, is briefed to defend him. Quinn claims he is innocent, but Alison is not so sure. The background becomes increasingly murky as she penetrates a wealthy and ruthless circle who cannot risk their secrets — sexual perversion, drugs, blackmail, illegal arms dealing and major fraud — coming to light. Can Alison unravel the mystery in time to save Quinn?

MY FATHER'S HOUSE

Kathleen Conlon

'Your father has another woman'. Nine-year-old Anna Blake is only mildly surprised when a schoolfriend lets drop this piece of information. And when her father finally leaves home to live with Olivia in Hampstead, that place becomes, for Anna, the epitome of sinful glamour. But Hampstead, though welcoming, is not home. So Anna, now in her teens, sets out to find a place where she can really belong. At first she thinks love may be the answer, and certainly Jonathon — and Raymond — and Jake, have a devastating effect on her life. But can anyone really supply what she needs?

GHOSTLY MURDERS

P. C. Doherty

When Chaucer's Canterbury pilgrims pass a deserted village, the sight of its decaying church provokes the poor Priest to tears. When they take shelter, he tells a tale of ancient evil, greed, devilish murder and chilling hauntings . . . There was once a young man, Philip Trumpington, who was appointed parish priest of a pleasant village with an old church, built many centuries earlier. However, Philip soon discovers that the church and presbytery are haunted. A great and ancient evil pervades, which must be brought into the light, resolved and reparation made. But the price is great . . .

BLOODTIDE

Bill Knox

When the Fishery Protection cruiser MARLIN was ordered to the Port Ard area off the north-west Scottish coast, Chief Officer Webb Carrick soon discovered that an old shipmate of Captain Shannon had been killed in a strange accident before they arrived. A drowned frogman, a reticent Russian officer and a dare-devil young fisherman were only a few of the ingredients to come together as Carrick tried to discover the truth. The key to it all was as deadly as it was unexpected.

WISE VIRGIN

Manda Mcgrath

Sisters Jean and Ailsa Leslie live on a small farm in the Scottish Grampians. Andrew Esplin, the local blacksmith, keeps a brotherly eye on the girls, loving Ailsa, the younger sister, from afar. Ailsa is in love with Stewart Morrison, who is working in Greenock. Jean is engaged to Alan Drummond, who has gone to Australia, intending to send for her when his prospects are good. But Jean shocks everyone when she elopes with Dunton from the big house . . .